Shanghai

Shanghai

a novel by

WILLIAM MARSHALL

Holt, Rinehart and Winston
New York

Library of Congress Cataloging in Publication Data
Marshall, William Leonard, 1944–
Shanghai.
1. Sino-Japanese Conflict, 1937–1945—Shanghai
—Fiction. 2. Shanghai—History—Fiction.
I. Title.
PZ4.M372Sh   1979   [PR9619.3.M275]   823   78-14178
ISBN 0-03-021031-3

Printed in the United States of America
1 3 5 7 9 10 8 6 4 2

for Mary

Shanghai

To the nineteenth century mind nurtured and kept prosperous by the Churchblessed twin notions of enterprise and export, the issue was a simple one. If the picturesque Chinese emperor of a nation of four million yellow heathens obviously created by God to be fed by British goods and clothed by British cotton intended to continue spoilt and intransigent like a petulant child about increasing imports of British opium from India then, in the name of common discipline and good manners, the Chinese emperor needed a short sharp lesson in the shape of a flotilla of men-of-war. The finest modern product of British shipyards, the iron-clad sidewheel paddle steamer, Nemesis, armed with the latest thirty-two pounder guns from British foundries, would lead this flotilla.

A long ground war would be costly in terms of Chinese consumer casualties and property and it was decided in Calcutta and London, following consultations with interested parties in Bristol and Birmingham—merchants and investors—that a series of naval actions in the vicinity of the Woosung forts protecting the city of Shanghai on the Yangtse river might prove sufficient to teach this lesson. For the Emperor—the Heaven-born, as he called himself—to take the line that an unstoppable flow of opium would turn his people into mindless obedient slaves was patently absurd; if there had been no demand for the stuff then obviously it would not have been worth his while attempting to regulate it. People had a right to be free to choose. There should be no government interference in their enterprise. That this was true for the Chinese peasant as much as the Bristol merchant was natural law approved by God. Settled.

In the early hours of June the 11th, 1842, the fleet opened fire on the Woosung river forts leading into the Yangtse river.

Sufficient. The barrage ceased fifteen minutes after it had begun and the fleet sailed the twelve miles up-river to Shanghai, landed Colonel Montgomerie and a thousand men from the 55th Regiment on the foreshore, took control of the one great building in the city (an

1

enormous public ice-house), collected a £145,000 ransom from the city treasury, raised the British flag, and moved on to Nanking.

Two years later, when a treaty to grant an 'Open Door' trading lease to the West through an International Settlement of 5000 acres on Shanghai's riverfront was granted, the Nemesis' guns and steam paddles were still objects of great interest and curiosity. It was asked if the secrets of their manufacture were fit to be known.

The secrets were not.

In the magnanimity of victory however, it was hinted that the Emperor might be permitted to inspect the vessel at the time of its next tour. The Emperor, for reasons of face, declined, and the British, anxious on their parts as victors to suggest something that might be acceptable as an alternative, offered not to execute any Chinese criminals they might catch in the course of their tenancy in the city. The Emperor's representatives looked worried. Surely the Western view of punishment did not include the forgiveness of—

What the British had meant was that the Chinese themselves could execute them.

Accepted. It was felt there could, from this omen, be understanding on both sides. The Emperor's representatives made a statement that could, when read in translation in Bristol or Birmingham, be taken as an apology for their thoughtless action in provoking war, although in China, the language of the Court being what it was, it could equally well be read quite a different way.

The conference broke up in the final weeks of 1854. On Christmas Day the first of the opium clippers tied up alongside the East India Company dock in the newly dredged river.

1923

The Condemned Man

Behind the barbed wire fence that squared off the killing ground two of the Chinese soldiers were digging a grave. They had their coats off and they shivered slightly in the morning cold as they worked. Both of them looked equally undernourished: their brown hairless arms were sinewy and thin. One of them had shaved his head some time ago—there was a dark shadow on the dome of his skull where the black hair was beginning to grow back again and he kept pausing to run his fingers across it. The constant flicks left smears of yellow earth on the stubble. The bald soldier glanced back to the officer and the rest of his section warming their hands by an oildrum brazier and continued digging.

Down from the killing ground and the track that ran to it, through the barbed wire, you could see across the Nantao farmlands all the way to the Yangtse River. The river was a snail's track of silver light framing the farmlands and their wooden huts and warehouses in a long unhurried semi-circle. Moving in amidst the silver light there were cargo junks coming down from the north towards Shanghai and the sea beyond it.

The sky above the fields of matured rice was dark and close, the fields and the raised earth levees that divided them into family plots empty and still.

Edge, dressed in the thick dark blue winter uniform of the Shanghai Municipal Police, shivered. Some of the Chinese soldiers around the brazier were heating pebbles and rubbing them between their hands—their uniforms looked thin and patched and the butts of their rifles, instead of having the rich deep warmth of good wood treated with linseed oil, looked grey and second rate, like old palings.

Edge glanced over at Constable Singh standing next to Superintendent Moffatt. He stood, six feet two high, next to Moffatt's diminutive frame, gazing at the gravediggers impassively. Edge thought he would have stood like that—like granite—if ordered until the winter snows came and covered him up. In all the time he had known him, in blazing Shanghai summers or in the depths of winter, Edge had never once seen him either sweat or shiver. Each of his brass buttons shone, his shoes were always mirror polished, his beard always combed, his shoulders square and his face with its hawk nose below glittering eyes impassive and solid. He had his candy-striped Constable's quarterstaff held loosely in his left hand.

Edge looked at his watch. It was six thirty-five in the morning. He put his gloved hand back firmly into his overcoat pocket and looked over towards the brazier. A little behind it guarded by two more soldiers, there was a young Chinese in shirtsleeves. This morning, a few days before Christmas, 1923, in the eighty first year of the western occupation of Shanghai, he was the one to be shot.

Moffatt called, 'Sergeant Edge,' and Edge turned and went over to him.

The condemned man was weeping. He was in his mid-twenties and his face was still smooth and unlined. His black hair was uncombed and grew down the back of his neck. In places it stuck out in tufts. The condemned man wore no shoes: his feet were calloused and gnarled like an old woman's. They were smeared with the yellow earth. The condemned man sat on a rock a little distance from the officer by the brazier and looked at his hands, turning them over.

Moffatt patted his pencil line moustache, and then touched at the flattened oiled hair on his temple below his cap. He was a man who liked uniforms: he resquared his cap and flicked at an imaginary speck of dust on one of the epaulettes on his shoulders. He touched at the thin moustache again and then sniffed hard in order to turn the dainty, precious movement into a manly annoyance.

The condemned man's mouth was quivering: the salty tears turned into little rivulets of ice on his face. He looked very small and brittle—the bones in his wrist were like a bird's. The condemned man turned his head to look at the grave.

Moffatt said quietly, 'I expect you're wondering about your promotion.' He looked around furtively to make sure none of the Chinese were within earshot, 'I think you can probably expect some welcome news on that front.' He had a Scottish burr to his voice. 'In fact, all things being equal, if I were you,

Jack, I'd be saving my pennies to buy drinks all round at the Shanghai Club.' He looked and sounded exactly like a provincial grocery salesman, 'If I were a member.'

Edge said, 'I'm not a member.' He looked over at the condemned man and then to the Chinese officer. The Chinese officer seemed to be waiting for something. He lit a cigarette and puffed it carefully over the burning oildrum as if he expected to have to extinguish it at any moment. 'I'm grateful if you put in a good word for me, Superintendent.'

Moffatt touched at his moustache and looked out over the rice fields. The farmers and their families were beginning to congregate around their huts. Some of them were carrying large rattan cages full of captured birds. They put the cages down near their fields and began removing the fluttering little birds one by one. Moffatt said, 'Rice birds. The farmers put bamboo reeds on their claws so when they release them the screeching will scare away the evil spirits from the harvest. It's a very ancient custom performed at harvest times.' He had learned it from a guide book to put it into one of his weekly letters home to Scotland. 'Things are changing, Jack. The sort of behaviour from white men that, say twenty years ago, might have been considered totally unacceptable—' He paused, then said quickly, 'New people are coming up, Jack. People are beginning to look on police service in Shanghai and the Treaty Ports as a career. Oh, I know, Jack, there's a lot to be said for your average Chinaman. God knows, we'd have a hard enough time without him, but—' he stabbed his gloved finger in the general direction of the nation that contained a quarter of the entire population of the globe, 'God knows equally well the Chinee'd have an even harder time without us.' He looked upwards into Edge's face, 'The point is, Jack, a white man has to be prepared to fit in with other white men.' He gazed expectantly, 'Do you understand me? If he wants to succeed.'

'You know, sir, of course, that I'm married to a Chinese woman.'

'Yes, we do know that, Jack, and to be brutally frank with you, we were hoping that in the fulness of time—but that of course is your own affair. In fact, the determination you've shown in standing by your decision to marry this lady in the face of. . . Well, I for one put in a word for you. On your record.' He said quickly, 'The way things are going politically, whatever our separate views of moral matters may be, we all have to stick

7

together. We certainly don't want the Chinks thinking that if they start threatening us, we'll all just pack up and go. We have to be all *united as one*.' He said humanely, 'That way no one gets hurt—neither us nor them.' He moved a little closer and said quietly, 'One of Chiang Kai Shek's people from Canton has been in the area here for the last few days trying to talk the local warlord into throwing in his lot with them. That's who we're waiting for now: the local *tuchun*. The reality of this chap's coming up here is that for the first time since the fall of the Emperors it looks like China might be able to form some sort of rough and ready European style government. In some ways that's a good thing, both for them and us. But in others—'

Moffatt interpolated suddenly, 'You see, Jack, what with you being born and raised here in China, growing up with the Chinese as if they were your equals and never knowing the company and comradeship of white children, and, and well, speaking the language as it were like a native—'

Edge said, 'My father was an American missionary. He and my mother were posted up country—'

'Jack, Jack, we know that.' Moffatt said, 'No one's suggesting for a single solitary moment that it was *your* fault—'

Behind the barbed wire the two soldiers completed the grave. They glanced at the officer by the brazier, then down into the rice fields. The farmers and their families had finished wiring the spirit-scaring reeds to the rice birds' claws and stood in groups surveying their rice and looking up into the sky. The two soldiers tapped their spades clean and put their uniform coats back on. The officer's cigarette was a little over half smoked: the two soldiers moved respectfully slowly towards him at the speed of the burning tobacco. The officer finished the cigarette and dropped the stub into the fire in the drum.

The condemned man looked down at his hands. They were blue veined with the cold. The pulse of his life force drummed at the side of his neck: he heard his heartbeat there.

The two soldiers put their spades neatly on the ground near the brazier. The officer looked at his watch. The condemned man's hands began trembling.

Moffatt said finally, 'Jack, to put it into plain language, the powers-that-be have left it entirely in my hands to decide whether you're promoted to command rank or not. The decision is up to me.'

The officer leaned forward and flicked a tiny shard of yellow earth from the bald soldier's pate. He said in Shanghai Chinese, 'Put your cap on,' and turned to look up the track.

Moffatt said, 'Did you hear what I said, Jack?'

'Yes, sir.'

'We have to know whose side you're on. Theirs or ours. *I* have to know. I want to recommend you. I've told them as much. I've gone and put my head on the block for you. Now it's up to you. It's your choice and yours alone. I'm being more than fair to you.'

The condemned man looked at the soldiers' rifles stacked against the barbed wire fence. Everyone except him was in uniform. They wore shoes and leggings. Their buttons were all hard and unbreakable. The condemned man thought of his wife. There were hard grey men everywhere around him.

Moffatt said, 'If we all behave ourselves, the trouble will pass. The Chinese always have some jumped-up firebrand telling them the Europeans in the Treaty Ports are the cause of all their troubles. This year it's this Canton fellow. Next year it'll be someone else. All we have to do is stick together.' The condemned man's tears had gone dry. His eyes flickered back and forth. His wrists and arms were twitching. Moffatt said, 'You can be one of us, Jack.'

'Thank you, sir.'

'The name is Alec, Jack.'

The officer took out another cigarette and put it in his mouth. It was a Russian one with a long cardboard tube. He consulted his watch, then examined the tube end of the cigarette. It was chewed away and soggy: he dropped it into the fire and reached into his top pocket for another. He was a very slight man in his late twenties, the son of a local small landowner: he looked up the track again for the *tuchun*'s procession.

The officer shouted at the soldiers in Chinese, 'Ready!' and the soldiers caught hold of the condemned man, bound his hands quickly behind his back, and took him into the killing ground.

Constable Singh caught Edge's eye.

There was the sound of horses being ridden fast over hard earth coming down from the other side of the hillock, then, a moment after it, a bell.

Moffatt said warningly to both Edge and Singh, 'The first time's the hardest. Stony-faced. All right?' He said to Singh, 'Understand the expression "stony-faced"?'

'Yes, sah!'

Moffatt nodded. He raised his gloved finger and glanced over at the Chinese officer. He looked at Edge's eyes watching the condemned man, 'Jack—'

The eyes came back.

Moffatt said, 'It's only a bloody Chink.' He touched at his moustache. 'With us or against us, Jack—one or the other.' The Chinese officer glanced at his watch for a final time and, with his soldiers shouldering their rifles and following him, went past the barbed wire through the open gate into the killing ground.

Edge said, 'I would like a successful career in the police, Alec. I realise that my background and my marriage is—'

The condemned man stood above the open grave. His chest was palpitating like a bird's. He looked up at the bald headed soldier.

'Jack, that's what I've been waiting to hear.' There was a new tone in Moffatt's voice. There was a tight gratified smile at the corners of his mouth. He touched at his moustache and the smile widened an intimate, conspiratorial fraction, 'Thank you, Jack.'

The bald headed soldier forced the condemned man to his knees and ripped away his shirt collar to expose his neck as the policemen went forward. Up on the hillock, you could hear the horses and the bells coming.

The sky had turned slate grey: in the valley the farmers peered into the approaching clouds for the signs of the evil spirits with burning eyes. The *tuchun*'s procession halted outside the barbed wire and the *tuchun*, a squat, well-fed man in a richly carved sedan chair, wearing rich Chekiang silk and a skull cap, folded his hands into his sleeves and remained seated. He turned his eyes to the man from Canton and nodded. There was the suggestion of a benign smile on his face. The discussion—the alliance of forces—had gone well. The *tuchun* moved his head past the man from Canton standing beside him in the direction of the soldiers: the soldiers were now also the property of the man from Canton. The *tuchun* gazed at the two European policemen and the Sikh without expression. A bearer brought a wooden stool and he rested his black slippered feet on it and straightened his back.

The Cantonese was no more than five feet tall, wiry. He touched at rimless glasses above a lined face and lit a cigarette, considered it for a moment, and then ground it out on the earth. His fingers were stubby and nicotine-stained. He hooked them into the leather belt around his shapeless khaki tunic and gazed at the assembled soldiers. One of the *tuchun*'s equerrys offered his master a sweetmeat from a silver box. The *tuchun* declined with a movement of his hand.

The man from Canton lit a second cigarette and kept it in his mouth. A cone of ash fell from his cigarette onto his tunic. He drummed on his belt buckle with his fingers. Outside the compound one of the horses snorted anxiously and then, except for the wind gathering strength across the flat expanse of the valley below, there was an uncanny silence.

Moffatt looked at his pocket watch and said to the benign smile on the *tuchun*'s face, 'Tuchun, muchee fear soon makee rain,' and glanced significantly towards the sky. The *tuchun* glanced at the Chinese officer near his men and made a barely perceptible shaking motion with his hand. The Chinese officer looked in the direction of the man from Canton and then back to the *tuchun*. He buttoned his pistol holster and looked relieved: the visitor would be doing the killing. The Chinese officer fixed his gaze with new interest on the bespectacled little man.

Moffatt said for the second time, 'Tuchun—'

The *tuchun* smiled at him expectantly.

The man from Canton took his thumbs from his belt and brought out something from inside his tunic. It was a small British flag. He looked at the soldiers and laid the flag on the earth in front of them. The flag was perhaps two feet square. He took another from his tunic—an American Stars and Stripes and arranged it carefully to the British Union Jack. The corners of the flags fluttered and he anchored them with pebbles and looked up at the soldiers. The soldiers watched. The Chinese officer glanced anxiously at Moffatt, Edge and Singh, then quickly to the *tuchun*. The *tuchun*'s face said the display had his approval. The man from Canton laid a third flag on the ground—a French tricolour—and anchored the corners of that as well. From his squatting position behind the three flags he raised his finger. The soldiers all knew the three flags represented the joint rulers of the International Settlement of Shanghai—they leaned forward to hear what the man from Canton was about to say.

Moffatt looked at Edge. He narrowed his eyes.

Edge said softly, 'He doesn't speak the local dialect—' He watched as the finger made a slow turning movement and pointed hard across the fields and valleys where, for over three quarters of a century round-eyed men with steel ships and guns had held inviolate as their own the centre of the greatest city in China.

The man from Canton made a short hissing noise. He raised his finger to the soldiers for them to return their attention to him and took out something else from his tunic. It was one of the *tuchun*'s personal standards, a yellow flag with a purple dragon embellished on it. The man from Canton like a magician demonstrating an empty top hat to a spellbound audience, held it up for the soldiers to see. Then laying the flag carefully on his knee, he produced a second flag, blue and red, with a white multi-pointed star—the flag of the Nationalist party of China. He gazed at the soldiers' faces and then looked to the *tuchun*. The *tuchun* nodded: the soldiers knew the flag. The bespectacled man produced two other flags: of other provincial governors and their forces and he indicated with a sweep of his hand that they were from provinces to the north and west. He stood up and in one movement (there must have been little hooks and eyelets sewn into them) joined the four flags into a single four foot square standard. He swept his hand in a wide arc: the flags joined together represented all China.

For a single moment he held the banner aloft. He hesitated, then let it fall. Weighted at each corner, it went down to the earth like a blanket and covered over the flags of the foreigners.

Moffatt said softly to Edge, 'The stupid little dwarf doesn't even speak Pidgin.' He sighed with boredom and the approaching cold weather.

Edge glanced at the condemned man. Bent down over the open grave with his wrists behind him, he looked like a crippled swimmer about to dive carefully into eternity. The muscles of his back contracted and expanded in spasms through his thin shirt. He was shivering.

Moffatt said softly, 'If it isn't one damned alliance or intrigue it's another.' He glanced at the *tuchun*, 'It's about time we brought pressure to bear to get rid of him.' He glanced at the sky, 'I've got an appointment with the Commissioner at ten.' He watched as the Cantonese came slowly towards him, 'Talk to him in his own dialect, Jack, would you, and let him know in a subtle way we haven't got all morning.' He greeted the man politely in Pidgin as he stopped a few yards away, 'Chin-chin.'

He whispered to Edge, 'Say good morning to him in Cantonese.'

'*Jo san.*'

The man from Canton inspected them both carefully.

Moffatt indicated the sky, 'Muchee fear makee rain—' He smiled politely.

The Cantonese looked at him. He said in English with a faint American accent, 'Why do you expect the *tuchun*'s forces to shoot your criminals for you? Why don't you do it yourselves? Inside your own Settlement?' He looked at Moffatt.

'All time thing.'

'I speak English.'

'Jack, tell him that the Chinese authorities and the authorities in the International Settlement have an agreement that Chinese criminals sentenced to death in the Settlement must be tried for a second time by a Chinese court and the sentence of death carried out outside the Settlement.'

'He—'

'Tell him in his own language please, Jack.'

Edge began, '*Ying gwok yan—*'

'And what if I happen to refuse to execute your man? What if I decide to consider him an unfortunate victim of European greed and corruption and let him go?'

'No can do.' Moffatt glanced at the *tuchun*.

The man from Canton looked hard at Moffatt. He held his eyes for a moment. (Moffatt feigned boredom and looked away.) 'O.K.' the bespectacled man said, 'I gave you a chance, but now, God help you!'

Moffatt looked at him. There was a faint smile on his face. He watched as he went determinedly towards the soldiers. He shook his head in mock-despair. 'Do you think they'll ever learn, Jack?' He said to himself wearily, 'No, they'll never learn.'

The man from Canton took a rifle from one of the soldiers and went towards the condemned man.

It was 7:30 a.m. and the clouds were closing in quickly. Down in the valley the farmers looked anxiously at their fields of rice. The long ripe wands were beginning to feel the cold fingers of evil spirits moving amongst them. From the dark sky invisible ghosts without feet slid with the hissing wind into the rice. The farmers nodded to each other and went to ready the ghost-frightening birds in their rattan cages. The birds fluttered in panic. There were little thumping sounds as their wings hit

13

the rattan bars and tiny peepings as stray bubbles of wind blew through the reeds on their claws. En masse, the farmers moved in a line towards their fields carrying the cages of rice birds.

The condemned man closed his eyes. At the small of his back all the fingers of his bound hands were twitching. It looked to Edge as if he was trying to locate a support—something thin and strong like a metal rod anchored into the ground—to hold himself back. There was nothing. At the gunshot, the empty grave would take him. A muscle in his left temple flickered back and forth: the nerves and junctions inside his brain were rushing and panicking chaotically. His mouth trembled and there was a spasmodic sniffing sound. His feet were bare: where he kneeled you could see the callouses from years of hard work. A long time ago, perhaps when he had been a little boy, one of his toes had been broken—it had healed at an odd angle.

Moffatt said in an undertone without moving his head, 'Keep an eye on this bastard, Jack.' He fixed his gaze on the man from Canton examining the rifle behind the condemned man. There was the sudden clatter of a cartridge being driven into the breech.

Moffatt said, 'Just see he doesn't forget his place. All right?'

Edge swallowed. The wind had jagged edges to it. He shivered a little below his shoulderblades.

The man from Canton raised the rifle. There was a dull click as he thumbed the safety catch forwards and rested the black muzzle against the condemned man's naked neck. A shiver went through the condemned man. The man from Canton moved forward a step and brought the stock of the gun up to his shoulder. In his hands the rifle looked enormous. He rested his cheek against the stock and peered through the sights. They terminated in a Vee on the flesh of the condemned man's neck just below the base of the skull.

The man from Canton glanced out of the corner of his eye to the seated *tuchun*. The *tuchun* was choosing a sweetmeat from his bearer's little silver box. He decided on one and popped it into his mouth. The *tuchun* glanced at the two Europeans and the Sikh and settled back on his wooden chair to chew the delicacy carefully. A second bearer brought an embroidered rug and spread it over his legs to keep him warm.

The man from Canton looked at Moffatt through his rimless glasses. There was a faint smile at the corner of his mouth.

There was a silence. Moffatt made a soft, unsurprised

grunting noise. He was aware of the Sikh leaning forward: without turning he shook his head so only Singh could see him. Edge was aware of Singh tensing.

The man from Canton smiled again.

Moffatt said softly, 'Nothing. Say nothing. . .' The man from Canton had his finger crooked around the curve of the trigger. He touched it carefully and the springs made a faint creaking noise. He released the pressure and then took it up again. He was waiting for Moffatt.

Edge moved forward.

'Stand still, Jack.' Moffatt's voice was soft. The man from Canton saw his mouth move. He squinted down the gun barrel for a moment.

The condemned man's mouth was moving. It formed a loose O. His two lips kept touching each other and then moving back into the O shape. Edge swallowed. His hand lay along the seam of his coat. He moved it upwards and felt the weave of the material through his fingertips.

Singh said in an undertone, 'Jack? Why doesn't he—'

Moffatt's whisper hissed, 'Be quiet!' The man from Canton raised his cheek from the rifle stock and gazed lazily at Moffatt. Edge glanced at the *tuchun*: the *tuchun* was pretending not to notice. The Chinese officer tensed to make a move forward, but the *tuchun* stopped him with a single shake of his head. The *tuchun* had a vague smile on his face. He considered a second sweetmeat between his thumb and forefinger.

Edge moved his face a fraction towards Moffatt. 'Tell him to shoot—!'

'Be quiet, Jack.'

The man from Canton smiled, waiting. Moffatt looked at him with an expression of disappointed boredom. The rifle must have been heavy for the tiny man—he held it as if it were a feather. He was going to hold it forever.

He was waiting for the Europeans to break first.

In the valley the farmers set their cages down urgently. The wind was rising. It whipped in among the birds and set them twittering in fear.

Edge glanced at Singh. Singh's face was a mask. He had the striped quarterstaff ground into the earth and he was pushing, pushing on it.

The man from Canton's eyes followed Edge and Singh. He looked back at Moffatt. He made a satisfied, expectant sound.

The smile widened. He pressed on the trigger until the creaking sound came and then, slowly, released the pressure again. The condemned man was shaking like a leaf.

Edge thought—

The man from Canton peered at Moffatt over the stock like an imp watching his mischief from the cover of a tree.

Edge saw the condemned man.

Moffatt said almost inaudibly, 'You don't face me down, you little Chink bastard. . .' The wind was strengthening in layers: it came as a deep, steady humming. The condemned man's breathing came in gasps. The man from Canton was smiling—

The birds came up from the valley in a single scream of sound. They shrieked over the hillock and tore the humming to shreds. There was a shot. A detonation. Recoil.

The man from Canton looked at—

The rifle had gone off. His glasses were gone. They had fallen off. The rifle was loose in his hands. The man from Canton—

There was a terrible howling sound. It went on and on.

Edge saw the condemned man. Half his neck was shot away. He rocked back and forth on the edge of the grave. Blood began pumping out like a fountain.

The man from Canton scrabbled at the rifle bolt. It was jammed. His glasses were gone—he touched in panic at his face. The bolt on the rifle was stuck fast. He—There was an intake of breath from the soldiers: a hissing, spitting sound. The condemned man rocked back and forth on the edge of the grave. The man from Canton fell to his knees and ripped at the hard earth for his glasses. The rifle barrel ground in the soil and stuck. He wrenched at it with his free hand. The condemned man howled in dying pain at the edge of the grave. His eyes came towards Edge. Edge's hand was spreadeagled against the seam of his coat: the fingers were rigid locked. The eyes came towards him. Edge's voice said, 'Oh my God—' He was above the condemned man with his pistol in his other hand—the pistol thrust itself at the side of the condemned man's head.

The eyes met his. The condemned man made a noise like a baby. His eyes were—The squat black shape of the pistol's muzzle exploded flame and sparks.

It was quick, sudden—two shots. In the thin morning air they came together: *bangbang*! and the condemned man, released, fell easily and limp into the open grave.

A long way off there was the faint sound of the rice birds,

high and moving away. He heard Moffatt's voice say softly, 'You're finished.' The voice said, 'My God, Edge, but you're finished now!'

Moffatt's voice shrieked across the killing ground at the man who had made his choice, *'You lying yellow Chink-lover, but you're finished forever now!'*

1941

1

Over the land and the river a great winter darkness had descended. It hung black and impenetrable in the granite cold folds of mountains to the north and in the ragged craters of shell-holes on the plain. It merged with the surface of the river in inky chill rivulets—the night drew the wan light and warmth of the day and enfolded it into its black immensity, like a sinister cloud. In the desolation of the Chinese city of Greater Shanghai surrounding the International Settlement held by the Japanese since 1936 irregular rows and clusters of street lights glowed on reduced power, some of them flashing and dying as the filaments grew weak and lit areas of torn-up streets and curbs as the wet fur of night creatures scuttled and scavenged deep in ruined cellars and dark deserted ruins of rooms and buildings. There was the long, raw throated howl of a domestic dog gone mad and vicious with hunger and loneliness, then abruptly, a single rifle-shot that shattered its brittle rib cage as someone—a Japanese night patrol in search of curfew breakers—destroyed it. From somewhere on the outskirts of the Japanese occupied section there was a surprised human shout, then a scream as a long bayonet was rammed through clothing and flesh into the hard ground. There were more shots—a series of rapid pops from an automatic pistol and then, as a group of stalkers and their victims met somewhere in the glow of a street lamp a volley of rifle fire and the eruptive burst of a hand grenade. For a long moment there was a scream that carried on across the darkness then suddenly, as a raised sword glittered in the street, muteness. Through the shelled and desolated suburbs and along the perimeters of wire fences, gangs of silent men flittered through alleys and lanes carrying weapons, searching and glancing back over their shoulders. Men in heavy hobnailed boots listened for the sound of sandals and bare feet of looting Chinese in rags, while men in rags finished off their victims silently in doorways and culs-de-sac and listened and watched for patrols of squat Japanese carrying flashlights and sniper rifles.

In the remains of the greatest city in China old scores were paid off in the silent geography of night. The stealth and fear and sweat on the palms of the hands, the prickling at the back of the neck, were living things, serpents.

On the Bund, along the foreshore of the river, all the great buildings of the International Settlement were grey and still, shuttered up. There was a young man on a bicycle piling up cardboard boxes in front of the Russo-Asiatic Bank, rugged up against the cold in a bear's fur of three or four woollen sweaters. He worked hurriedly, placing marked boxes below the brass nameplates of the various tenants of the building. There were lights along the foreshore and in the centre of the wide road—he tilted the tops of the boxes to read the pencilled characters on their lids. He was delivering severed heads as messages of warning—he had to get the correct message below the correct nameplate. The messages were, politically, a matter of indifference to him—he ran a clearing house industry.

He set the last box below the nameplate of its intended recipient and cycled by into a knot of refugees by a tram shelter. There was a thump as they killed him for his clothes. Someone rang his bicycle bell and then dropped the machine with a splash into the river.

A police armoured car came by at top speed, its blacked out lights casting rectangular prisms of light on the grey macadam. Eyes from inside surveyed the locks on buildings. The vehicle went by the naked corpse and did not slow down. From somewhere inside the steel cabin there was the crackle of a radio message being received, then the clang of a hatch being bolted down as the vehicle turned off quickly into the darkness of sidestreets.

It was said that for the first time in a hundred years, alligators had come down the river into the mudbanks. They had black reptilian Japanese eyes. It was said you could hear them scrabbling on their strong claws along the edge of the embankment. It was said during the day they sank below the surface of the mud and waited. You could hear the popping of their air bubbles just as it became dark.

No one had seen them. It was said they were there. It was said they multiplied. It was said their young were born old and full-size. The Japanese had lists of ordinary people. It was said no one—not even the Japanese soldiers—knew what the lists represented. The lists came from Tokyo—it was said the Emperor had magic powers and he went into a trance and made the lists.

In the suburbs outside the International Settlement all the buildings and streets had been bombed and shelled to rubble. At night, rats scrabbled audibly to get out from under the bricks.

It was said that everyone on the Emperor's lists was to be shot.

Hiding in their houses, families heard the sounds of the wind as it blew down deserted streets and overturned baskets and boxes outside their doors—or was it the sound of a footstep? Sounds tapped and scraped, magnified—the sound was something moving in the corner of the room, or downstairs. They tensed. The wind howled and meandered through holed and shattered buildings like lost souls in a labyrinth of brick connecting rooms: they heard the wind whispering at tiny cavities in the mortar, they heard it hissing down the sides of buildings like poisoned water. In the darkness, families sat in secret rooms; they heard muffled screams in houses down the street: they heard the snapping of birdcage bones as amok broken electric cables slithered and jumped in flashes of blue flame: they heard, frequently, the shrieks of the cornered—they heard shots or the thud of a long knife. Their mouths were dry. All the saliva in their mouths had become arid. They listened and trembled.

They heard a single aircraft pass quickly over their roofs: a Japanese night fighter looking for lights. Far away, up on the darkened hills, they heard the ragged eruptions of bombs as the aircraft dealt with a single yellow campfire where none should have been.

The night went on endlessly. The families dropped off luxuriously to a heavy lidded, irresistibly closing-in sleep. They jerked awake, terrified, their eyes staring out into the darkness.

Constable Singh stood rock still at the intersection of Gordon and Outlands Road on a raised white platform, his white gloved hand resting on the controls of the metal box that activated the traffic lights. He pulled the lever down to turn the lights on Gordon Road to green.

At the corner of Gordon Road an American Marine raised his head above a heavily sandbagged gun emplacement and peered across the road to the Japanese side. The Japanese side was quiet—there were a few bored sentries sitting on stools on the other side of the wire making tea. They, in turn, peered at the Marine. The Marine stretched hugely with boredom and lit a cigarette. Constable Singh raised the lever and turned the traffic lights to red. There was no traffic coming—people stayed away from the perimeter areas—he waited the required length of time and lowered the lever.

Gordon Road paralleled the perimeter. Everything was early morning quiet: Constable Singh switched the lights there again to red.

Thirty feet from him on Outlands Road which ran directly into the Japanese occupied suburb of Yangtsepo, there was another identical signal box controlled by a Chinese collaborator in Japanese uniform. The Chinese collaborator had his lights set permanently on red. He watched the steady changing of the Gordon Road lights without interest. He looked over at the American Marine and made a half-smile. The American moved the barrel of his Springfield rifle a few inches to the left on the sandbags and the Chinese collaborator looked away. One of the Japanese soldiers noticed the movement and stood up, went towards a pyramid of stacked Arisaka rifles and took one up. The Marine cocked his head to one side and did something to his Springfield that made a sharp click. The Japanese soldier paused for a moment with his rifle held loosely in his hand, pretended to rub a speck of dust from its stock with his finger, then replaced it. Behind the tea drinkers, stretching away down the road into the centre of the Japanese-held territory there was nothing but shelled and bombed-out desolation. The Japanese soldier glanced at it significantly. Singh heard a voice behind the sandbags say, '*Dirty sonofabitch. . .*' and then Singh turned his lights back to red again.

There was nothing much doing this morning: the Chinese collaborator—a member of the Tao Tai, New Way organization formed by the Japanese, decided to stroll over to his friends the Japanese for tea. Half way, he stopped. There was the sound of sirens coming. The Tao Tai policeman went quickly back to his control box. The Japanese sentries on the other side of the wire stood up and retrieved their rifles. There was a heavy double-clicking noise from the Marines' position.

Singh turned his lights to red, glanced down the road and turned them to green again.

Two police trucks led by a 1938 black Nash flying the pennant of the Shanghai Police came into view. The Tao Tai policeman left his lights on red and put his hands on his hips. The convoy swept past him without pause and halted momentarily beside the Japanese soldiers. A piece of paper was produced (Singh heard Deputy Assistant Commissioner Moffatt's voice), the Japanese soldiers saluted, and the convoy went quickly along the desolated street towards Japanese military headquarters with their sirens still blaring.

Two of the American Marines watched as the Tao Tai policeman scuttled angrily towards the Japanese sentries to protest that his red light had been ignored. One of the Americans grinned at Singh.

Singh moved his lever to reset the traffic lights to red. The American's face grinned at him expectantly.

Constable Singh, stone-faced, looked down Gordon Road for traffic.

The American said angrily, 'Son of a bitch!'

The sound of the sirens died away.

2

Edge, still dressed in pyjamas and dressing gown, sat at the set breakfast table in his fourth floor apartment. By the table there was a large picture window overlooking the Bund and the river: he watched a little biplane gliding above the grey water like a model. The aircraft made no sound. In the banks to port Edge could see the wooden propeller locked off. He thought up in the morning air the wind would be making a whistling sound. There were a few heavy clouds in the sky—the little grey biplane sailed beneath them. Edge had a morning chill in one of his shoulderblades. He rotated it and made a grunting noise of relief. He touched his face with the hand holding the cigarette and felt lines and wrinkles on his face. The newspaper was full of news of the continuing American economic blockade of Japan and the Japanese-American peace talks in Washington. The headline said there had been no progress.

He lit his second cigarette of the morning and watched the airplane.

He touched his shoulder, massaged it, and wondered about things.

Edge's Number One Houseboy, a slight wizened man of indeterminate sexagarian age wearing silk trousers and a white servant's jacket, stood at the kitchen door and surveyed the room disapprovingly. He sniffed at the smell of Virginia cigarettes before breakfast, glanced down at the tray in his hands, came forward to place it noiselessly on the edge of the breakfast table and, in one deft movement replaced the ashtray and burning cigarette significantly with a full coffee cup and saucer, waited until Edge took a sip of the black coffee and then, and only then, moved sugar and milk towards it. He cast a surreptitious glance at Edge's dressing gown and pyjamas, at the progress of the morning light through the window, looked disapproving, and stepped back a pace out of direct view and waited. The airplane over the river was going round and round.

Edge said over his shoulder, 'He hasn't enough petrol to fly with the engine on.' He touched at a piece of bacon with his fork.

The houseboy looked uninterestedly at the window.

'It's Mr Hooper.'

'Breakfast b'long number one good?'

'Breakfast is fine.'

He looked out the window again. Edge heard him making a clucking sound. 'Master, you thinkee Japs fight bang-bang Melicans and Blitish—come this side bang-bang? Come chop-chop soon?'

'Probably.'

'Why Master thinkee that-fashion?'

'Master thinkee that-fashion because Master—' Edge said irritably, 'Why the hell don't you speak proper English?'

'No savvy ploper English.'

'Yes, you do.' Edge said in Shanghainese, 'Or Chinese.'

'Master, Boy talk-talk Pidgin talkee. Master no savvy Chinee.'

'That's a bloody lie for a start.'

'No savvy, Master.'

'Master savvy Chinee. Savvy?'

'No savvy, Master. Talkee only Pidgin.'

26

Edge said in Chinese, 'Pidgin is for ordering people about. There are things you cannot say in Pidgin.' They had had this conversation before. 'You pretend you don't understand proper English when, since I taught you myself, I know you do.' He glanced out the window and added, 'And since I speak Chinese at least as well as you do—'

Lee said, 'Not ploper talkee Chinee with—'

'Then why did you ask me to teach you English?'

'Better Number One Houseboy. Savvy quick-time orders from Master—good face for Number One Houseboy talkee Blitish-Melican—better all time Blitish-Melican Masters—not got to workee for Chinee Master—'

Edge said in Chinese, 'Heaven help you with your imperial mentality when the Japanese come in.' He used the slang expression "dwarf bandits".

Lee said, 'I stay with you.' He asked abruptly, 'Why you long-time same thing Sergeant? Why you no Inspector?'

'That's none of your damned business.'

'When Jap man come we go catchee ship home side.'

Edge put aside the plate and touched at his coffee cup.

'Go catchee Missy all go home side.'

'This *is* home side.'

'Go catchee Missy—'

'Missy is gone.'

'Missy come back.'

'Missy is not coming back. My wife has left me. Understand?' He looked suddenly out the window, 'Anyway, your takings from the household expenses are a damnsight better now than they used to be. Missy kept your squeeze down to five percent.'

'Missy Chinee lady. Savvy squeeze percentage. Missy—'

Edge said, 'I don't want to talk about Missy. She's gone. If the Japanese come you'll be all right. They're even worse snobs than you are. As much as they hate the Chinese they can't help themselves thinking that because it's an older civilization the Chinese still know more than they do. So if you play your cards right, you can tell them how to behave and when to smoke cigarettes at breakfast and the correct language to use between master and servant and, provided they don't shoot you for insolence, they'll probably make you a General.' Edge said, 'But until they do, I don't want to hear any more talk about Missy, all right?'

'Missy make you sad man.' Lee said, 'Houseboy at Master

Deputy Commissioner Moffatt's house say you do something keep you all-time Sergeant. What you do? Get big squeeze money from Police job? O.K. We all go catchee ship home side.'

Lee said, 'Brothel lady Saturday night-time no same as Missy—'

'That's enough!' Outside the window the plane was circling. Edge said softly, 'It takes a lot of money to buy a passage out at the moment.'

'Takee big fashion squeeze.'

'I should have taken big fashion squeeze long ago. No one bribes the police any more. They're all saving their money for the Japs. Even if I had anywhere to go.'

Lee said enthusiastically, 'I loan you money—'

'What did you say?'

'I loan you money. Very small interest.'

Edge said, 'I have to go to work.'

He stood up, went towards his bedroom, and closed the door behind him.

Above the river David Hooper was gliding. At five hundred feet, with its engine turned off, his biplane whistled above an abandoned extinct collier caught in the rising mud. The air rushed back over the nacelle of his engine, over the cowling, and pressed against the windscreen on the open cockpit. He heard the air rushing through the wires and supports between the wings, pinging at them like piano keys. He banked a fraction to the right and as the wings came up he saw the collier's smokestack, tall and soot encrusted, cold and dead. There was a single motor patrol boat at anchor in the centre of the moving mud. He saw its plywood bridge and white-painted deck.

He touched at his goggles. The wind flowing over the canvas-covered airframe set the leather of his flying helmet flapping. The airplane bobbed against a rising air current and he turned its nose and slid silently through the air above the Bund, the shoreline of the International part of the city. He passed over the sandbag emplacements at the fenced-off perimeter of Gordon Road. He saw soldiers and steel helmets and black guns poking out from cover. There was a No Man's Land that separated the Settlement fences from the fences of the Japanese: he saw people looking up at him from inside concrete bunkers. He saw Japanese flags on flagpoles. He leaned the stick to the right and he was out over the river again and moving silently, like a ghost. The wooden propeller on his patched-up first world war Nieuport 17 was stopped and parallel to the earth: the air rushed over it and set it vibrating. He made a gentle descending turn and passed again over the dead and extinct collier.

He tilted his helmeted and goggled head back in the cockpit and drew in clean, free air.

Far out over the river, Hooper switched on his engine, and with the noise of the pistons drumming in his ears, pulled the nose of his aircraft up to prepare to land. Rising two hundred feet to get the approach path right, he went reluctantly down towards the reality of the morning.

It was 7:30 a.m. Friday the twenty-eighth of November, 1941, and the all-conquering, ever victorious Japanese Army of Occupation in China had been poised at the gates of the International Settlement for almost five years, awaiting their chance.

3

Captain Masonobu Isogai of the Imperial Armoured Corps in China stood in the centre of the deserted road like a sentinel, looking up. There were Japanese tanks and the three vehicles from Moffatt's convoy parked at various points against the pavements, but they were stationary. In the grey morning mist that still hung in layers about the leafless trees and stumps and rubble of the street Isogai was a single figure in a landscape. There were minute shards of ice about his black leather boots where he had strode over puddles: he stood with his legs a little apart in an at ease position and directed his gaze upwards. He was immobile. He wore no gloves—his hands, clasped together behind his back, were steady and still. His eyes, unblinking beneath their hoods, stayed unyieldingly on the building in front of him.

The building, standing alone in the desolation of the bombed and shelled-out street, was a granite seven storey monolith that before the 1937 fighting had been a Chinese department store financed by Europeans from the International Settlement. Now it was the Greater Shanghai sector headquarters of the Japanese Army; Isogai's eyes stayed fixed on a curtained window at the centre of the fifth floor. There was a white flagstaff protruding at an angle from a lintel under that window—the Rising Sun on it was icy stiff and folded back on itself. There were no sentries on the building. It looked deserted, like a pyramid.

The folds of skin under Isogai's eyes contracted minutely. They were hard and unmoist, slanted, like a cat's.

Isogai waited. His breathing came regularly and lightly. There were tiny white ice flecks on his eyebrows—his mouth was hard set and emotionless.

There were Japanese tanks and the three vehicles from Moffatt's convoy parked to one side of the building. Behind his fogged glass one of the Shanghai police drivers started his motor and let it tick over to keep up the engine temperature. It made a regular, well maintained idling sound that went on for a few moments until the gauge read correctly and the driver was satisfied or until he was embarrassed by the sound in the silence and turned it off. The exhaust gases combined with the mist and drifted over towards the stone steps to the entrance of the building. Outside the building, at the base of the steps, lying side by side, were the bodies of two dead men on stretchers, covered completely by Japanese flags. The flags were tucked in under the length of each body and again under the backs of the heads and heels. The mist floated over the mounds and dissipated at the top of the steps.

The driver of Moffatt's Nash, parked at the head of the convoy, wound down his window and glanced out. He had a burning cigarette in his hand. He looked at the line of tanks and peered slyly at Isogai. Isogai stood still. The driver tapped the ash from his cigarette carefully onto the flat roadway. A momentary muscle flickered at the meeting of his cheekbone and eyesocket and he looked away, took his arm and cigarette back inside the car, out of view, and wound the window up.

Somewhere far off, in a street or an alley in the Chinese city, away from the sealed-off and deserted military compound, there was a ragged series of shots, like firecrackers, then silence.

Someone coughed. It was one of the tank crew clambering from a hatch in his tank carrying a greatcoat. He manoeuvred himself carefully down the steel sides of the tank and started to come over. He stopped for a moment, thought Captain Isogai saw him out of the corner of his eye, and raised the folded grey coat on his arm to offer it.

Isogai's eyes stayed on the window. He shook his head once, slowly. No other part of his body moved. The tank man swallowed and glanced back at his tank. He looked back to Isogai. The tank man stood in the cold mist, still holding the coat. He became motionless.

Fifty feet from the flag covered bodies Moffatt had brought in from inside the International Settlement, Isogai waited.

In the fifth floor room Commander Nobata's hand suddenly tugged decisively at the edge of the curtain. For an instant, his eyes travelled to Moffatt, then continued about the small office. He blinked. There was an angry tightness to his mouth.

Moffatt enquired, 'Is there anything wrong, Commander?' He had a sheaf of papers on his lap. He leaned forward in his chair and put the top document on the leather bound blotter on Nobata's desk.

Nobata was sixty years old, a soft-faced man. There was a gold decoration on the right breast of his dark blue naval uniform, rubbed down at the edges from years of polishing. He touched it the way a woman might put her hand to her throat. He was used to wearing soft white gloves with his uniform: his hands were podgy and very clean. Still standing by the curtained window, he glanced down at the floor.

Moffatt said, 'Commander—?'

'Are those the death certificates?' Commander Nobata's English was careful, precise. It had a faint croak to it.

'Yes.' One of the buttons on the waistcoat of Moffatt's three piece suit had become undone, the second from the top. He did it up casually, with one hand, then let his thumb and forefinger hook themselves into a fob pocket. He leaned back in the chair. 'They're in order, of course.'

'A good physician?' Nobata's eyes strayed to the curtain. His braided blue cap lay upside down on the desk. The remaining hair above his ears was stubby and grey.

'Yes.' Moffatt released his finger from the pocket, 'Naturally, we regret the occurrence of the incident, but as you will appreciate—'

'And the list of personal effects found on the bodies.'

'Is attached. As I was saying—'

'Yes.' Nobata came and sat down at his desk, facing the

European. His fingers came up under his chin thoughtfully. 'It is assumed they were both dead when found?'

'They were dead on arrival at the hospital.'

'Oh? Does that mean—'

'They were both dead when found.'

'I see. The form of the matter.'

'The formality, yes.' Moffatt said, 'You will appreciate, Commander, that although both bodies were found inside the International Settlement and the likelihood is that they were killed where they were found, even out of uniform they had no right to be there.' He studied Nobata's face carefully, 'It is entirely likely that they were recognised by Nationalist or Communist guerillas as Japanese military personnel and on the spur of the—'

'What were they doing inside your Settlement? Have you any notion?'

'I have no idea.'

'A matter for us, rather than you.'

'I should have thought so. With respect.' There was a framed portrait of the Japanese Emperor on a white horse on the wall behind Nobata's desk. (All the other walls were bare and, except for the desk and two chairs, there was no furniture in the room.) 'The Shanghai Municipal Police have no jurisdiction in the case of members of the Japanese forces. In the same way that your forces have no interest in non-Japanese residents of the International Settlement.' Moffatt said, 'The incident is very regrettable.'

Nobata glanced at the curtain.

Moffatt said, 'You will find all the papers completely in order.'

Nobata nodded.

'This incident, Commander, particularly in view of the current peace talks between the Japanese and American governments in Washington, which, in my opinion—'

Nobata said, 'There is no need to labour the obvious. I am aware of the current situation.' He said, 'It is the official view of the Japanese government that with good will on both sides the Americans will suspend their economic blockade of Japan and, in turn, the Japanese government—'

'Yes?'

'In turn the Japanese government will see to the people's best interests.' Commander Nobata glanced unconsciously at his cap on the desk. It bore the Japanese naval emblem above its peak.

32

'As a naval man I was depressed by the sight of so many ships leaving anchorage in the river in your International Settlement. Shanghai, up until recently, was one of the great ports of the world—certainly the largest in Asia.' Nobata said, 'I believe the river silts up very quickly at this time of year.'

'Normally, the Whangpo River Conservancy Board keeps it dredged. Their equipment was confiscated.'

'Yes.'

'—by the Japanese Army. Their offices and equipment were situated outside the Settlement in Greater Shanghai—'

'Which the Japanese Army now controls.'

'Just so.' Moffatt said, 'I suppose in time of war, one must—'

'One must, Mr Moffatt.' Nobata nodded pleasantly, 'Those of you remaining in the International Settlement must sometimes feel like a flea riding on the back of a tiger.' He glanced at his soft hands and brushed them on the surface of one of the documents.

'I was not under the impression that tigers were prone to fleas.'

Nobata said, unperturbed, 'If you know anything about Asia you will know that the two great forces contending for it have always been China and Japan. China and Japan have been at war, in one way or another, for the last forty or more years. Foreign nationals resident in Treaty Ports like Shanghai and Hong Kong are in rather a paradoxical position in the light of Japan's present ascendancy in China.'

'By your use of the word "present" I assume you envisage the possibility of the situation being reversed.' Moffatt said blandly, 'Your English, by the way, is extremely good.'

'I learned my English in England in the diplomatic service. You agree your situation is—delicate?'

'The situation of the Shanghai International Settlement remains, as it has always been, founded firmly on law. As you say, it is a treaty port.'

'But of course your licence to occupy a small part of China—a foreign country—was granted following a war.'

'As indeed is your licence to occupy it all.' Deputy Assistant Commissioner Moffatt said plainly, 'I am aware that the deaths of these two soldiers might be thought sufficient provocation for the Japanese Army to invade the Settlement in order to "pacify" it. Since you, Commander, are the senior officer in the area immediately adjacent to the Settlement I can only ask you directly if that is your intention. The display of coiled aggressiveness presented to me in the street outside could hardly have failed to instil certain doubts as to your peaceful intentions.'

'The sovereignty of the International Settlement is recognised by international convention.'

'Indeed it is.' Moffatt said, 'However, the subject under discussion has been international warfare, has it not?'

'Only in passing.' Commander Nobata said quietly, 'We all have to justify the form rather than the shadows of our actions to our superiors.'

'I'm sorry, my mind fails to comprehend subtlety in cold weather.'

'Then you are a poor diplomat to send in November.'

'I am a policeman. There is no question of diplomacy involved, frigid or otherwise. Two of your people entered sovereign territory illegally and were, just as illegally, murdered by persons unknown. We return the bodies to you in a respectful and ceremonial manner—'

Commander Nobata said suddenly sharply, 'You have left them out in the street!'

'Your second in command *ordered* them left there. It is not for me—on what amounts to foreign soil—to question his directions.'

'What is the possibility of your apprehending the murderers?'

'I couldn't say. In any event, since the crimes were committed on sovereign neutral territory the perpetrators could hardly be handed over to—'

'Is that to say they would escape punishment completely?'

'They would be punished according to law.'

'So I can put that in my report to my superiors in Tokyo.' Nobata smiled. 'Good.' He asked lightly, 'Do you happen to have a hobby, Mr Moffatt?'

'I beg your pardon?'

'I mean, do you, um, collect stamps, or learn languages, or—'

Moffatt said uneasily, 'Well, I—Well, I'm a great letter-writer, as a matter of fact.'

'Oh, yes? To, um—' Nobata's soft face creased for a moment to find the word, 'To *penpals*?'

'To my family in Scotland.'

'Indeed?' Nobata smiled again. (Moffatt tried to read his face.) 'When I was at the London Embassy, Scotland was one place I never managed to visit. Perhaps being young I always thought there would be another time.' He said, 'As I approach retirement age I find myself a man totally without outside interests. I thought perhaps your hobby might be something unusual that might appeal to me.' He added quickly, 'You are about the same age as me so it must be a common problem.' He asked, interested, 'Do you intend to publish your letters?'

'I thought I might. At the appropriate time.'

'Very good.' Commander Nobata said, 'My second in command, Captain Isogai, is very much his own man. His display of coiled aggressiveness as you term it is not meant to intimidate *you* at all. If the chances of apprehending the murderers are slim I would appreciate your candour.'

'Then candidly, they're not good.'

'Ah.'

Moffatt said warningly, 'The International Settlement is sovereign territory. It is conducted jointly by more than a dozen nations, including Great Britain and the United States. To attempt an invasion on the pretext of—'

Nobata raised his hand, 'I am satisfied to tell my superiors that police enquiries into the matter are proceeding and that no punitive action is called for.'

'That seems eminently sensible.'

'You appreciate, of course, however, that regular reports should be made concerning that progress, and that they should be made personally to me by a police officer of equivalent rank. That is, by someone of command level. Either yourself or the Commissioner.' He paused. 'While I, at the same time, appreciate that both you and the Commissioner would be far too involved in daily administration to be able to execute such personal reports.' His face remained pleasant and soft. The eyes were a little different. Moffatt furrowed his brow. 'Tokyo, Mr Moffatt, requires assurance. My report will assure them. Should someone of lesser rank than yourself or the Commissioner be detailed to head the investigation I could hardly, as a matter of rank, allow myself to see him. He would therefore deal with only junior members of my staff. Reports from junior members of my staff often disappear without trace into the mire of bureaucracy. Possibly for years. . .' Commander Nobata suggested, 'Perhaps a Constable?'

'All my Constables are either Indian or Chinese.'

'Then a Sergeant?'

'It's a possibility.' He indicated the drawn curtains with a sweep of his hand, 'That officer outside in the street—'

Commander Nobata said, 'Mr Moffatt, Japan could not survive a war against England and America. Simply, we do not have enough oil.' He glanced at the curtains, 'And tanks and ships, unfortunately, do not run on blood and determination. It is important for us all not to be overtaken by events. That is surely the one lesson older men can have for youth.'

'I take your meaning.'

'Someone of unnoticeably low rank.' Nobata asked, 'Is there such a person?'

'I can find someone.'

Commander Nobata closed his eyes for a moment. He seemed like a man with, as he said, no interests in life. When he reopened his eyes Moffatt thought for a moment they seemed to be moist. Nobata said, 'No one wants war, Mr Moffatt—no one.' He said suddenly in an informative tone of voice, 'The Emperor's hobby is fish.' He turned quickly to the portrait and nodded to show he meant the Emperor of Japan, 'Yes. He is an accomplished marine biologist. He has written several scholarly monographs. It is an abiding passion with him.' He said, almost to himself, 'Wonderful.'

In the street, with the mist moving hissingly in currents above the two flag-covered bodies, Isogai nodded to the crew of the lead tank watching him anxiously through steel slits in the armour and, cautiously and without making a sound, they came out and stood in a line on the road.

There was a muscle going in the side of Isogai's face. The barbed wire perimeter of the International Settlement was less than a mile away, a glittering prize.

He watched while the tank crew lifted the stretchers and took them towards their tank for transport.

He gazed up at the curtained, secret room with hatred.

4

Noise and movement and colour, sounds, turmoil, the crushed, crowded comings and goings of over four million ragged people—it was only suddenly, when he stopped, and listened, and gazed at it, that Edge heard or saw it. People. Pressing and pushing their way through the narrow, basket lined streets, streets where even more people slept in doorways, pushed gigantic wooden wheelbarrows, grunted with loads of rice, cotton, food or livestock on poles across their shoulders, argued, cajoled each other, sold their strength, begged for alms and compassion in the gutters, or shouted or swore at each other. The Chinese. A convoy of wooden one-wheeled carts went into the thick of the forest of people, the pushers crying: 'Hai yo! Hai yo!' while hawkers shouted discounts on goods stacked in doorways and up dark precarious staircases. There was the cry from somewhere of 'Shang hei tz! Yao ma shang hei tz! Children! Children for sale!'

Behind him, rickshaw drivers and owners were arguing at the top of their voices with some decision of the Rickshaw Licensing Clerk as a chill, head high wind whipped at cotton clothing—blue jackets—and at black silk gowns and skull caps. The clerk, in turn, was kicking hard and loudly at a tinplate fender on one of the vehicles to prove graphically that his description was a fair one. The noise went on like mad static on a wireless, at top volume. If you ever lost control and clapped your hands to your ears there was the clammy sweat fear that, in that instant, you might go mad. There were smells, smells of all the sweat and movement and noise. They rose up like an aura of human body warmth and mixed with all the other things and objects and activities of the Orient and became something your body could not do without.

Standing at the edge of the rickshaw compound with fifty rickshaws from The Steam Train Company (each rickshaw had a little metal locomotive plaque affixed to the rear of its seat), with all the sounds and smells of an international city crushed too full of life and refugees, Edge thought, "What the hell have I done with my life? Since Missy left, what the devil have I done with each day except live through it?" He glanced towards the entrance to the compound where rickshaws were entering and leaving as their licences were either renewed and they could return to the streets to ply for fares, or had not been renewed and had to be returned to the rickshaw company for repairs, and wondered what his parents would have made of him. He thought, "They believed in a life of service to God." Edge thought, "I'm as old now as they were when they died and I don't feel as young and happy as they seemed to be." He thought, "Maybe it would have been better if Missy had stayed. Lee thinks I'm turning into an irascible old man who smokes before breakfast."

He asked himself, "Am I?" He thought abruptly, "Maybe I am" and went towards the clerk and the half-blind ageing harridan who, on licensing day, represented the interests of The Steam Train Company and asked her in clipped Shanghai Chinese, 'How are you, Mrs Hzu?'

The harridan looked up at him. There were cataracts on her eyes. At least a foot shorter than Edge in his uniform greatcoat cap, she took a step backwards like a ragged, sinewy bantam hen, and glanced down at her gnarled fingers. The odd thing was that she always wore a brand of very expensive French perfume. 'Not so blind and so old that it isn't clear to me that your clerk is trying to cheat me.' She turned her milky gaze onto the unfortunate Chinese, a young police clerk in a drab Winter suit of poor cut and cheap lining, 'This'—she indicated a rickshaw at the head of the line-up of some thirty such vehicles—'is in perfectly good condition to carry fat Europeans with big behinds.' She stabbed at the clerk with an accusatory finger, 'He is taking more responsibility upon his sparrow shoulders than his position warrants. A dented fender is not grounds for taking the sole support of its puller and his family off the road for repairs.' She put her head to one side and gazed up at Edge in a way that suggested grandmotherly ire, 'Sergeant Edge, I appeal to you to display your well-known sense of fairness.'

'What does my clerk say?'

The clerk said, unintimidated, 'In my opinion, Mr Edge, the vehicle is unsafe.'

Mrs Hzu said, 'What does he know? Is he in charge?'

'Have you tested it, Mr Wong?'

'No, sir.'

'Give it a few good kicks and then see if you can wrench the fender loose.' Edge warned Mrs Hzu, 'If my clerk detaches any part of the vehicle by ordinary force then the Regulations deem it unsafe for public conveyance and the detached parts are confiscated.' He asked Mrs Hzu, 'Or do you abide by my clerk's decision on a cursory examination and accept his ruling that the licence will not be renewed until the vehicle is deemed by repair or adjustment to be fit for public use?' He thought suddenly, "Is this how I end up?" He cautioned Mrs Hzu, 'I should remind

38

you that, in law, a rickshaw so deemed to be unroadworthy should be transported to a place of repair on another conveyance.'

'The Steam Train Company appreciates that you allow us to take the rickshaws back to the factory under their own power, Sergeant Edge. It is a financial saving.' Mrs Hzu said suddenly, 'The Japanese aren't so particular about licences in the rest of Shanghai!'

Edge said wearily, 'Do you accept my clerk's ruling or would you prefer—'

'I have another thirty-six rickshaws to be licensed today! I can't waste all morning on one!'

'Yes or no?'

'I have to accept it!' Mrs Hzu said, 'In any other branch of the police, a clerk and his—'

Edge said quietly, 'I don't allow my clerk to take bribes.'

'You have a perfectly good office above the compound warehouse, why don't you go and rest in there like—'

'This is my job. When I decide to give it up and sleep away the days in an office I'll let you know. Can my clerk get on with it now or not?' A rich merchant came along the crowded road in his private rickshaw, his puller wearing an expensive gown of Canton silk to break in for his master by drenching it in human sweat. Edge said, 'I'm sorry about what appears to you to be the iniquities of the system, but the major concern is to protect the lives and welfare of the people who pay to travel in these vehicles.' Near the compound warehouse a foreman from one of the other rickshaw companies was beating a rickshaw coolie with a long stick to extract a confession that he had held back a portion of his takings. 'The world is full of iniquities. I regret that you'll lose your licence commission, but that's the law.' He said finally to fix the point that debate was concluded, '*Me yu fa tz*—there's nothing to be done.' In the street and in the compound, the noise went on and on. 'Mr Wong, please continue the inspection of the other vehicles.'

Mrs Hzu said acidly, 'When the Japanese come—'

'When the Japanese come you'll still be in work.' He glanced across at the coolie being beaten. The foreman was lashing him about the shoulders. 'And the coolies won't change their situation either.'

Mrs Hzu said with grandmotherly concern, 'That poor man is probably in debt with money lenders and in debt to his rickshaw company for the rent of his rickshaw. He makes ten coppers a day and he's lucky if he can afford a bowl of Grade B rice—and you don't give a piss!'

'No. And neither do you. The foreman of The Steam Train beats people too. And for exactly the same reasons.'

'Then why don't you take bribe money? Aye?'

'Because I don't have anything I want to buy.' Edge said, 'This has turned into a personal conversation and neither of us is here to discuss personalities.'

'When the Japs come, all this will change!'

'Nothing will change.'

'You wait until the Japs come!'

'If you like.' He turned to address his clerk.

Mrs Hzu shouted in a sharp, cracked voice, 'You people won't be able to corrupt the poor Chinese then! You people won't be able to draw the life's blood from the working masses and take it away in sacks of gold to the counting room at the Shanghai Club! When the Japs come the poor people of Asia will hurl you into the sea! There'll be no more crushing poverty for honest Chinese driven to debt and death by the Europeans—'

Edge said with a faint smile, 'Grandmother Hzu, if the Japanese hear you talking like that, they'll shoot you as a Communist.'

Near the warehouse, the coolie fell to his knees as the foreman rained blows down on him. Edge said, 'You're wasting my time—'

'You think you're so smug because you won't take bribes, because you never go into your office, because you stay out here in the compound and spoil business for everyone else! Where's your compassion for the poor people, for the—'

Edge said, 'Mrs Hzu, shut up.'

'Where's your profit? Where's your soft job and a soft woman? Where's your—'

'Shut up! That's an order!'

'How can a poor coolie make a living when people like you—'

Edge took a step forward.

'Go on! Strike a poor old blind woman!' Near the warehouse, the coolie's head was down. He had his hand behind his back trying to ward off the blows with his palms.

'The Japs will be here tomorrow or the next day! Maybe in three minutes, and you take the sole means of people's support off the road! Where's your—'

Edge shouted to the foreman near the warehouse, 'That's enough!'

Mrs Hzu said, 'I hope when the Japs come, that you *die!*' A tiny blue Topolino Fiat came to the edge of the compound and stopped. Against the warehouse the foreman stopped beating the coolie and looked across at Edge curiously. Mrs Moffatt got out of the car and locked it. Coming across the compound, she gazed at the line of rickshaws with a strange, sad look on her face. She was a tall, thin woman in her forties who had once been very beautiful. Mrs Hzu said in an undertone, 'I hope that when the Japanese come—'

Mrs Moffatt said quietly, 'Hullo, Jack.'

'Kate.'

Mrs Hzu said, 'Oh, I know who she is all right—'

Kate Moffatt's voice, like her eyes, seemed a long way off, distant. She asked softly, 'Can we walk, Jack?'

Mrs Hzu looked at her, trying to work out the meaning of the English words.

'Please, Jack.'

Mrs Hzu said evenly and flatly, 'Everything is going to change—' It was obvious the European Deputy Assistant Commissioner's wife didn't understand a word of Chinese. Mrs Hzu said, 'You'll see, everything is going to change!'

'Can you spare me the time, Jack?'

'Yes.'

Kate Moffatt said, 'I'd be so grateful.' She had a sad, mad look in her eyes. She asked, 'Can we find somewhere quiet?'

'All right.'

Kate Moffatt said again, 'I'd be so grateful.' She brushed a strand of long brown hair from her eye. There was a faint, hopeful smile at her lips. She said, 'Thank you very much, Jack.'

For her, one day, the noise had simply grown too loud.

5

Once, Shanghai had its walks and promenades and moments of tranquility and elegance, a sort of wonderful, unchanging almost courtly sense of slow movement and grace. Once, it had had the river, gently lapping at dusk with a wonderful cool breeze moderating the heat of the day, all the lights and bunting on ships and vessels twinkling and reflecting, stars everywhere in the giant night sky, and the sound of dance music and laughter drifting across moonlit water from the cruise liners farther upstream. The International Settlement. Bands and orchestras in Jessfield Park—the professional musicians, playing *Eine Kleine Nachtmusik* and Strauss as couples dressed in freshly laundered shirts and starched and scented dresses wandered together among the trees or along little well laid out paths, talking in whispers and dreaming, making their plans. The smell of flowers and tended grass, cooling night breezes and perfume, clear, young, strong skin and women's hair. Cigar smoke and gold watch chains across waistcoats.

The recently arrived colonial *riches* prospering, the rustle of fine clothing, the faint tinkle of fine bone china near the entrance to the park as ladies and their husbands took tea with silver pots and milk jugs in rustic wooden gazebos.

Secure, safe, thought to be immutable, protected by a high locked fence and prominent wooden signs that read in all the languages of the ladies and gentlemen, and more prominently in Chinese, NO CHINESE OR DOGS ALLOWED.

Now all such a long time ago. . .

Katherine Moffatt said quietly, 'Do you remember when they used to hold races here?' They were walking on one of the old roads that led from the park to the racecourse—a bridle track overgrown with brittle Winter grass—and she paused for a moment to smile at the memory of a day long gone, 'In May and September, wasn't it?'

'Yes.' There were circles of deep muddy water out in the empty training paddocks where shells fired over the International Settlement towards either the Japanese or the Nationalist lines had fallen short. 'The last time there were horses here was during the fighting in 1936.' He remembered someone from the Shanghai Jockey Club telling him that when the shelling was over he had had to destroy so many wounded animals that in the end his rifle breech had jammed with the heat. 'They used to be quite a social occasion, the races.'

'And the ladies used to wear their very best hats—imported.' There was a bitter wind blowing across the waste ground that caught Katherine Moffatt's hair and blew it briefly across her eyes before she brushed it aside with an abrupt gesture, 'I've heard Alec talk about the day with you on the hill. I've heard him talk about it again and again. About the shooting.' She said quietly, obscurely, 'But it's all too late now, isn't it?'

'It was a long time ago.'

'You and he were friends once, Jack.'

'No.'

'But you might have been. If things had been different.'

'Maybe.'

'—we could have all been friends—Alec and you, and me—and your wife—' She said earnestly, 'I'm sorry she left you. In a way, Alec holds himself—'

Edge said quietly, 'It was between her and me. My wife didn't feel she could continue to be tied to someone who had run out of ambition.' He asked, 'When are you leaving Shanghai?'

'Alec wants me to stay.' She looked up into his face. The corner of her mouth ticked once and then stopped. 'You and I—'

'There was never anything between us, Kate.'

'Not because I didn't want there to be. I felt sorry for you. I felt Alec had—Jack do you think they'll really come? The Japanese. Do you honestly believe they'll come?'

'I don't know. It depends on the Americans.'

'Why would the Americans want them in here? Their own people are here—people like Mr Hooper and—why would the Americans have put the Marines in here to guard us if they intended to let those yellow devils get in?' Her voice dropped suddenly, 'Jack, you know what they do to people.'

After the battle for Nanking in 1936 the victorious Japanese troops had been turned loose by their officers. The orgy of bayonetting and rape that followed had sickened an entire world. 'We're only one little part of China, Kate. The—'

'But we're Europeans! We're not Chinese! The British wouldn't let them into Hong Kong and Singapore! The British are reinforcing Singapore and Hong Kong. Alec says they're pouring men into India and—'

'I don't know, Kate. If your husband wants you to stay he must think you're safe. I'm only a Sergeant. I don't know any more about the diplomatic aspects of it than you do.'

'I wanted to be your friend, Jack. When your wife left—'

'I know that.'

'That was all. I just wanted to be your friend.'

'I know.'

Kate Moffatt said desperately, 'If you felt you couldn't trust yourself with me—'

'You're another man's wife. Your husband is third in charge of—'

'Jack—' Her voice changed, 'Jack, you know things. Everyone says so. Even Alec. Alec especially. That's why you make him uneasy. You know things no one else does.—About *Orientals*. About the way they think. About the way—' Her voice faltered. She halted him with her gloved hand on his arm, 'You were born here. You speak the language the way they do. Why, someone once told me he heard you talking to a Chinaman and unless he had been watching—if he'd heard the two voices in a room or—or somewhere—he wouldn't have been able to tell the difference between you at all. You—you're resigned to what's going to happen because you *know!*' She said very urgently, 'Who do we know? Who can we talk to? Chinese servants or a few overseas educated people—and they wouldn't say. And they know what's going to happen and we don't because there's a—there's something they listen to that we can't hear. Like a—like a secret harmony.'

'No.'

'Yes! Can't you see how alone we are? The Europeans—'

Edge took her by the hand, 'Kate—'

'Please, Jack. Can't you tell me? Just me. For old times? Because I once—' Her eyes were glistening with tears.

'Kate, I—'

'I read in a book once that Alec had said that there were hidden secrets in Asia that—they *know*, Jack, they know you understand them. What you did at the execution that day proves it. You wouldn't have taken pity on that man unless you felt you were one of them—if you didn't feel that you were—'

'Kate—'

'But it proves it, Jack! You know things! You—'

'Kate! *I would have done it for a dog!*'

'No!' Her voice echoed across the flat land.

'Yes, Kate!'

'There's more to it than that!'

'It was nothing but pure Christian charity!'

'You ruined your entire—'

'Then it was a mistake!'

'No! You don't think it was a mistake!'

Edge took her by both shoulders.

'Do you? You don't think it was a mistake, do you?' Her face grimaced. She felt very frail under Edge's hands, 'You're hurting me, Jack.'

'I'm sorry.' Edge dropped his hands. He stepped back. She was wearing shoes with high heels. They seemed very thin and feminine, not made to support someone on ground that had seen explosions and death and neglect. He tried to remember what her hands looked like without gloves. He remembered them as long and fine. 'I'm sorry, Kate.'

She forced a smile. 'Alec thinks you know something. I know that.' She glanced away, 'And he's going to do something about it too.'

Edge nodded.

'But it's a secret.'

'Listen, Kate—'

'No.' She looked like a little girl at a birthday party, 'No, it is. It's a secret.' She nodded to herself, 'And I'm not supposed to tell.'

'All right.'

'But if you ask me, I will.'

The wind across the area was bitter and chill. Edge said softly, 'It's getting cold.'

'I do know a secret. I do.' She put her hands in her pockets.

'I don't know what to say.'

'Say you want to hear my secret.'

'All right.' There was that strange light in her eyes. He asked gently, 'Please tell me your secret, Katherine.'

'Don't call me that! He calls me that! You have to call me "Kate"!'

'All right, Kate.'

She glanced down at the ground quickly, then back up again. She nodded, then said very quickly, 'The secret is that he's going to get you to save us.' She looked up to Edge's face and smiled. 'There.' She nodded again and smiled to herself, 'Alec is going to get you to save us from the Japanese because he knows you know things and he's a Deputy Assistant Commissioner and you can ask him because, by God—' (the tears were at her eyes again)'—because, by God, Katherine, your bloody husband is never wrong!' She said, 'I've begged him, Jack, but he won't send me home!' She almost shouted, 'Can't he understand I want to go home?' She put her hand to her face and said, 'Oh my God—!'

45

Edge said softly, 'We had better get back now.' He laid his hand on her shoulder.

Kate's eyes behind her black gloved hand stayed on the ground. Her voice said softly, 'He's going to have you find out who killed those two dead Japs so there won't be an incident. I heard him on the phone to the Commissioner. He said he was going to pick you.'

Edge drew her a little closer. 'If they come I'm sure your husband will—'

She looked up. Her face was instantly bright, 'Oh, but they're not coming now, Jack. He's got you. And he knows you know things. We'll be all right now.' She nodded to herself happily, 'We'll be all right now because we've got you.' She shook her head definitely, 'No, they're not coming now, are they, Jack?'

'No.'

'No. That's right. They won't come now. And Alec did the right thing making me stay because it sets a good example, and if he and I know that we're not really being brave because you're going to save us, then there's no reason why anyone else should know. Everyone will just think how brave we are.' She said, 'It's all like a trick really. It's a harmless little subterfuge that won't really hurt anyone.' She said with determination, 'And I was being silly to worry about it.' She threw her head back and then nodded. 'Yes.' She asked lightly, 'Do you remember when the Hunt Club used to ride past here?'

'The Paper Hunt Club?'

'The Paper Hunt Club. You were never a member because you had more time for the Chinese than us, but, yes, it used to come by here. Of course, in those days, before those boorish people, the Japanese, came we could ride out of the Settlement and through the Chinese city and out into the country, but, of course, I suppose we'll just have to wait now until they're gone and we can organize a new Hunt.' She said in a bored tone of voice, 'I don't suppose the Japanese have things like that and they'd never understand if we wanted to carry on while all this nonsense at the moment lasts.'

Edge rested his hand gently on her shoulder.

'No, they wouldn't!' She thought for a moment carefully, 'All the best riders have gone away anyway, at the moment—certainly the lady riders—' She asked, 'We couldn't get them back, I suppose? I suppose the Japs would be all silly about it, wouldn't they?'

46

'I suppose so.'

'I'm sorry your Chinese woman left you but if you must marry a Chinese I suppose you must be Chinese yourself.'

'Come on, Kate.'

'In a minute, if you please!' Kate Moffatt said, 'I'm not afraid, you know, not really—I just miss some of my friends who have gone home. Ladies.'

'I know that, dear.'

'I just don't think it's fair that Alec doesn't even think of that. But it's all right now because he's picked you. And Alec's always right. Isn't he?' She said abruptly, 'You and I could have been lovers, Jack. You and I. That's true, isn't it?'

Edge did not reply.

'When—when your wife left you and you were—' She said, 'I know you wanted to fall in love with me but you were too much of a gentleman. I was beautiful. Wasn't I?'

'Yes.'

'I was! I've looked at old photographs and—'

'You were very beautiful, Kate.'

'And it wouldn't have taken much encouragement on my part—'

'Not much.'

'I appreciate the fact that you were a gentleman. Deeply.'

Edge smiled at her.

'You do know secrets about the Orientals and I can respect your reasons for not telling me, just as after your wife left you respected me. I can appreciate that, Jack.' Her mouth began to tremble, 'It's just that I've never been to bed with anyone except Alec and—' Her voice was strained and staccato, 'And—and that—and that, you see—' She touched her eyes with her hand, 'And that seems really—awful, Jack, because now—'

Edge took her gently into his arms. The wind blowing across from the desolate, ravaged ground was boney-fingered and bitter.

Her voice pleaded suddenly, 'Oh dear God in Heaven, Jack, please don't let them rape me!!'

6

Hooper said evenly, 'Mr Chan, I'm just a small-change disbarred lawyer who happens to have a way with money and engines.' He stood, a slight, fair haired young man still dressed in flying boots and leather coat, watching his Number One Mechanic draining oil from the Nieuport's sump on its makeshift runway between two enormously long wooden warehouses. 'If a truck you supplied and I filled with some of the contents of one of my absent principal's warehouses gets itself blown up by a landmine in Japanese-occupied territory on its way to the Nationalist forces you represent, then all I can say is that I regret that the Nationalists are going to have to stand the loss.' He watched critically as a thin stream of oil flowed down from the engine of the tattered plane, 'I'm sorry that one of your drivers lost his life, but you'll appreciate that my principals still have to be paid.'

'Your principals are patriotic men. They are Chinese Nationalists themselves.'

'My principals are a consortium of Shanghai importers who have now moved their financial base of operations to the United States. The contents of the two big warehouses you see here represents their entire capital.' Hooper watched as the plane bucked a little in the cold ground wind that gyrated across the macadamized private road between the buildings. 'My principals, through their various families, have been involved in trade in the International Settlement for the past sixty years. As much as they may believe in the final victory of the Nationalists over the Japanese, they have to live in the commercial here and now. I promised to liquidate their holdings for them and they rely on me to do it, if not at a profit, then at least not at a loss.' Moses Chan was a short, balding Chinese wearing a black glazed gown with an embroidered waistcoat. He touched at his round framed spectacles anxiously. 'I'm sorry you lost one of your drivers, but smuggling materials like machine tools and engine parts is a dangerous business. Nevertheless, it's business. So I'm afraid you will just have to be prepared to bear the loss. The money you paid has already been transferred through Hong Kong to America.' Hooper caught sight of his mechanic gazing interestedly into the bucket of sump oil and called out, 'All finishee now, Henry! Go catchee new oil!'

Moses Chan paused for a moment. His English, like his forename, was the outcome of a transaction made some forty years ago that required on his part as a seven year old orphan that in return for an education he need only accept for the rest of his life a Baptist God and the attitudes that went with it. 'You are not suggesting, Mr Hooper, that you would sell the goods to the Communists?' He watched as the mechanic brought out a tin of oil from an open door in the left hand warehouse, 'Your principals would certainly not accept that? That would not be your advice to them? As a man who owes his second chance in life to China?'

'My advice to my principals was and still is, that to maximize profits, they should have shipped their seven hundred tons of stored goods directly to India. If, through patriotism they want to see the goods in the hands of the Chinese Nationalist forces then I'll do what I'm told.' He said suddenly, 'You're getting all this stuff: machine parts, tractor and marine engines, silk, everything at a highly competitive price—'

'I am doing this solely from love of the Nationalist cause—'

'I believe that. As I told you, I'm just small-change and gullible.'

'You think that I personally—?' Moses Chan began to raise his hands in horror.

'I don't give a damn. All I want is to empty the warehouses, crate my airplane out of here before the Japs come, and get out to Australia as quickly as possible.'

'Your old aircraft appears to mean a great deal to you.'

'All it means to you is that your people ship it overland to Hong Kong or Macao when the time comes. It isn't much for an entire Nationalist Army and a country full of guerillas to manage and it's part of the deal. Written in.' Hooper said abruptly, 'For your sake, it had better be.'

'Maybe one morning before breakfast the Japanese will shoot you and your airplane out of the sky.' He said, smiling, 'It's cold. Can we go inside one of the warehouses?'

'No.'

'I see.'

'No, you don't.'

'But you and I have been doing business together for over—' Chan said curiously, 'Why does it mean so much to you? The airplane?' He asked, 'If it does why do you not paint it?' He glanced at the patches of grey and green paint on the fuselage and the fading, almost indecipherable registration number on the tail, 'There must be ample paint in the warehouses?'

'More than ample.'

'Then why not paint it?'

'Because I prefer it the way it is.'

'Why?'

Hooper asked, 'When will your trucks be here?' He said quietly, 'The Japs won't shoot me down because, like the stocks in the two warehouses, they fondly imagine it'll be here for the taking when they arrive. The Japanese have a great love of machines and equipment. They don't understand them, but they collect them as symbols of the West and the twentieth century.' He asked again, 'When will your trucks be here for the next consignment?'

'Is it true that your principals left a quantity of industrial diamonds in your keeping as payment for your services?'

The Number One Mechanic had brought out a small wooden stepladder. He stood on the top rung pouring oil into a funnel inserted in the Nieuport's Le Rhône engine.

'What is true is that part of the deal was that you take out my plane when the warehouses are empty.'

Moses Chan said, 'I believe, Mr Hooper, that you are still wanted for embezzlement in New York—'

'You don't believe it at all. You know it for a fact. Otherwise you wouldn't have talked about second chances in life.' Hooper said, 'For the record, I was innocent and it wasn't embezzlement. It was a prospectus fraud issued by someone else and signed by me as their company secretary. I was guilty of not bothering to read what I was signing.'

'But you cannot go back to New York.'

'I can go back to certain conviction and up to twenty years in prison. If there are any industrial diamonds maybe they're to give me a new start in another country. Maybe they're to make sure of your continued co-operation.'

'About your aircraft. Which, of course—'

'Which of course would not be a matter of patriotic duty, but a matter of profit. And a separate financial arrangement.'

'I see.' Moses Chan nodded thoughtfully.

'If there *are* any industrial diamonds.'

'But there is most assuredly an airplane.'

'Most assuredly.'

'Then in that case the Nationalists will bear the loss of the truck.' He put his hands in his sleeves again. 'It is a question of enemy action.'

'I knew you would be reasonable.'

Moses Chan said, 'The trucks will be here Tuesday night if your amenable friend in the American military is on border duty.'

'My amenable friend is on duty.'

'Have you heard how the Washington peace talks progress? I heard that two Japanese soldiers were killed inside the Settlement yesterday. The bodies have been returned to Yangtsepo and the trucks carrying them have come back without incident, so presumably it was not the excuse to invade the Japanese seem to be looking for.'

'In that case, no doubt your trucks will be here Tuesday night.'

'Yes.' Chan frowned momentarily. 'With my driver dead, I will expect you to drive one of the trucks yourself.' He glanced at Hooper's eyes watching the mechanic work on the plane, 'Tell me, Mr Hooper, is there no aviation fuel in the warehouses?'

'Some.'

'Then why not use it?' Moses Chan asked curiously, 'Rumour has it that you buy what little fuel you can privately. If you have so little interest in China why not use what is here?' He put it to the young American, 'Or is it that secretly you do believe in China and hate the Japanese?'

'I'll see you Tuesday night.'

'I am most sincerely curious.'

'Are you?'

'I am, yes.'

Hooper smiled at him.

'About that and your funny little second-hand airplane. I really am most—'

Hooper said, 'You go to hell!' He stuck his hands in the pockets of his worn leather flying coat and clumped off to consult with his mechanic.

Chan watched him go. He had an amused private expression on his round bland face.

He touched at his spectacles thoughtfully.

The Japanese military hospital in Yangtsepo had been sited in a wired-off exclusive compound in the centre of the Chinese city. Silent and grey, on two stories, it looked out across the Whangpo River towards the mouth of the Yangtse River, twelve miles away. All the buildings within a radius of four hundred yards around the hospital had been first, bombed and mortared in the 1936 fighting and then, when it had been taken over by the Japanese Army and the few unevacuated Chinese patients put out in the streets or shot by the Kempetai—the Secret Police, razed to the ground by dynamite and flamethrowers. The hospital and the Japanese Army Headquarters a mile away stood tooth-like, like two sentinels on flattened waste land.

Inside the hospital, the two dead soldiers would be processed by respectful hands, their names and ranks noted, effects and family objects collected and placed in appropriate ceremonial boxes, consecrated by their service to the Emperor, and their ashes returned safely across the water to Japan. In Japan, candles would be lit in the houses of their families. Mothers and sisters would gather around the family shrine, kneeling with their heads bowed and, entering quietly and respectfully through little gardens, neighbours would wait silently at the steps of houses to be called in.

The two bodies had been taken up the steps of the hospital. They were inside, already part of the soil and history of Japan, like its mountains and rivers, inviolate and eternal. Isogai touched at his sword and, after a moment, standing alone on the steps, motioned for his waiting staff car.

He said softly to himself, 'No'. He touched again at the hilt of his sword.

He said to himself for the second time, 'No.'

He made a decision to act.

8

Hooper came out from a little wooden door in one of the warehouses and paused. Dressed in identical brown heavy duty coveralls as his Number One Mechanic, he stood with his hands in his pockets admiring his airplane. It was a sesquiplane—a one and a half winger, the lower wing thinner and shorter than the upper surface, almost like an extra forward elevator—eighteen feet long, eight feet high from the ground with sixteen and a half square yards of total wing area. Built in France at the Nieuport factories in Issy-les-Moulineaux in 1917, and powered by a hundred and ten horsepower Le Rhône 9J engine, it could give a top speed of 110 miles per hour at a top ceiling of eighteen thousand feet and it could keep that up for almost two hours. Hooper looked at it. It had taken him and his mechanic almost five years to restore and every part in it was original. He grinned to himself. Here and there were even traces of the original Great War colour scheme: patches of sky blue and black. The plane sat exactly true on the flat macadam, vibrating along the camber of its upper wing in the slight headwind between the warehouses. The wooden twin bladed airscrew was perfect in its chord: it had a wonderful warm patina where Hooper and the mechanic, night after night, had treated the wood with linseed oil.

It was his. Hooper went towards his Number One Mechanic grinning to himself. The mechanic, on a stepladder, finished pouring the fresh oil into the engine and grinned back at him, 'Airplane all number one order.' He was a young man about Hooper's age, a thin Chinese with small features, named Henry Chu, 'Special number one apple-pie order.' He grinned again and patted the nacelle. He asked, 'Putee away time?'

'Pipee-thinkee-lookee time.' Hooper drew two curved pipes from his coveralls, one from each pocket, and passed one to the mechanic as he came down the steps, then squatted with him on the ground beneath the locked propeller to fill them from a leather pouch. 'Gas tank empty?'

The mechanic nodded. He filled his pipe, lit it using a permanent metal match, and passed the flame in his cupped hand to Hooper. Clouds of smoke enveloped them. The mechanic said appreciatively, 'Apple-pie smokee.' He grinned again. 'Wantee look-see carburettor, David?'

'First look see airframe.'

'O.K.' The mechanic stood up and set his pipe firmly in the centre of his mouth. He asked as Hooper did the same and glanced exploratorily along the curved configuration of the tiny fuselage, 'David, you see muchee Japan man upstairs?' He pointed upwards with his index finger.

Hooper nodded.

'No shootee at Bert Hall?' The mechanic touched a wheel strut protectively, 'No bang-bang miss-miss Bert Hall? All apple-pie? Good apple-pie?'

'Mother's apple-pie.'

'No shootee one bang?'

'Not even a loud handclap.' Hooper said, 'Old Bert Hall flew over them and they just watched.'

'Bert Hall good top number one airplane.'

'You're a good top number one mechanic, Henry.'

The mechanic smiled. 'Good pilot man, David.' His face clouded, 'That man just gone, Chiang Kai Shek Nationalist man, all things still good order?'

Hooper nodded and bent down to tap out his pipe on his boot.

'Bert Hall still go safe?'

'Yes.'

The mechanic paused. He asked softly, 'Me too, David? Bert Hall, you, me, all go?'

'Yes.'

'Ah!' Henry said loudly, 'Good! Apple-pie number one! All go—good!'

Hooper said softly, 'We all go together: you, me and the Nieuport. You, me and Bert Hall.'

'Japan man no get plane, David. Melicans, Blitish, French, all go soon now. All go home-side. Japan man come and—'

Hooper said, 'You're going with me, Henry.'

'Number one best mechanic, David.'

'I know that.'

'Bad if Chinee helpee Melican if Japan man come. Wantee all machines, bang-bang!'

'By the time the Japs come everything will be gone. Including Bert Hall and us.' He said, 'We go Australia-side same time.' He looked hard at Henry's face, 'All time together. O.K.?'

'O.K.'

Hooper touched his mechanic on the shoulder as he turned to

look at the engine. 'You takee my word, Henry. O.K.?'

'O.K., David.'

Hooper said, 'Trust me.' He said softly, 'I promise you I won't let you down.'

'Good! Good!'

Hooper said, 'O.K. Now—'

'Smokee-lookee-thinkee Bert Hall time.'

'Right.'

The mechanic grinned at him.

They took out their pipes to refill them as they admired their airplane.

9

Isogai strode purposefully down the length of the fifth floor outer office towards Commander Nobata's room. Clerks stood to attention as he passed. He reached Nobata's receptionist's desk and returned the man's salute. The receptionist, a portly, middle-aged Sergeant with failing eyesight behind thick rimmed glasses, touched unconsciously at forms and files on his desk as he rose.

Isogai glanced back to the expanse of the outer office. There must have been fifty or sixty desks. A phone began ringing on one of the desks and the clerk standing at it—a dumpy uniformed woman wearing her hair in a bun—moved her hand surreptitiously to silence it. Isogai said in a clear, unraised voice, 'Carry on with your tasks,' and as one, the clerks returned to their seats. The phone stopped ringing as the woman took it up.

The fat clerk had sat down. He seemed poised to rise again.

'Inform Commander Nobata that Captain Isogai is here to see him.'

'Yes, sir.' The clerk started to rise, looked anxious and uncomfortable, and sat down again. He pressed a button on the internal telephone on his desk and relayed the message carefully, listened for a moment, and then replaced the receiver gingerly. He paused for another few seconds to eke out his time. He began to rise.

Isogai said irritably, 'Sit down!'

'Commander Nobata regrets he—' the fat clerk said, 'He regrets he cannot—at this time—'

Isogai looked at the sweat on the man's forehead. 'Contact the Commander again and inform him that as his second in command in the Shanghai sector I respectfully request a few moments of his time.'

'Yes, Captain.' The clerk did as he was told. Isogai watched while the inaudible reply came back through the earpiece. The clerk said, 'Commander Nobata says that if the matter is urgent he requests you to wait for a moment or two.' The clerk said on his own initiative, 'He is on the phone to Tokyo.' He half-rose again in his chair, 'If you would care to have my chair, Captain—'

'What is your name, Sergeant?'

'Onuki, Captain! Sergeant Clerk, Grade One!'

'Why did you lie?'

'Sir?'

'If the Commander was on the telephone to Tokyo you would not have dared interrupt him. Not even for me. Why did you lie?'

'I'm—'

Isogai said acidly, 'You are only a fat clerk. If you had been a soldier and you lied you could expect punishment. A soldier would not have lied.' Isogai said, 'If you lied to spare my feelings I should tell you that a soldier has no feelings. A fat clerk may have feelings, but fat clerks do not go into battle.' His voice stayed toneless and even, 'Do you understand what I am saying to you?'

'Yes, Captain.' The telephone buzzed and he stood up erect and listened in the earpiece for a moment. He informed Isogai efficiently, 'The Commander is free now, Captain.' He said suddenly, 'I apologize, sir.' He said as Isogai went towards the office door, 'I volunteered, Captain, but my eyes were too bad.' He said desperately, 'If you would have me, I would be honoured to give my life for Japan!' He said, 'Sir? Captain?'

Isogai stopped and looked at him.

The Sergeant clerk said, 'Please, sir—' Behind the pebble lenses of his glasses his eyes were large and pleading. A buzzer on his desk rang urgently. All over the room there was the

56

organized ant-like shuffling of paper and ringing of telephones.
Isogai said, 'Japan does not need your life.' He said with
vehmence, 'You fat, squinting man!'
He went into Nobata's office without knocking and closed the
door behind him.

10

In Washington, the Japanese peace negotiators Kurusu and
Nomura called on President Roosevelt at the White House.
People had gathered outside in the street and they watched as, a
little after midnight, the official cars passed the Marines on duty
at the White House gate and turned down Pennsylvania
Avenue towards the Japanese Embassy.

Two hours later, from another official building in the Capital,
a coded message was sent by the U.S. War Department to the
Commander of the Army forces in the Far East in Manilla,
Lieutenant General Douglas MacArthur. The message read in
part: NEGOTIATIONS WITH THE JAPANESE APPEAR TO BE
TERMINATED TO ALL PRACTICAL PURPOSES WITH ONLY
THE BAREST POSSIBILITIES THAT THE JAPANESE GOV-
ERNMENT MIGHT COME BACK AND OFFER TO CONTINUE
X JAPANESE FUTURE ACTION UNPREDICTABLE BUT
HOSTILE ACTION POSSIBLE AT ANY MOMENT X IF
HOSTILITIES CANNOT REPEAT CANNOT BE AVOIDED
THE UNITED STATES DESIRES THAT JAPAN COMMIT THE
FIRST OVERT ACT X THIS POLICY SHOULD NOT REPEAT
NOT BE CONSTRUED AS RESTRICTING YOU TO A COURSE
OF ACTION THAT MIGHT JEOPARDIZE YOUR DEFENCE
STOP

At the same time, the Naval commanders in the Pacific,
Admirals Hart and Kimmel, received their own version of the
warning, Hart in the Philippines and Kimmel at Pearl Harbour
naval base in Hawaii. THIS DESPATCH IS TO BE CON-
SIDERED A WAR WARNING X NEGOTIATIONS WITH
JAPAN LOOKING TOWARDS STABILIZATION OF CONDI-
TIONS IN THE PACIFIC HAVE CEASED AND AN AGGRES-
SIVE MOVE BY JAPAN IS EXPECTED IN THE NEXT FEW

DAYS X THE NUMBER AND EQUIPMENT OF JAPANESE TROOPS AND THE ORGANIZATION OF NAVAL TASK FORCES INDICATES AN AMPHIBIOUS EXPEDITION AGAINST EITHER THE PHILIPPINES THAI OR KRA PENINSULA OR POSSIBLY BORNEO X EXECUTE AN APPROPRIATE DEFENSIVE DEPLOYMENT PREPARATORY TO CARRYING OUT THE TASKS ASSIGNED IN WAR PLAN 46 X

That same evening, from the Japanese Embassy in Washington, Kurusu telephoned the Tokyo Foreign Ministry and spoke to Kumaichi Yamamoto in the American Bureau there. Every word of the clumsily coded conversation was intercepted by American Intelligence, and at 8 a.m. the next morning, President Franklin D. Roosevelt sent a personal message to the Japanese Emperor warning him that war was imminent and expressing the continuing desire of the United States Government for peace.

The Japanese negotiators telephoned Tokyo for further instructions.

11

On the road back from Jessfield Park, Edge looked out across the river. It was silting up faster each day. Along the banks and wharves even the fishing boats and sampans had been abandoned; already it was almost impossible to get a vessel of medium draft up from the mouth of the Yangste. Soon the mud and silt and desolation would flow over the tiny International Settlement from the river like primaeval ooze. He looked at Kate's face for a long moment.

At the rickshaw compound, they found Deputy Assistant Commissioner Moffatt waiting for them.

12

Isogai stood in Nobata's office, waiting. His eyes were narrowed: he watched while Nobata gathered confidential documents from his desk and, moving back in his chair, locked them away securely in the centre drawer. Nobata glanced up at the younger man—the papers did not concern him. He considered his bunch of keys for a moment and then, opening a side drawer, put them out of range of the coming conversation as well. Nobata selected a Corona cigar from a box also hidden in the key drawer, snipped its end with a silver cigar cutter and lit it carefully with an English Dunhill lighter. He took out an alabaster ashtray from the same drawer, placed it exactly in position on the desk and snapped the drawer closed. He puffed exploratorily lightly at the cigar, considered the colour of the ash, and, taking a final, full puff, rested his smoking hand a few inches from the ashtray and tapped the grey ash gently into it. He asked Isogai quietly, rotating the cigar in his mouth to put a thin film of saliva on the mouth piece, 'In view of our respective ranks and responsibilities, Captain, should I offer you a cigar or not?' He looked at Isogai blandly, like a religious Master testing a novice, 'Is yours the sort of family background where you would have learned to appreciate good food and conversation and cigars, or is it merely the background of a—'

Isogai said, 'My father was an agricultural clerk.'

'Oh. Then you are not from a military background.'

'My father was an agricultural clerk. My family sword comes from my mother's family. Her father was a—'

'I see. Then the answer to my question is that—'

'Who were they?' The tone was flat and direct.

'Who?'

'The dead.'

Nobata said, 'Would you care to sit down?'

'No. I would care to know, Commander, why you allowed the deaths of two Japanese soldiers to go unpunished. I would care to know why at this moment our troops are not in the Shanghai International Settlement restoring peace and order.'

'Because, my dear fellow, peace and order has not been lost.' Nobata glanced unconsciously at his chrysanthemum decoration. He flicked a speck of cigar ash from the tunic above it. 'And because we do not happen to be at war with the British and Americans and the French and further, because I have no intention of putting us into such a war through an error of judgement.' Isogai opened his mouth to speak, but Nobata went on over the top of him, 'The matter, in my opinion, is not a volatile one. This is not yet Manchuria where wars are instigated and won by junior officers. And for your information, the two dead men were spies. They were found in civilian clothes in foreign territory. By rights, if they had caught them, the Settlement authorities could have stood them up against a wall and shot them.' He added a little too quickly, 'In the event, they didn't. They were murdered by guerillas or criminals. They were not even regular troops, they were members of the Kempetai: the secret police.'

'The Settlement authorities told you all this—'

'No, I am telling you all this. As far as the Shanghai authorities are concerned they were shop-lifters or looters.' Nobata said, 'With an army recruited largely from the lower classes of Japanese society—from the ranks of agricultural peasants—it surprises no one that some might find the temptation of western goods too much for them.'

'You refer, I assume, to items like cigarette lighters and cigar cutters.'

'You are attempting to be insolent.'

'I am attempting to be a soldier.'

'And you do that best by striking melodramatic poses outside my window, do you?' Nobata said, 'You may think me a weak, insipid old man, Captain Isogai, but I am a weak, insipid old man who survived the campaigns of assassinations in Tokyo in the twenties and thirties and no doubt I shall also survive your posturing.' He said flatly, 'It would be a mistake to use the deaths of two spies as an excuse to send Japan to war. There are, you may know, negotiations going on in America at this very moment for the sole purpose of keeping Japan *out* of war.' He said quietly, glancing at the cigar, 'I talk to you in this fatherly way because, although you are a man of apparent military zeal and honour, you do not seem to have found the time to be equally zealous in the practice of political reality.'

'Japan is ready for war.'

'Is it?'

'Yes!'

'With everyone? With the entire world? With the British and the Americans and the Australians and the Indians—with everyone? Never mind that we are an island nation totally dependent on the imports of raw materials for our survival or that less than a hundred years ago we were a feudal country without a single breech loading rifle, let alone heavy armaments, Japan is, nevertheless, ready to conquer the entire world. Is that correct?'

'That is correct.'

'Is that what they teach young officers these days?'

'That is what Manchuria and China have taught us! That the Japanese army is invincible!' Isogai said tightly, 'It is only a matter of weeks until we are at war with the United States.'

'Is it?'

'Yes!'

'Unlike you, I am not privy to the intentions of the War Cabinet.'

'Your duty—'

'My *orders* are to garrison this sector of Greater Shanghai and put down any local opposition from the remaining elements of the Chinese Army and guerillas. My orders are to strip whatever valuable materials I may find here and ship them back to Tokyo. That is what I am doing—I have no brief to enter the International city; and unless there is a provocation of such flagrant proportions that it does not require justification of my actions to Tokyo, I shall not do so. And I do not consider the killing of two *spies* to be such a provocation.' Nobata raised his head a fraction, 'I have the traditional military caste's dislike of people who skulk in corners out of uniform and do their work by stealth.' He said with contempt, 'For all I know, off-duty, they *were* shoplifters. With scum like the Kempetai, nothing would surprise me.'

'General Tojo was the head of the Kempetai in Manchuria. Do you also call the Prime Minister of Japan scum?'

'Whatever I may think of General Tojo is none of your business. My duty is perfectly clear and I am executing it.' He said darkly, 'There are also other, more practical considerations against a full-scale invasion of the Settlement. Known to the Cabinet. But not—I regret to have to say—to junior officers.'

'You refer to the purchase of strategic goods from traitors there.'

'Do I?'

Isogai said suddenly, 'When I was posted to China, my mother stood in the market place of our village with a thousand stitches *obi*. One thousand people who passed by put one stitch into it, so I might wind it around my belly as both a protection from the cold and as tangible evidence that the wishes and hopes of my nation went with me. Like my sword, I wear it always—'

Nobata nodded. He examined his cigar sadly. It had almost burned away.

Isogai said, 'It is meant for war!'

'I am aware of the tradition—'

'It is meant for conquest and honour and blood and endeavour!'

'I am perfectly aware of the—'

'It is not meant for fat old men smoking cigars! If you wish to be safe, then stay safe—I will supply your cigars personally—*but let young men go into battle!*' He asked, 'Did you never fight? How did you earn the honour of your medals?'

'I fought the Russians in 1905! My ship was one of the first to engage their fire!'

Isogai said, 'Then give me Shanghai!'

'Times change.'

'Japan does not change!'

'Japan *has* changed! Young men like you have taken it over. Blood and enthusiasm for blood has changed Japan! A world war is—'

'A world war is Japan's destiny!'

Nobata said abruptly, 'The Shanghai Police have the incident well in hand. I will not be intimidated into rashness by you.'

'If you are a man of honour and a hero in battle, why do you not have your own ship?'

Nobata blinked.

'I do not accuse you of dishonour. I only ask why you do not command a vessel of war—'

The cigar had gone out. Nobata glanced down at his chrysanthemum decoration. It had been polished over the years until some of the plating had gone. It looked old and tawdry.

Isogai said, 'I will *share* the glory with you. The conqueror of Shanghai need not be a young man. Old men can do deeds of daring.' He waited, moving his head in tiny movements, looking for an opening, his eyes examining Nobata's face microscopically. 'Commander?'

Nobata closed his eyes. 'Back home in Japan—'

'Will you do it?'

'At home . . . in Japan, the—the Imperial Navy will—They

62

will not give me a ship.' His voice sounded a long way away, like an echo, 'I have asked them and they—it's a question of age and—and they don't trust me any more—' He said suddenly, 'I'm just an old man who's been left alone and no one cares about me any more.' He counselled Isogai abruptly, 'Marry young and have children—' Nobata said desperately, 'No one in the world gives a damn about me! Can you understand how that must feel?'

'I can understand it.'

'Can you? Can you really understand that?'

'Yes.'

'Can you?' Nobata said, 'My God, what a sorry pass I've come to!' He fell silent with his hand over his eyes, staring down over the years at the empty desk.

The little room was soundless.

Nobata said softly, 'My God, it's all so disgusting!' Behind his hand, he shook his head in emotion.

Unconsciously, Isogai touched at the hilt of his family sword. There was a faint smile on his face.

13

Three miles away, in the French sector of the international city, in a windowless stone room in the cellars of the Shanghai Catholic Mission School for Chinese Children, Father Olivier Duras of the Society of Jesus in China stacked the last of seventeen plywood tea chests neatly against a wall and listened. Above the room there was a corridor that led to one of the small chapels at the rear of the building. He listened without interest to the sound of small children there chanting a catechism in Chinese and thought that it had often been suggested by his superiors that by true vocation he was an archaeologist and his priesthood merely a convenient profession in which to practise it. Born in Paris fifty-eight years ago, he had spent almost his entire adult lifetime in China and he thought he was too old to change now.

He walked the length of the room, a tall, powerfully-built

man in clerical collar and suit, touching at the lids of the frail boxes with his fingers. Each of the chests had metal supports along their sides: Duras touched at one and pushed it. It was a light silver tinplate, nailed down. The dampness lay heavy in the pores of the thick walls and he thought, "The treasures stored in these boxes have endured two thousand years of climate, some of them, and the dampness of a few months more in this room isn't going to make much difference one way or the other." A faded typed note was glued to the top of the chest in question—the letters showed uneven pressure on an old and rickety portable machine—that read in French, *Pottery, blue glaze, Szechuan province, gathered during 1921–26. Ming?* and a typed signature *Fr. O. Duras S.J.*, and on another, *Shensi province, tomb ornaments, Chou dynasty, 5th–3rd Centuries B.C., excavated Feb–March, 1920.* He brushed a speck of grey dust from the words. He could still hear the steady chanting as the Chinese children, under the direction of the Dominican nuns, went through the unceasing business of learning what to say to God and he thought, "The Japanese, when they find this room full of my lifetime's work, are going to rip open the lids with the points of their bayonets and hurl the paper packing about in the air like coloured ribbon."

He touched at the Shensi box. "They'll put the little statues and ornaments in their pockets and trade them for cigarettes or *sake*. Or, because the boxes only contain useless treasures, they'll disintegrate them on the cement floor with the butts of their rifles."

He looked at the box by the rear wall. It contained a collection of old manuscripts saved from destruction during the Boxer Rebellion, each carefully catalogued by antiquity and subject and separately wrapped in oil cloth. He thought, "Not even useful for toilet paper." He thought, "They'll burn them."

He thought, "If only some of the things were useful." He squinted his eyes. He had a migraine coming. He could feel the damp sweat on the palms of his hands. He said aloud, with sudden vehemence, 'If only they were useful!'

He wondered what to do.

14

Commander Nobata composed himself. He waved his hand a little above the desk to dismiss something trivial and unimportant from ever having momentarily existed. 'Forgive me, Captain. I would ask you to forgive a tired old man an uncharacteristic display of emotionalism. To get back properly to the business at hand—' He said, shaking his head in self disapproval, 'Stupid and childish.'

'I am not the sort of officer to underestimate the strain of leadership, Commander Nobata. There is no need for apologies.'

'I—I appreciate that, Isogai.'

'It is hardly an enviable task and, taken over a great number of years of service, it would be surprising if, in the privacy of two officers talking together, the temptation to relax a little might not be . . . present.' He glanced at the curtained window, 'Modern times must be trying for you.'

'You must understand, Captain, that I am in no way attempting to denigrate or ridicule your personal appreciation of the current situation, it is simply that there are things—considerations—you may not have taken into account.'

'Because of my lack of experience.'

'Yes.' Nobata said in a kindly tone, 'Experience, unfortunately for the young, only comes with age. I was the same at your age.'

Isogai came to the desk and sat in the chair facing him. He rested his elbow against the edge of the flat surface and tapped his finger on the leather bound blotter.

Commander Nobata said, 'I too was eager for glory.'

'And honour.'

'Yes. These things come at—'

Isogai said quietly, 'It is my opinion that Japan cannot continue to survive as an autonomous nation.'

'Agreed. But now we have China and—'

'Japan cannot survive without oil. And the Americans have embargoed all supplies of oil to us until we give up all our previous Asian conquests. If we do they will sell it to us.'

'That is a reasonably accurate—'

'And if we do withdraw in order to get oil then we are back to being what we were before: a second rate feudal power with no foreign territories or possessions to finance our purchases. Of oil.' He said sarcastically, 'No doubt, however, in their magnanimity, the Western nations would be only too pleased to loan us money to pay them. But then, in order to guarantee our repayments of the loans. . .' Isogai said, 'I do not believe the true will of the Japanese is that the Europeans should take over our country the way they took over China. I believe the will of the Japanese people as personified by the Emperor is that *we* should be the masters.' He said without varying his tone, as a statement of fact, 'As a man of honour I know you believe that the greatest fate that can befall a Japanese soldier is to die in battle for the glory of the Emperor.'

Nobata did not reply. His face hardened.

'I know you believe that. Your chrysanthemum medal proves it. You are a man of sincerity and iron. In my opinion you have been given command of this sector—a Naval officer—over the heads of Army commanders of equal rank because your heroism and single-mindedness of purpose have been previously proven in battle. I, as an officer untried in blood, have respect for you. As the authorities intended.' He looked at Nobata with unblinking dark eyes. 'No doubt there was an overwhelming reason for not honouring the deaths of two Japanese soldiers.'

'They were not soldiers. They were Kempetai men.' Nobata gritted his teeth. His eyes narrowed.

'Whoever they were. Carrying out the will of their Emperor on foreign soil.'

'There were reasons, yes!'

'Overwhelming reasons, I am certain. Of course, I apologize for my earlier outburst. My only personal excuse is that of my youth. I am sure your interpretation of the current feeling in Japan is the correct one. Naturally, so that the Japanese people did not appear to be totally compliant fools to the Europeans you set some sort of limit to the affair?'

'The murders are being investigated by the International Police.'

'And they have how long to solve them?'

Nobata did not reply.

'There is talk, both at home and here, of a single mighty blow against the English and the Americans. One that would decide the outcome of the war.'

Nobata said, 'There *is* no war!'

'—of the inevitable war. A single decisive move: perhaps the invasion of Singapore, or an enormous seaborne landing on the

American Pacific naval and land bases—the Philippines. You, sir, perhaps, have the knowledge in the back of your mind and your actions—'

Nobata said, 'You have no understanding of the British and the Americans at all.'

'No?'

'No.'

'I understand that a crippling blow of merciless proportions—'

'You understand nothing! I lived in England! I know the people there—I understand them. I have seen their industries. The Americans and the British are backed by a machine culture. They have massive, unthinkable resources—'

'The British are at war in Europe—'

'But the Americans are not!'

'The Americans do not have our sense of purpose. They are weak and degenerate. They *rely* on their machines. We do not.'

Isogai said, 'Blood and destiny.'

'*It is not as simple as that!*'

'I shall deal with the Americans and the British in Shanghai easily if you—'

'If you invade the International Settlement in Shanghai you will set Japan at war!'

'And is that not what Japan *wants*?' Isogai said abruptly, 'Tell me, sir, with great respect, what exactly did you mean when you said Japan no longer trusts you?'

'That is none of your affair!'

'I assume that in the case of the two dead soldiers you have set a limit of say ten days for the Europeans to satisfy us?'

'I have not!'

'Less?'

'I have set no limit!' Nobata shouted, 'They were *spies*!'

'And in the Imperial Navy, no doubt, where clean sheets are the order of the day, therefore of no account!'

'You are being insolent!'

'I am defending the role of the Army! It is the Army who must fight this battle—the battle for China—it is the Army who have endured the winters and the heat and the desperation. It is the Army whose officers and men have died and suffered in—'

'And it was the Army, was it not, that fell upon Nanking like the horde of murderous raping peasants that they are—it was the Army, was it not, that brought the horror and disapproval of the world upon us all. *Was it not?*'

'Japan does not consider the opinions of anyone but the Japanese!'

'Do they not?'

'No! The Army is a machine to bring war down on the heads of lesser nations! The Army does not take itself along to cocktail parties and exchange small talk with degenerates and sycophants and—'

Nobata said, 'That is enough! Captain Isogai, if you are as determined in battle as you appear to be in—'

Isogai said, 'I assume that to be a word of encouragement from a senior officer and I am appropriately satisfied.'

'Nevertheless, my young hero, the British and Americans—'

'The British and the Americans are—'

'How could *you* possibly deal with them?'

'I have no intention of *dealing* with them. My intention is to *kill* them!'

'If only it was that simple.' Nobata said, 'Young men have nothing to lose but a few years of enthusiastic life. Older men—'

Isogai said, 'A life is a life. It is only precious to the Emperor. And then, only in the way he can dispose of it.'

'You are—'

'I am Japanese!' Isogai said, 'I love my country as you do. All I require from the Anglo-Americans is a single provocation.'

'*You* couldn't even *talk* to them!'

'I would have given them a time limit of ten days and then my tanks would have levelled their abscess of a border and their defences to the ground!'

'Well, *I* did not! How long do you think we would survive? Have you considered what might happen if the British and the Americans and all the Allies they might find—the Indians, the Australians, the French—what might happen to the Japanese race if all those people took it into their heads to eradicate Japan and its people from the face of the earth! Is Japan prepared to occupy *America*?'

'That is defeatism!'

'That is reality! I know! I know the European mind! What do you know? You? A peasant!'

'I am a soldier!'

'You are a peasant! A looter and a rapist! A wild dog!'

'And the Emperor whose will it is that we go to war, what is he?'

'That is none of your affair!'

'The Emperor is none of my affair?'

'It is not appropriate for a peasant even to enquire about the Emperor!' Nobata said, 'The Anglo-Americans do not even deign to learn the *languages* of small nations—You may think me a tired fool and the Cabinet may think me a man gone soft on Western attitudes, but at least I understand them! They understand *me*!' Nobata said, 'Tell me how you would give them ten days and I shall give you Shanghai!' He said, 'I will be retired soon enough—left alone to rot—and I will not bring a war down on the Europeans, or on Japan with my last arthritic gasp!' He shrieked at Isogai, 'Tell me where your strength lies! Tell me how you could do anything but shoot and stab! Tell me how you could even *talk* to them in their own language and I will give you—'

'I attended Staff College, Commander Nobata, and it was the opinion of my superiors that I was a very good pupil. It was their opinion—the opinion of the Army—that a war was inevitable.'

Commander Nobata shook his head. He closed his eyes for a moment. He heard Isogai get up and open the door.

Isogai, smiling, said in perfect, almost unaccented English, 'Since you have made the offer, Commander, may I assume the ten day limit?' He waited at the open door.

A few of the dozens of clerks in the outer office glanced up.

Nobata shouted at Isogai in Japanese, 'You damned fool, the Emperor is a narrow, untravelled man! Japan cannot win!' He shouted at the top of his voice, '*The Emperor is a fool!*'

The clerks stopped, paralysed. They stared at Isogai in disbelief.

Isogai stepped quietly back into the Commander's office and closed the door.

15

'It's been a long time, Jack.' Moffatt looked him up and down, like a schoolmaster. He looked at his wife and pursed his lips, 'I saw your car parked out of the way, Katherine.' He had one hand pushed loosely into the pocket of his British Warm topcoat, 'I thought you were going to be at home today. I telephoned this afternoon and the houseboy said you'd gone out in the car.' He said again to Edge, 'It's been a long time.' He touched at his face with a black gloved hand, 'You look a lot older, Jack.'

'So do you. You used to have a moustache when I knew you. You used to wear it to make yourself look authoritative.'

'There's no familiarity between us, Jack.' Moffatt glanced at his wife. 'You made a mess of all that.' By the little blue Fiat, the cacophony of the rickshaw compound went on as background noise only, 'I gave you a chance and you let me down.' The Scottish burr, renewed every three years on home leave was still very strong. Moffatt said to his wife, 'I was disappointed you weren't at home to receive my call, Katherine. I don't see much of you these days and it was more than a little disappointing for me to find you'd seen fit not to wait in.'

'I came here, Alec.' She looked away.

'I can see that, Katherine. I can also see you've been out walking. I can see you wore your heavy coat in expectation of walking somewhere.' He said easily to Edge, aware of their relative positions, 'I don't believe you should have encouraged my wife to go out in the air where she might easily catch cold, Sergeant.' His face made a tight little smile, 'You haven't been filling Mrs Moffatt's head with all that rubbish about the good Orientals, have you?' He glanced at his wife, 'Sergeant Edge has a pet hobbyhorse about how much better the Celestials are than us clumsy Europeans, but he sometimes takes it too far. Don't you, Jack?'

'If you say so.'

'Sergeant Edge has a habit of losing his perspective on reality.' Moffatt said to his wife, 'I don't think even Sergeant Edge would expect everything he said to be swallowed hook, line and sinker. Especially by an impressionable woman.' He glanced back at the business of the rickshaw compound, 'How many of those silly contraptions do you examine these days? A hundred a month?'

Edge nodded. 'More or less.'

'I suppose someone has to do it.'

'I suppose so.'

Moffatt continued looking at the rickshaws. He turned back to his wife, 'Time for you to go home, Katherine. I imagine things can get pretty boring here—' his eyes were on Edge '—what with the same thing day after day. If it were me, I'd look for a diversion of some sort. Did you remember to put petrol in the car, Katherine?'

'Yes, Alec.'

'She sometimes forgets. You know what women are like, Jack.'

Edge said evenly, 'You've got it wrong.'

'Have I?'

'Your wife happened to be passing. I haven't seen her for some time. The only topic of conversation was the situation with the Japanese.' Edge said, 'And her car, as a matter of fact, is parked in full view of the main road. It isn't, by a long stretch of the imagination, parked out of the way.'

'I stand corrected, Sergeant.'

'I was simply stating facts.'

'I don't give a damn if she spends *all* her time with—'

'Be that as it may—'

Katherine Moffatt said suddenly, 'Alec doesn't think the Japanese will invade us, do you Alec?' Her face shone hopefully, 'And I told him that you're always right in your judgements, Alec—'

'Time to go home, Katherine.'

'No, Alec, I want to—'

'The Sergeant and I have police business to talk about. It doesn't concern ladies. So you go and wait in your car and then I'll see you get escorted straight home.'

'Jack says, Alec, that the Japanese—'

'I'm not really vitally interested in what Jack has to say, Katherine. "Jack" has had a nice, inconspicuous station here for quite a long time. He's been quite happily hidden away presenting the uniform to a bunch of rickshaw coolies and their masters for quite a considerable length of time and he's had a very good run for his money, all factors taken into considera- tion. And he knows it. But now the time has come—'

'His wife left him, Alec. I was just trying to—'

'I believe that was more than some time ago, Katherine. It certainly didn't happen this morning or even last week or even last year. As I was saying, your friend's time has come to contribute a little more to the cause than he's been doing for rather a long time.' He said to Edge, 'I'm sure you'll welcome the opportunity, Sergeant Edge.'

Edge said evenly, 'I try to do as I'm told.'

Moffatt's face made a bitter smile, 'Not always, Sergeant. Not always.' He said to his wife as a warning of things to come if she continued to refuse to obey his request to go home, 'It concerns the murder of the two Japanese in the warehouse district. I've been down to see the local Japanese sector commander and—'

Katherine Moffatt looked at him. She was about to say something.

'—and *he* says, also, Katherine, that the chances of a Japanese invasion of the International Settlement are remote, so Sergeant Edge's historic moment of crowning glory—when the Orientals all mass together to take over the world—hasn't come just yet.' He said to his wife, 'Now go.'

'Alec, I—'

'Please do as you're asked, Katherine.'

'I just want to know if—'

'Sergeant Edge is going to investigate the murders. Are you happy now? Now you can wait in the car while I discuss the details with him.'

'I told him you were going to give him a second chance, Alec. I told him you weren't like the others—I was only telling him that—' She said, 'Alec, we were only just talking about *you*!'

Edge looked at her. Her face was mobile, flickering back and forth with the minute changes in her husband's expression. She said desperately, 'What you're thinking isn't true—Jack and I—when I was—' She said urgently, 'He always behaved like a gentleman!'

'*Wait in the bloody car!*'

'No, Alec, it isn't like you think!'

'Woman, I gave you an order.'

Edge stepped forward. He said quietly, 'Do as he says, Kate. Please.'

'You keep out of this, you Chink-loving, ruined bastard!'

'You've got it all wrong, Moffatt—'

'It's *Mr* Moffatt as far as you're concerned!' Moffatt glanced back at the rickshaw compound. People had stopped. They were listening. 'Where's your office?'

Edge jerked his head to one of the warehouses.

'Then I'll continue this conversation with you there.'

'I haven't used the office for—'

Moffatt looked at him hard. His gloved hand raised itself. The black leather index finger laid itself on Edge's chest. 'I don't *care* what you may or may not do or have done, Edge. I give the orders and you obey them.' He turned back to his wife and stared hard at her, 'And you—' the finger indicated a point just above her eyes, 'You wait in the car.' His face changed. He said softly, 'Look at them.' He turned his head to the mass of rickshaw coolies. He nodded to her, 'Yes. Look at them looking at you.'

His wife stared at them.

Moffatt said, 'Think about them.' He glanced at Edge. 'The Japs aren't the only ones.' He ordered her, 'Think about them, too.' His face stayed hard and unmoving. He said tautly, 'Now wait in the bloody car while I'm away.' He turned his gaze to Edge, 'Where you'll be safe.'

The light in the compound was fading. An early winter's dusk was drawing in as he went into the darkness of the open warehouse.

16

In the fifth floor office there was only the framed picture of the Emperor of Japan on the wall. Nothing else. The picture showed the god-king of the Chrysanthemum Throne, alone, on horseback, reviewing his troops. The picture showed a slight man wearing glasses. Japan was an ancient island wherein the Japanese Emperor descended in an unbroken line from the gods.

Nobata thought sadly, "I am almost sixty years old." He glanced down at his hands on his desk. "One does not speak of the Emperor in such a way and continue living on the same earth as—" He said softly to Isogai, 'I had nothing to look forward to anyway.'

'As your next in command I shall act for you should you require assistance when the time comes.'

'I shall not require assistance.'

'However, at the moment, your life is still temporarily required by your country.' Isogai said evenly, 'Ten days, that is what we agreed, was it not?'

'For the International Settlement?'

'Yes.'

'To apprehend murderers long gone—'

'That is what we agreed.' Isogai said, cautioning, 'You are still officially the commanding officer here—'

'Am I?'

'So your permission is required. The order must come from you.'

'I was an easy victory for you, Captain. . .'

'Do I have that permission?' Isogai said, 'In your name, I shall issue the order. It will be transmitted to the Shanghai police and—'

'In my name?'

'Yes, in your name.'

'Have you left me any name to have?'

'That is your personal concern, not mine.' Isogai said, 'Japan still requires your service for a limited period.'

'*You* require my services—' Nobata said, '*You* have taken all my honour away and now *you* tell me I am not permitted to kill myself until after you have decided to dispense with me. I ask you again, Captain, have you left me any name to have?'

Isogai's face hardened. 'You weak old man!'

'Yes.'

'I require you to set a limit of ten days!'

'And if I refuse?'

Isogai shook his head. He smiled.

Nobata said softly, 'Captain, may you, one day, yourself grow old. May you—' He said, suddenly vehemently, 'I hope you grow old, Captain. I hope you grow old and lonely and useless, and I hope one day—'

'I shall not grow old.'

Nobata looked at him. Nobata's eyes were soft and fluid. Commander Nobata said, 'No. You will not.'

He looked away towards the desk top, at his soft hands.

17

Moffatt said, 'God in Heaven!' He stopped in the centre of the high warehouse in a circular pool of light from an opening in the curved corrugated iron roof—like a monologist in a spotlight— and looked around quickly, 'God in Heaven!' There were people in the semi-darkness—he saw hundreds of them: dark eyes watching him. Hundreds of silent eyes staring at him. And possessions: mattresses, cooking pots, chairs, tables, suitcases, clothes—they were piled up along the walls: bundles of people, knots of them, chaotically spreading along the length of the warehouse and in the high corners of it like a breeding colony of ants, shadows and forms, silhouettes. He heard them breathing like a single giant dark animal. Here and there there were little makeshift lanterns and around them, more people. People in suits and gowns, rags—he felt them moving, heaving—the smell of all that humanity prickled under his armpits, sent invisible minute scrabbling insects moving in the thick serge of his suit. He had an overwhelming urge to scratch. He exclaimed, 'God in Heaven! Who the hell are all these people?' His eyes flickered down the length of the warehouse, following the misshapen backbone of a supine breathing dragon made up of nothing but breathing, reeking Chinese, 'Who the hell let these people in here?'

'They're refugees from across the wire.'

'I know who they are! How did they get in *here*?' He caught sight of a woman in rags trying to stifle her baby's cries with her hand. There was a pot cooking on a tiny paraffin stove. The grandmother of the child hunched over it to shield its light from him, 'They've set up house in here! Don't these people know this shed is police property?' A thought struck him, 'My God, what sort of things do they do in here at night?' He demanded, 'How many of them are there?' He said again, 'My God, what sort of things do they do at night?' He turned on Edge, 'In front of the children?'

'We can talk outside.'

'We can bloodywell talk in here!'

A baby at the far end began wailing, and then another nearby. Moffatt saw the mother staring at him in terror. Moffatt said suddenly accusatorily, 'You've done this to spite me!' He stared at Edge's tall form in the gloom, 'Did you show this to my wife?

Is this where she comes with you?' He said, horrified, 'This isn't where you and she—'

'Don't be absurd!'

'The place for these people is on the streets with the other refugees! My God, did you bring my wife in here to see *this*?'

'It doesn't concern your wife. I do my job and that's all that counts. I didn't invite these people in here and I—'

'But you bloody help them! Who *feeds* all these bloody Chinks?'

'They feed themselves.'

'Then how the hell did they get in here?'

'They appeared.' Edge said, 'They crossed over the wire to avoid being killed in the fighting and they came here to avoid freezing to death on the streets.'

'So they freeze to death in here! On police property!'

Edge glanced at the woman shielding her baby. He said something quickly in Chinese then turned back to Moffatt. 'The warehouse is warm. If they want to shelter here it's none of my concern.'

'You're their bloody leader, are you? Their spokesman—lord of all the shivering bloody Celestials—'

'I've told you, it's none of my concern.'

'Don't you realize that if we grant shelter to one of these people we have to grant it to everyone?' Moffatt said, 'My God, we'd have them feeding out of their rice bowls under the long bar in the Shanghai Club if we did that! Is this what's been turning my wife against me? *This?*'

Edge said softly, 'Your wife should be sent home.'

'Is that your opinion?' Moffatt's eyes stayed riveted on the undulating mass of people, all silent, all staring at him, 'Other policemen—good men—are pestering me day and night to be sent home so they can fight Nazis threatening their homeland and what the hell do you do—?'

Edge said, 'England isn't my homeland.'

'—you compromise us all by stealth!'

'I've told you, I didn't encourage these people to come here.'

'But you didn't send them away when they did! They'll be pouring in here like ants—'Moffatt said abruptly, 'Just where the hell *is* your homeland, Edge?' He pointed an accusing gloved finger, 'Here? Is this where your patriotism lies? In a bunch of ragged bloody coolies? How dare you expose my wife to this sort of thing!' He paused. 'You hate us, don't you? The

Europeans. You hate us all.' He glanced at the dark mass against the far wall, '*This*—these second rate . . . *Chinese*.' Moffatt said, 'That's it, isn't it? That's the key to your character, isn't it?'

Edge said nothing.

'Isn't it!'

'*Yes!*'

'You damned traitor!'

'You go to hell!'

Moffatt stepped forward a pace. His voice dropped. 'Is this what your parents taught you—your missionary parents—oh, I know all about them—is this what they told you—one of them English, and the other American—that your duty lay in supporting the Orientals against your own kind? Was that their message to you, *Jack*?'

'My parents taught me that life was a gift from God.'

'Was that before they were slaughtered by the Chinks in the Boxer Rebellion or was that after? As they lay chopped to pieces and dying, killed by Chinks from their own congregation—was that before or after? Tell me that.'

Edge said quietly, 'They died in the service of their God.' His voice was very soft and tight, 'You said you had a job for me. If I can carry it out, I will.'

'As a matter of duty?'

'Yes, as a matter of duty.' Edge said barely audibly, 'China is eternal. It will survive me and it will survive the Japanese.' He fixed his eyes on Moffatt's face, where the moustache had once been, 'It will certainly survive you.'

Moffatt's eyes stared at him, then moved along and down the huddled outlines of the refugees against the dark mass of the far wall. Then the eyes came back. 'Out of a sense of pity I wasn't going to tell you this, but I picked you for the job—investigating the deaths of the two Jap soldiers—in consultation with the Japanese sector commander for the simple reason that I knew you didn't have the staff to do anything about it. You'll have to report to his underlings that you haven't found out anything and his underlings will press you for more efficiency, but at base, both he and you—you'll never meet him because he refuses to associate with failures—will know that you're nothing but a uniformed marionette dancing to strings.' Moffatt said, 'Tie that in your China is eternal shit and see where you come up.' He added, satisfied, 'You may be able to pull the wool over my wife's eyes with all your China talk but you don't convince *me. I* still give the orders around here and people do as *I* say.' He ordered abruptly, 'And I want these people out of here and onto the streets where they belong!'

'They'll die on the streets!'

'Good! The more the better!'

'Your wife isn't my mistress.'

'The subject is closed.'

'Your wife is ill!'

'That's none of your concern.'

'And she believes you when you tell her that the Japanese won't invade the Settlement. All right, it's none of my concern, as you say, but she is ill and you should get her home. There's a ship due on the 8th and if I were you, I'd—'

Moffatt said, 'But you're not me, are you? You're a second-rate Sergeant who's just been told that the greatest contribution he can make to his fellow man and his comrades is just to carry on botching-up his already botched-up bloody career. You may be able to impress silly women with a load of airy-fairy Chinese half-truths and mumbo-jumbo, but you can't impress *me*—or any other real man.' Moffatt said intimately, 'If I were you, Jack, I think I'd try and be a little bit humble.' He said with mock concern in his voice, 'It might sit a lot better on you when you're ten or fifteen years older and silly women don't fall for you any more. Then it'll come to you that all your life has been wasted—'

'Like yours?'

'Oh, no.' Moffatt made a satisfied smile, 'No, Jack, I've amounted to something. I've associated with important people and made important decisions and my place in the history of the European settlement in Shanghai is quite secure.'

'In twenty years no one except a few old men will even know the Europeans were here.'

'No, I don't think so, Jack.'

Edge said evenly, 'Do you still write letters home? Do you still ask your correspondents to keep them for you?'

'Oh, yes, I do, Jack. You see, you remember everything about me. In twenty years who will want to remember you?'

'Probably no one.'

'Shanghai will prosper again. You take my word for it. After all this Japanese business is over the money'll come back. People'll start investing here again. People see realistic facts: the market here in China for goods is an insatiable one and we're right at the centre of it. The ships will come back and all the people with them. Society will begin again—'

'And you'll be thought of with affection.'

'Yes, I will, Jack. Yes, I will. And people like me who served the cause through the hard times—'

'They might even build you a big house on a hill.'

'They might, Jack. But they won't build you anything. Nothing at all except a—'

Edge said softly, 'I'd appreciate it if you didn't have these people in here put out on the streets.'

'Would you, Jack?'

'Yes.'

Moffatt nodded. 'All right then.'

'Thank you.'

'Oh, I can see reason. I'm not a hard man. If you're offering to strike a sort of bargain with me, then I can see compromise. I can do that much for you out of a sense of past comradeship. In the event, with the curfew starting soon, there won't be much call for rickshaws and we'll be closing this place anyway. I don't see why I can't just forget that a few illegals have taken up residence here.' He added, suddenly coldly, 'But then, of course in return, you have to make a certain allowance to me.'

'I've already told you that your wife and I—'

Moffatt said quickly, 'A certain allowance, that's all. There's no need to go into details. Just a certain allowance. That's fair, isn't it? That's understood.' He glanced towards the line of people against the wall, 'In India, even today, the tea planters upcountry still go in for the practice of flower girls. Do you know what flower girls are, Jack? They're pretty little things who tend the gardens and if the *sahib* rides by on his horse and touches one of them with his riding crop—'

Edge said, 'I know what flower girls are.'

'No decent European woman will have anything to do with a man who's soiled his character by taking a Chinese girl in off the streets. You know that, don't you, Jack? Certainly no wife of *mine* would, and that's point enough—' He called out loudly to the refugees in English, 'I've got a warm house and good food for a woman who speaks English!'

'This is a waste of time—'

'Is it, Jack?'

'Yes.'

'Then it's my time.' He called out again, 'Do you people hear me? A warm house and regular food—' His eyes roved across the nearest knot of people. Eyes stared at him in terror. 'Well?'

'There is absolutely nothing between your wife and me!'

'Do you want them out on the streets, Jack? Do you? An allowance, Jack. *Any of you people?*' His eyes settled on a woman by the corner, out by herself, 'You. Are you of good companionable stock? Are you the sort of woman who could put up with an irascible old policeman?' He grinned happily at Edge, 'Nothing personal, Jack old man, but I've got to prepare the poor recipient of your favours for her fate, haven't I?' The grin turned bitter at the edges, 'Are you, dear? Are you the sort of—' He asked loudly in Pidgin, 'Likee eatee, keepee bum warm, all-time good fashion fuk-fuk? Yes?'

The woman's face came up from the darkness. She was southern Chinese. Moffatt said, 'You want go eatee this man's food? Thinkee now chop-chop quick.'

The woman's eyes gazed at him.

'You savvy, woman? What name you? Doesn't speak a word, Jack.' He looked her up and down, 'About thirty-five, Jack, would you say? Good peasant stock.'

Edge looked at her. Something about her cheekbones reminded him of Missy. He looked at the woman's hands in the half light. The fingers were long and slender. The fingernails had been kept trimmed. He said warningly, 'This woman comes from a good family—'

'Rubbish.' He pointed a gloved finger at the woman. For a Chinese she seemed very tall, 'You, you're saved through the grace of the Shanghai Police and in the name of a continuing peaceful accommodation with the Japanese. Aren't you lucky?'

The woman looked at him.

'Better give her a bath when you get her home.' He turned suddenly back to Edge, 'No, Jack, I don't feel I'm playing the whoremaster because, you, as a man of proven moral principle, probably won't sleep with her.' He said with disgust in his voice, 'God, I know I wouldn't. But the point is that certain other people won't believe that and that's our allowance. So it's settled.' He said loudly to the standing woman, 'You don't know just how lucky you are.' He shouted at the top of his voice out the open door of the warehouse, '*Rickshaw*!!' He saw Mrs Hzu peer into the gloom, 'You! Getee rickshaw!' He turned back to Edge. 'My office will tell you who to report to.' He glanced back at the woman in the shadows and said before striding out,

'I'll wait in sight of my wife's car for ten minutes.'

Mrs Hzu came in leading her best rickshaw coolie. She paused for a moment watching Moffatt's retreating figure. She asked Edge in Chinese, 'Is that man the one?' She pointed outside in the direction of the condemned rickshaw, 'Is he the one I complain to?' She hobbled up quickly to Edge and caught him on the sleeve with a gnarled finger, 'Is he the one who'll solve my problems with you?'

Edge looked at her. His face was ashen.

Mrs Hzu said, 'Well?'

Edge glanced back at the woman. He shook his head. In the semi-darkness his voice said quietly in English, 'Grandmother, your problems are all but over.' He looked back sadly to the woman and then in the direction Moffatt had gone, out into the bitter night wind of the open cement compound. He said to the woman softly in Chinese, 'Do you have a name?'

Mrs Hzu said, 'Aye? Aye? Is he the one?'

The woman looked at him. She came forward, tall and very straight of carriage. Edge saw her long fingernails. He said to her in English, 'I'm so sorry.' He asked in Chinese gently, 'What's your name?'

Mrs Hzu protested in a cackle, 'Why are you talking to her? Is that the man? Tell me before he gets away!' She asked loudly, 'Is that him— Don't ask her name—tell me what that man's name is! Is he someone in charge?'

The woman paused. She said clearly to Edge in English, 'My name is Ling Fan Su. Europeans call me Barbara Ling.' She said, 'I'm cold and hungry and I can't afford your scruples.' She glanced at Mrs Hzu. She said, again in English, 'I haven't ridden in a rickshaw for a long time.'

Mrs Hzu screamed at the top of her lungs, 'Why don't you tell an old woman what she wants to know?' She drew in a deep breath, and howled, 'You bastards, why don't you speak Chinese?' She caught sight of the look on Edge's face and the way the English-speaking Chinese woman with cared-for fingernails was watching and shrieked in frustration, 'All anyone ever does is think of themselves!' She shouted, 'You bastards, doesn't anyone ever consider a sick old woman?' She cursed the entire shed full of people, 'You illegitimate scum of toeless dwarfs!'

She clenched her claw-fists into tight balls of fury and fell silent, panting and shaking her head.

18

At the War Ministry in Tokyo, General Hideki Tojo, Prime Minister and Minister for War, began dealing with the single item on the Imperial Conference Agenda for that day. In the presence of Foreign Minister Togo, the Navy Chief of Staff Admiral Nagano, the Ministers of Finance, Agriculture, and several others of lesser rank, he read out the proposition in his sibilant, monotonous voice, from time to time touching at the bridge of his spectacles and the crown of his shaved head.

He read, to respectful attention: '*Agenda:* Failure of Negotiations with the United States based on the essentials for carrying out the Empire's policies concerning United States oil embargo on Japan. *Proposal:* Declaration of War on the United States, Great Britain and the Netherlands.'

It was the evening of November the twenty-eighth, 1941, and a Japanese naval task force of aircraft carriers and escorts whose mission it would be to attack the American base at Pearl Harbour in the Hawaiian Islands had been at sea for almost five days.

19

As the rickshaw carrying Edge and the Chinese woman passed close by the little Fiat Topolino and moved off into the darkness, Moffatt nodded to himself. He glanced across to see the look on his wife's face. It was too dark. He made a tight smile.

The police driver started the engine of the black Nash. Its exhaust made a spume of grey smoke in the cold winter night.

20

At the corner of L'Avenue du Roi Albert, in the French section of the International Settlement, Hooper called out from the crowded bright din of 'Jean-Claude's', 'You're late.' He called out, marginally drunkenly as Duras pushed his way through the Saturday night throngs of people in search of night-life, 'In your opinion, Father, can an unconvicted embezzling unrepentant shyster find forgiveness in a degenerate French-Chinese restaurant on a Saturday night and thereby discover the peace and tranquillity of God?'

Father Duras pushed and eased his way through the milling pedestrians. He arrived a little breathless inside the cacophony of the establishment. The casino on the ground floor was in full swing and upstairs on one of the other floors there was a band crashing out their rendition of *Together* on old brass instruments and, somewhere higher up, a Chinese orchestra with cymbals. Duras said, 'I'm the last to arrive. I had to walk. Someone murdered another Triad man somewhere on the Bund a bit earlier and the rickshaw pullers have gone on a twenty-four hour strike until they get the protection from the secret societies they pay for.' He called out above the din, 'What did you ask me?' He saw Hooper set his face for a long question, 'Oh that? Definitely not.'

'I'm glad that's settled. I'm the host tonight and I'm buggered if I'm going to end up drunk and depraved if in your considered opinion I'd be better off spending my time praying for forgiveness.'

'In my considered opinion, David, we're all better off getting pissed.' He managed to manoeuvre his overcoat off in the crush and hand it over the heads of people to the cloak room girl, a Chinese girl of perhaps twelve or thirteen. He pointed at the coat as it reached her hands and shouted to her in Shanghainese that there was a coin in the pocket. He had a woollen scarf on over his clerical collar. He moved forward past the gaming tables, 'How's your airplane? Still running?'

Hooper, being propelled in a knot of anxious gamblers, pushed out to the edge of the crowd and made for the wooden stairs. There were two sing-song girls down from the upper floor taking a cigarette break against the varnished bannisters. They chorussed out a greeting. Hooper winked back at them and they tittered and went into an animated discussion about some well-remembered aspect of his anatomy or performance. He called back over his shoulder to Duras, 'We're drinking Scotch tonight. Does that suit you? The Gindrinkers' Club has run out of gin. I bought a case of Johnny Walker Scotch whisky— O.K.?' He glanced back and saw Duras nod. 'Edge has taken in a woman. It'll be good for him.'

'Yes.' Duras glanced back down to the casino.

Hooper said, 'I've invited a friend along. A fellow American. Do you mind?'

'Not at all.'

'He's one of the Marines on the wire.' Hooper lowered his voice, 'After all, it's an unofficial drinking club and—'

Duras said, 'Forget it.'

'—and he's been useful to me.'

Duras nodded.

'But if the other members don't agree—'

Duras said, 'Always glad to have another connoisseur of good food and drink, David. In any event, it's your turn to pay—'

Abruptly, there was an unaccountable lull over the entire establishment as if everyone waited for something. The silence held another moment, then all at once, it began again louder than before. Hooper said, 'I don't think we're going to be able to get together too many more times.' He looked at Duras' face, 'Next month it'll be Charlie Singh's turn to pay and I have a strong conviction that the Japs are going to see to it that he saves his money. Do you agree with that estimation?'

'Yes.'

'I thought you might.' Hooper said mysteriously, 'I've asked the waiters to leave the empty dishes on a side table. Is that all right with you?'

'You are the host, David, not me.'

Hooper said quickly, mounting the next flight of stairs, 'My pal's name is Clarence Dubrinski. That's an American name, believe it or not.'

'Originally Polish?'

'Not according to Clarence. According to Clarence the first book of Genesis was set squarely on Ellis Island.' He said, 'He's pretty new to this part of the world.' He added, almost apologetically, 'He's a great believer, like you, in the ultimate triumph of good over evil.' Hooper asked, 'There's a ship leaving on the eighth. Probably the last before the river silts up.

Have you heard anything from your superiors about leaving on it?'

'I shall probably stay. Listening to the woes and confessions of peasants will give me humility again.'

'Is that what they say?'

'That's what I say.' Duras said, 'The vice of my Order is snobbery.' He said lightly, 'I may even get the chance to learn Japanese.'

'Classical or otherwise?'

A faint smile moved across Duras' face.

'Unfortunately, David, otherwise.' He smiled again, sadly, at his own Jesuit's disappointment.

Upstairs, in the private dining room, Hooper, after a respectful pause, eulogised grandly, 'To Jean-Claude, our mentor, who used to run, this, the most ferociously obscene cabaret in Shanghai, of late and lamented memory.' He was seated at the head of the rectangular lacquered table fanning up the live coals in a tall, minaret-like earthenware vessel, 'This hot pot furnace is all we have to remind us of you—Jean-Claude of the famous two-ladies-one-cat-and-rolled-umbrella-trick, we, the social outcasts of the Gindrinkers' Club salute you!' He glanced mock-concernedly at Duras, 'Although, possibly, there may be some among us who do not approve of the wasted vessel of your life, there are all of us who approve of your magnificent Semi Mongolian Peking Hot Pot maker, bought at an auction of your possessions for one dollar, and this—' he fanned reverently, intoning in rhythm, 'glorious and ancient vessel we hold dear in our hearts rather than the memory of your fishy green body hauled out of the river with a sailor's knife wedged firmly between its shoulderblades.' Hooper said mournfully, 'Dear Jean-Claude, your cabaret turned into a common eatery by dreary and unappreciative businessmen. Clarence, this beautiful utensil holds one of the great secrets of the East: the famed Semi Mongolian Peking Hot Pot.'

Edge said, 'Of famous memory—'

'Indeed, sir.' Hooper looked at Singh, 'You there, the coloured gentleman with the bushy beard, place a cigar firmly between that drunken flatfoot's drooling lips. Clarence—' he looked hard at Dubrinski, like the others, in his shirtsleeves and already partially drunk, 'This Semi Mongolian Peking Hot Pot will be, to you and all who sail in her, one of the enduring memories of the exotic East when all but the memory of the last almond eye and slit skirt have long passed. You will sit in the autumn of your years dreaming of it while you fondle your medals and bore your grandchildren.' He took a quick swig from a half full bottle of Johnny Walker by his elbow '—This creation—which this month you have none to thank but the deep and generous pocket of yours, David J. Hooper, embezzler and swindler unconvicted—'

Duras said, 'No, David, not true—'

'No, no, Father, quite true—' Hooper hiccoughed, 'Bird man extraordinary, who one day will leap—' he reeled slightly, '—reel into his little aircraft and—'

Singh began booing.

'Who is that booing?'

Singh said blearily, 'Singh the coloured gentleman—'

'Charles Singh of the Punjab—?'

Singh said, 'The same.'

'You realise, of course, sir, do you, that this is a sacred moment? I am attempting to educate Clarence the Dubrinski' (Dubrinski, a thin young man with brown hair brushed back, smiled sheepishly) 'into the ways of the mysterious Orient—' He pointed down at the massive utensil with a badly aimed finger, 'I am attempting to explain to him that this famous Semi Mongolian Peking Hot Pot is to be eaten in the following manner—' He asked with a deadly serious eye staring at Duras, 'Father, as a cultured man do you ever feel you have fallen in with a bunch of loafs and poltroons?'

'Constantly, David, but the expectation that one month the speeches will finish early and I may eat encourages me to forgive them.'

Hooper asked Edge, 'Jack, as a man of some experience with the missionary class in China, may I enquire as to your opinion in regard to the French Jesuit branch of that—' He asked, 'What was I talking about?'

'You were giving our friend Clarence a lesson in the fine art of eating Eastern exoticies—'

'I was.' He asked Dubrinski, 'Well, fine, is that all clear then?' He addressed the gathering, 'Clarence is from New York City, from Queens.' He glanced down at the whisky bottle.

Dubrinski had an amiable drunk's smile on his face. He raised his bottle. 'Here's to New York.'

Hooper raised his own and halved the remaining liquid in a single gulp.

86

Dubrinski said again, 'New York City, U.S.A.' He smiled happily and looked at Hooper.

Hooper said, 'Yeah.' He looked down at the bottle, 'Give my regards to Broadway.'

He took another, longer drink.

The test of a good, satisfying Chinese Hot Pot rests almost entirely in the ability of the host, seated in front of the large vessel to keep the coals inside it alight and at an even temperature by fanning. With a delicately judged, constant temperature the two pints of thin soup in the moat around the central core of the kiln and chimney—the balcony of the minaret—simmer with a pleasant steady sizzling sound.

In a true Mongolian Hot Pot, the guests, using chopsticks, pop razor-thin slices of lamb about four inches long by two inches wide into the boiling soup to be cooked on the spot. A Peking Hot Pot, on the other hand, allows the addition of slices of pork, chicken, ham, liver, fish, shrimps, pork and even oyster flesh and the soup, which in a Mongolian Hot Pot can be dilute and simple to a fault, may be strengthened in the Peking version by spinach, noodles, cabbage and bamboo shoots.

To the cooked meats each guest adds his own particular recipe of sauce, combined alchemically on the spot from sauces laid before him containing hoisin, chilli, tomato, tangerine or soya sauce, depending on his palate, down to the more sophisticated concoctions containing sherry, ginger, chives or soya-garlic.

Steamed bread is provided to mix with the meat and its sauces and, usually, one or more raw eggs to be poached in the boiling broth or mixed raw in the bowl.

Such a meal, particularly if the various ingredients are pre-cooked the afternoon before the meal, involves very detailed and careful preparation and, to do justice to it, can take four or more hours to consume with full Epicurean honour.

The crowning moment is at the end, when the hot broth, enlivened by the flavours of a dozen different meats and vegetables, is poured into beakers and distributed.

In the Semi Mongolian Peking Hot Pot, the sole invention of the monthly meetings of the Gindrinkers' Club, inaugurated two years before, there were no such hard and fast rules. On at least two famous occasions, ending in the near total demolition of Jean-Claude's upper storey, the boiling soup had been replaced by hundred proof gin.

By midnight, there was a heavily glazed look to the film on

Clarence Dubrinski's eyes. He found difficulty holding focus. There were empty oblong Scotch bottles in unmilitary disorder on the inlaid lacquer table. The black wood of the table and clear glass of the bottles kept merging. Dubrinski clasped his hand around the body of his second half full bottle and pressed down to anchor both it and himself to something solid. The conversation had been about duty: he felt it was something he ought to have an opinion on. He tried to form one. None came. He had a picture of himself on parade in summer uniform, thin and tight and clear eyed and the smell of trees and gun oil and pressed khaki—it seemed to be himself in a photograph his parents had, after a graduation. He tried to recall the weight of his combat helmet on his head. He recalled a broad-brimmed hat with wooden toggles—it must have been a summer parade. He rotated his eyes slowly around the rectangular table and fixed on Singh's turban. The folds and windings in it confused him and he thought, "I'm the only one who's drunk." He looked at Hooper's eyes. Below them the mouth was moving animatedly as he told some witty and totally sober story to the priest. The priest was resting his elbow on the table, propping up his forehead. His elbow slipped and his head fell down. Dubrinski looked at Hooper. The mouth went talk-talk-talk unceasingly. The priest seemed to have gone to sleep. Edge the policeman was pushing his eyebrows down towards his eyes with great concentration, practising, it seemed, ferocity and Dubrinski thought self-consolingly, "Well, maybe they're a bit drunk." He moved his eyes to Singh, realised he had forgotten where he was, drew a breath, opened his mouth, and with an effort of will fired off into the void, 'The Japs are going to conquer India when they've conquered China. Is that right, Mr Singh, in your opinion?' He asked, still wondering where he was, 'Mr Singh?' He received no reply. He tried again after what he thought was a long time. 'Who were the two dead Japs anyway?' He found Edge's face, lined and bleary, looking at him, 'Jack? Who were the two dead Japs?' He thought, "I'm terribly drunk. I'm not making sense. Thank God I'm not in uniform." He thought, "My God, these people can drink." He asked, 'Jack, what do you think?' He thought, "David Hooper looks absolutely sober. He's carrying on a long important conversation with the Father who's fascinated by what he's saying." He saw Singh's face lean across the table towards Edge and say something about India and Edge begin to reply (Dubrinski thought, 'That isn't really fair. *I* started that conversation.") and then Duras look over at Edge and smile, shaking his head.

Hooper was talking about his airplane—the one he had rebuilt that had fought with the Americans in the Great War. He heard the words *Lafayette Escadrille* and lost interest because he and the French priest were obviously speaking French. Dubrinski thought, "I'll give them a burst of Polish." He thought, "I can't remember any."

Someone said, 'They were probably spies or looters. They were only found a hundred and fifty yards from your warehouse. You probably heard the shots,' and then Hooper said, 'Sure, which shots were they? Were they the hundreds of shots before midnight or the hundreds of shots after midnight?' Hooper went on to say to the priest, '*Lafayette, nous sommes ici*—Lafayette, we are here!' There were glistening tears of emotion in his eyes and then the priest said, 'David, you're a romantic.'

Hooper's voice said, '—with part of the original battle colours still on it. It was Bert Hall's. He was a weird character in the Squadron who brought the Nieuport with him to China after the war to train the—' Then his voice said, a little louder, 'You can't repaint battle colours unless you're going into battle. It's worse than wearing another man's medals.'

Someone said, 'You paint battle colours on it and the Japs will shoot you out of the sky.' It was Edge. Dubrinski thought, "These people have been boozing here in China for years. I'm making a fool of myself." He heard someone saying in the middle of a sentence, 'The British say they'll defend India and my place is there at home,' and he realised it was Singh answering his question. Dubrinski said, 'I see, Mr Singh.'

'Charlie.' It came out very friendly and as an aside in an interested reply to an intelligent question and Dubrinski thought, "I'm not drunk at all. They're as drunk as me. I'm doing O.K." He said, 'Swell.' He put in quickly to Singh (he found him sitting opposite him talking man-to-man) 'My name's Clarence, Charlie.'

Singh said, 'I don't know how far my duty in Shanghai is supposed to extend in these circumstances. Up to the end? I should be home with my family, defending them. Everyone's gone from here and now we're just looking after refugees. That's all right if you've got a stake in the country like Jack—'

Edge said (apparently he had been listening to Dubrinski's

intelligent question as well), 'I haven't got a stake in the country the way you have in India. You own land there. A man always feels stronger towards land and children.' He said to Dubrinski, 'Charlie has a triannual breeding session every time he goes home on leave. Good subjects of the British Crown.' He said hazily, 'The trouble is, Charlie, the British Crown we're talking about is the one Queen Victoria used to wear.'

Singh said, 'I don't want independence for India.'

'Then you're an idiot. The incorruptible British Indian Civil Service, the heaven-born of colonial administrations, are stealing your country from you. Just as we've been stealing it from the Chinese.'

Singh said, 'Except for your face, Jack, you might as well *be* Chinese.'

'You might as well be British.'

'I am British.'

'Well, I'm not Chinese. They wouldn't have me. I might have done well as an upcountry missionary but I'm no good to anyone as I am.' He said to Duras, 'If your God had a sense of justice I might still believe in him. Although he's sure as hell got a sense of humour.'

Hooper's voice said, 'The clerical gentleman here refuses to talk shop while I am explaining to him about the finer points of maintaining a Le Rhône aero engine,' and Dubrinski thought, "My question started that conversation. They must be glad they invited me." He took a deep pull from his bottle of Johnny Walker and asked, 'What's your opinion of the Japanese Army as a fighting force, Father?'

Duras stopped. Momentarily, there was silence.

Dubrinski said quickly, 'Have I said something wrong?' He thought, "David warned me not to ask him that."

Duras glanced at his hands. They were powerful and supple.

Singh's voice hissed, 'No—they murdered his congregation upcountry.' Singh said, 'I was telling Clarence, Father, about your collection of artifacts. I couldn't remember what dynasty they were from—I mentioned you'd—'

Duras said evenly, 'No, you didn't, Charlie. And I'm sure Clarence doesn't give a damn about artifacts. Clarence is a professional soldier and obviously he wants to know everything about a potential enemy that he can.' Duras said, 'In my opinion, Clarence, they are a race of evil, savage, totally uncontrollable barbarians. My personal feeling is that they

90

should be wiped off the face of the earth and their bones buried in primaeval slime, every record of their existence as a race eradicated, and their island poisoned by disease and pestilence and removed from every map and chart in the universe. That is my personal opinion based on my personal experiences. My military opinion of them is that they are a formidable force who never surrender. The consummate act of their lives is to die in battle. Their motto is *senko seisaku*, the three alls: kill all, burn all, destroy all and at that they are extremely efficient.' He paused and said, 'My opinion as a religious is that it should be possible for men of good will and understanding to forgive them. My prognosis as a realist is that they will enter the International Settlement and raze it to the ground and my personal fate is that I shall be here to see it, doing what I can for the few poor souls they leave alive.'

Dubrinski said very soberly and clearly, 'Sir, the United States of America will not stand by and let that happen.'

'I sincerely hope you are right.'

Dubrinski said, 'I apologise, sir, for bringing up—'

'My name is Duras. Or Father Duras. Or just Father. Or Olivier, whichever you prefer.'

Dubrinski said, 'I'm a Catholic myself.'

Duras smiled at him. He asked Edge, 'Any progress on your investigation, Jack?'

Edge shook his head. 'David—' Hooper looked over '—I'd like to go upcountry with you next time to talk to your Nationalists. Can that be arranged?'

'Sure.' Hooper nodded to Dubrinski, 'Can a trip across the border be arranged, Clarence?' He asked Edge, 'Can you drive?'

'I can drive.'

'The answer to a mercenary maiden's prayer. Tuesday night at eight.' Hooper asked, 'O.K., Clarence?'

Dubrinski looked at Duras. Dubrinski said, 'Sure. Anything I can do to help.'

'Good! Fine!' Hooper said happily, 'Now, since the Hot Pot is now officially out, I, who am the possessor of all dem bits and pieces dat I waz left by my Massas to sell down on de levee, propose since it is undoubtedly the last time we shall all meet at Jean-Claude's, that I open the magic black box beneath the empty case of empty Scotch, and from that black box brought by me for the occasion, pass out various gentlemen's weapons of destruction, to wit, five nineteenth century saloon pistols and ammunition for same, and then, being certain and sure to take careful aim, we—' He said, 'What the hell, I've already paid for the damage.'

Edge said bitterly, 'Haven't we bloody all!'

Singh said, 'Hear, hear!'

Hooper said grandly, rising from his chair to collect the mahogany box from under the whisky crate, 'Gents, let's now shoot the shit out of the place.'

He put the open box on the table to display a set of five single shot pistols hand made to special order in 1893 by the firm of George Gibbs of Corn Street, Bristol, nestling in velvet lined compartments. Set around the long barrelled guns were lacquered tins of Eley cartridges: bulleted breech caps firing a round ball six millimetre projectile, their labels certifying that the reduced loading—there was no powder in the cartridges and the propulsion came solely from the rimfire primer—made them ideally suitable for indoor ranges and gentlemen's gatherings. A full set of nickeled cleaning equipment accompanied the set, complete with tiny pewter oil bottles made to order by Hawksley of Sheffield. Set in the lid of the box was a circular brass escutcheon for the owner's name, regiment, crest or initials.

Hooper drew one of the pistols from its resting place, snapped open the drop-down barrel, closed it again, and tested its balance. He had an angelic drunk's grin on his face.

Dubrinski said carefully, 'What I still don't understand is why you call your dinners the Gindrinkers' Club when all you seem to drink is neat whisky—' He reeled backwards a few degrees and stepped back to regain his equilibrium.

Hooper said happily, 'The Shanghai Club ordered these from London to use in their private, select, and members-only shooting gallery for gents with Port and Havana cigars. I imported them for them, but don't ever seem to have gotten around to delivering them.' He spread the weapons out on the table by the window and upended a tin of two hundred and fifty tiny cartridges, slipping a round into place, and let fly at the table still grinning as, in the drunken rush to avoid flying debris from a porcelain sauce bowl, the other four guns found owners. Hooper said, 'The Hot Pot is mine!' He took aim at it and demolished an ashtray.

There was a ragged volley of shots as two sauce bowls, splinters from the table, and the neck of a Scotch bottle went skywards, then a heavy huffing and puffing pause as inebriate thick fingers shoved and pushed minute cartridges into impossible-to-locate tiny breeches, then another volley and the destruction of more glass and porcelain. Duras tried to focus his aiming eye and ripped a shard of wood from the floor. He reloaded, steadied the gun with two hands and demolished an ashtray. Dubrinski had a variety of Marine pistol hold on his weapon: a complicated knot of fingers woven around the butt. The bullet pinged off something metal in the back of a chair and lodged God knew where as Singh, Hooper and Edge fired off a salvo in the general direction of a half full Scotch bottle. The bottle exploded and sent a satisfying geyser of alcohol three feet into the air.

Dubrinski had his fingers untangled. He was firing and reloading steadily, working his way methodically through the detailed and orderly destruction of a flotilla of sauce bowls. They exploded one by one like rafts floating in puddles of booze. Hooper hurled a full tin of cartridges in the vague direction of the table and took aim. He heard someone say, '*Sat Sri Akal*—!' (It was Singh—a Sikh war cry) and before his very eyes some bastard got his shot in first and detonated the tin with a single ferocious shot. Smoke began to fill the room.

Duras had the knack. He was loading smoothly and efficiently, firing shots off into nowhere, fascinated by his own skill. He reloaded again, forgot to fire, accidentally ejected the live cartridge and, oblivious and happy, reloaded again. Edge had decided to shoot from the hip: he was making fast-draw noises and pinging the bullets off the wall. They left pock marks in the painted mortar: he lowered his aim and disintegrated a pair of wooden chopsticks with a satisfied grunt.

Hooper shouted, 'Shot, sir!'

'Thank you, my man!'

'Shot, sir!'

'Thank you, my—'

'*My* shot, sir!' Hooper banged a round off at the imposing minaret of the Hot Pot. It missed and a fusillade of bullets tore at the debris around it.

The smoke swirled about the room. Singh moved a little away from the window, manoeuvred his mouth into a determined marksman's configuration, and touched a shot off at a bottle top. The bullet caught the metal rim and launched it vertically straight up. He tried another at a second top and blew a hole in the table. Not a man to be trifled with, he blew another hole in the table, and then another. He muttered something dark and evil in Punjabi, fired again, and the elusive top took to the air.

Edge shouted something and, simultaneously with Singh and Duras, fired at a sauce bowl. The bowl seemed to vaporise into powder. Duras called out, 'Don't leave anything!' and then in case there were any French speakers within earshot distance, '*Déluge! Déluge!*' He fired and fired at the shattered whisky crate and succeeded in shattering a full bottle somewhere at the bottom. The whisky flowed out through the gaps like The Flood. He shouted happily, '*Déluge! Déluge!*' thought instantly to translate it, and cried above unceasing volleys of fire in English, 'Deluge! Deluge!' He fired again and tore a slat of wood from a chair, aimed again and blew the chair's leg off. He glanced at Edge, happily concentrating on something with the wandering barrel of his pistol, and ducked as some enthusiast fired too close to his ear. There was a series of fumbling clickings as besotted eyes tried to concentrate their fingers on the task of reloading and then a last shot that seemed heavier than the rest as Hooper drew a short barrelled .38 calibre Bulldog revolver from his hip pocket and detonated the Hot Pot into shards with a final fullsized bullet.

A smokey, acrid silence fell. Nothing was left in one piece.

Duras sat down on the floor. The smoke passed over and about him in layers. Somewhere outside in one of the streets or alleys there was a dull thump as a hand grenade or home made blast bomb went off and then, a few moments later, a few shots a long way off. The barrel of the pistol was hot in his hand. He laid it by his hip on the ground and watched as the others came to join him, sitting heavily and silently with their backs against the wall. A few stubborn shards of porcelain finally surrendered to the pull of gravity and gave up their hold on shattered porcelain, making a series of tinkling sounds as they struck the floor. Hooper reloaded his revolver and stuck it back in his pocket and patted the bulge.

Singh's eyes felt very tired and sore. He closed them against the smoke for a moment. The lids felt deliciously heavy. After a long time he heard someone say, 'Well, that's the end of that,' and someone else made a grunting sound of agreement. He felt so tired he couldn't work out who it was.

Edge said to someone, 'They've given us ten days. The news came through from their Headquarters this morning.'

Someone asked, 'Do you believe them?'

'Moffatt doesn't.'

Singh heard Hooper's voice say, 'Of the good old Shanghai Club—'

'There's a new man. Moffatt doesn't deal with new men.' It was Edge's voice, 'A junior man, Isogai, a Captain. Moffatt doesn't deal with junior men.'

Someone said, 'Do you believe them?' It sounded like Dubrinski. Then Dubrinski's voice (definitely) said, 'I'm sorry it's been the last get-together for you, but I was very honoured to have come and I've had a really swell time.'

Singh drifted off to sleep. Someone seemed to keep saying the same thing over and over. There was the acrid bite of gunsmoke in his wide nostrils. He heard the voice saying over and over, 'Do you believe them?'

Over and over, the voice said, 'Do you believe them?'

'Is it true?'

The voice said over and over, 'But do you believe them?'

He fell into a brief uneasy sleep wondering what it meant, wishing something were different. Befuddled, he found it impossible to fix his mind on just what it was he wanted changed. He thought it had been a hell of a good night and wondered whose turn to be host it was next month, in January, next year.

He thought sadly of his children, a long way away, in India.

21

Across the lit city, in the darkened area of the Japanese occupied night, Commander Nobata knelt alone in front of a small wooden altar, his white kimono flopping down over his wrists. Before him, at the base of a lacquered altar, his *daisho* of long and short swords rested in their ceremonial holders. The short sword—his *koto waki zashi*—rested beneath the long sword in its ornate scabbard, the kojiri hilt decoration heavy with engraving and fine chiselling. On the mirror bright blade there was an even finer engraving of a dragon rising from the sea and, on the tang, hidden, the signature of the bladesmith, Umetada Miojiu, and the date, in Western terms, 1546.

For once, these things offered him no comfort. He took his writing set from inside his sleeve and leant forward over a blank scroll to compose his apologies for demeaning the name of the Emperor.

That done, he trimmed his nails and left the parings in an ornate silver box as a relic of himself.

He leaned forward and withdrew the *kogai*—like a small metal skewer—from its pocket on the scabbard and used its point to unlock the short sword from its scabbard.

He thought with an old man's tears in his eyes of better seasons and trees and flowers in bloom, of warm breezes and days of suppleness and tranquility.

He replaced the *kogai* carefully. The short sword would stay in its appointed place, unlocked, until the quiet, chosen evening of his death.

He lowered his head to the sword and left the candlelit room silently, with measured, soft steps.

He had no wish to meet anybody and went quietly through his darkened house to his bed.

Away in the city there were the unceasing sounds and cries and shots as a new generation of his countrymen went about their business.

He thought of them not at all.

22

Dubrinski still in civilian clothes but wearing his coat, pistol belt and helmet, dropped into the sandbagged emplacement at the Gordon Road intersection. Along both sides of the wire there was complete darkness: he heard faint scrabbling noises coming from somewhere on the Japanese side. His section of Marines were all on alert, belts fed and ready into Browning machine guns and Springfield rifles laid across the sandbags. He manoeuvred himself into position next to his Sergeant and whispered, 'What's happening?'

'People on the wire.' The whites of the Sergeant's eyes were the only features discernible on his face. He smelt Dubrinski's breath, 'Good party, Lieutenant?'

'Japs?'

A Marine leaned over into the cramped emplacement, 'I heard a kid's voice. Chinese.' He kept his voice down low. There was a metallic snicking sound, 'Refugees. It sounds like they're trying to climb over the wire. Can we go forward and get them, Sarge?' The Sergeant shook his head. 'Lieutenant?'

'No.' The sounds stopped and they waited in silence. Dubrinski whispered, 'When did the lights go?'

'Couple of hours ago. There was only one left. A rock.'

'Are you sure they're not Japs?' Dubrinski tried to peer into the darkness. 'Who's got the flare pistol?'

The Marine whispered urgently, 'I heard a kid's voice. We were giving them a chance to—' He had a soft, Massachusetts accent, 'We thought we'd give them a chance, sir.' He paused before handing over the gun.

'I'll give them a couple of minutes.' He hoped he sounded sober.

'Thanks, Lieutenant.'

The Sergeant said in a whisper, 'I can't hear them anymore.'

'I'll give them a couple of minutes and then I'll fire the flare.' He heard the Marine begin to protest. 'We can't risk letting Japs through. We can't afford an incident. We have to keep the United States—'

There was a terrible shriek of discovery from out of the night then scrabblings and the clashing of metal.

Dubrinski said, 'Jesus, what was that?' The cocking bolt on the Browning came back. 'Don't fire! For God's sake don't fire!' There were grunting sounds then scrapings and a whining cry: he saw for an instant the flash of upraised polished steel. Dubrinski pulled back the hammer on the pistol and fired the projectile in a curving arc that exploded the magnesium light a hundred feet in the air and saw in the sudden light a section of squat Japanese soldiers dragging a woman and her five year old child—girl or boy, it was impossible to tell in the knot of helmeted figures—back from the wire. He saw a long killing sword come up as the soldiers pressed the woman down to her knees and ripped the collar of her quilted jacket away from her neck—in the gyrations of the falling parachute flare he saw a dead man (her husband?) twitching on the ground in a river of blood—and he shouted to the machine gunner, 'Give them a burst over their heads!' He saw the Japs turn and watch as a stream of bullets whipped over the wire. They seemed merely to be pausing. They watched unconcernedly. Almost smiling.

The Sergeant began to order the machine gunner to depress his aim. Dubrinski ordered, 'No!' The firing stopped as the flare drifted in spirals above the scene, hung motionless above it for the last moment, and then went out.

The machine gunner said bitterly to himself, 'They know we won't do anything.' His voice had a rising note of anger, 'They know we can't do a fucking thing—'

Dubrinski said, 'Sergeant, get the Engineers out here in the morning to rig out some lights on our side at least.' He still had the flare pistol in his hand and he put it neatly on a sandbag, 'O.K., Sergeant?' He thought, "We're not at a—I have to show them I'm still in command."

From across the wire in the blackness there was a decapitating whack! noise and then, an instant later (they must have readied the child in silence) another, and all at once Dubrinski was uncontrollably sick across the sandbag.

23

Edge, sitting on the corner of the bed in his curtained bedroom, looked down at the metal cabin trunk between his feet on the floor. Plastered with shipboard and train labels, it had a large dent in its top and marks of fire on one side. He leaned down and lifted the lid carefully and it came up, warped, with a grating sound. Inside the lid he saw his father's name in fading painted letters and below it—on a printed card cut from something larger, perhaps a programme or leaflet of some sort, *American Presbyterian Mission, Wu Chang, China.* The style of lettering looked antique and turn-of-the-century and the glued-in paper itself foxed and water-stained. Once, there had been a good strong brass lock set into the box—the box was about three feet long by two feet wide and three feet deep: and he touched at the exposed tumblers with his finger. They were loose and broken and there was no key. On top of the strata of objects kept there inside the box he saw his father's Bible.

After a moment, he took the Bible out and put it behind him on the bed. He lit a cigarette and bent down with it dangling from his mouth and undid his shoes and took them off. His father's old white canvas walking hat was packed in the box, folded next to a cracked leather guncase. He took the hat up and ran his finger around the sweat band. The hat had an old forgotten, musty smell to it. He opened it out with the Bible on the bed. There was a briar walking stick in the box with a silver presentation plaque set into the head inscribed from a missionary society in Philadelphia. Edge put it with the hat without reading it.

The cigarette in his mouth had gone out. He relit it and rested it in an ashtray.

His mother's white cotton gloves were there, in a tissue paper bag, smelling of camphor. He held them in his hand for a moment—they seemed fragile and weightless—and then placed them on top of the Bible on the bed. The smell of camphor and leather reminded him of wooden lecterns and pews. He closed his eyes for a moment and remembered voices singing and the freshly washed and starched dresses and shirts of enthusiastic Chinese parishioners.

He undid the two leather straps securing his father's long guncase and looked down at the dissembled English shotgun inside without touching it. There were still two ancient 12 gauge cartridges in a side compartment with little balls of birdshot spilling out from split wads. He put the case on the ground and heard the loose shot roll first one way and then the other. He found next his father's Sears, Roebuck American duck-calling whistle, fashioned in the craftsmanship of the late nineteenth century, all polished wood and ivory, with the maker's name in inlaid Gothic lettering. His father had had some theory about Chinese river ducks being totally and infuriatingly deaf and he smiled at the memory and put it on top of the guncase. He paused. There was next a plain envelope addressed to him containing a letter from the missionary authorities expressing their sympathies at the deaths of his father and mother during the Boxer Rebellion and the base ingratitude of people brought out of their heathenism into the light, but he knew it by heart and did not open it. Almost forty years later even its envelope had the look of a museum object. Under the letter there was a package of assorted tinted postcard views of Wu Chang. He leafed through them, but they had all been composed from artistic photographic angles and looked nothing like the place he remembered. He thought there might have been a view of the Mission, but all the pictures were of quaint Chinamen posing grit-teethed carrying sedan chairs or telling fortunes. There was a stamp on the back of one of the views but no address, inscription, or date. He thought someone in the Shanghai Philatelic Society before the Occupation might have found it vaguely interesting but it seemed an ordinary enough stamp to him.

There was a leather bound volume in the trunk, a little collection of Chinese proverbs translated into English and privately published by his father's predecessor at the Mission, William Scarborough, inscribed in his father's scholarly hand *To my Son, John, from his affectionate Father, on his twelfth birthday* above a series of Chinese characters quoting one of the proverbs, *Shou tu shên ssú: study thoroughly and think deeply*, and the page reference, *p.93*. The spine of the book was cracking. It would be worth getting it repaired. He put it to one side on the bed.

Nowhere—not in the letter or on the postcards or in the book his father had given him—did it say that when his parents had been killed he had run away.

Below the space where the book had been there were piles of photographs. Edge took up his cigarette, relit it for the second time, and looked at the drawn curtains in his room. The overhead light caught the rising grey smoke and billowed it upwards.

The photographs were all of Missy. He took them out without looking at them and put them face down next to a little wooden box containing his mother's watch and his father's plain gold ring. (He wound the watch and found it still worked.) The ring was plain, worn down gold with a thick square face to it. He slipped it on his finger and sat turning it around and around. It felt very heavy and unfamiliar and he wondered why he had always had it in his mind that his father, who had always seemed very tall, had had such enormous hands and fingers. He looked at the ring on his own finger: it was a perfect fit and seemed no bigger than any one of a thousand men's signet rings. He took it off and put it on the bed together with the ticking silver watch.

He knew each of the photographs of Missy, all of them—the pictures from the houseboat trip up the river, the ones taken walking in Jessfield Park on Sundays, the posed family portraits of her with her middle-class Chinese family in Peking, the ones outside their new flat on Nanking Road, him posing grandly in his brand new Sergeant's uniform, the ones taken by street photographers: Missy standing, walking, caught looking at something off-camera, smiling, laughing, looking coy or serious, him looking posed, rather silly, ungainly, and proud in the self-conscious posturing of youth. There was one of him sitting on a rug at a picnic on a hill somewhere outside of Shanghai wearing one of Missy's floppy Summer hats and making faces, and another taken on the same spot (before or after?) pointing at something unseen down the hill and guffawing like a donkey, Missy sitting on the same spot looking demure and yet, if you knew her face, just beginning to giggle at something. (The same thing? He wondered what it could have been.) In a cardboard folder there was a posed studio portrait done by a photographer in Canton from the year they had travelled overland to meet a friend of her father's. The portrait was all light and shadows and chosen angles and looked like a wonderfully beautiful Chinese girl who looked nothing at all like anyone he knew. Even the hairstyle was different. He remembered long black gleaming hair getting in her eyes and mouth when there was a wind. He remembered what her hair felt like. The eyes in the portrait were glassy and disapproving: he remembered what her eyes had really been like.

There was a single picture that looked like her, taken upstairs in the Chinese tea-shop in Sun Sun's shop on Nanking Road. She was at a table by a window and as she had turned to see him coming in to meet her one of the photographers employed there had frozen her in time with a look of joy and anticipation on her face.

He drew in on the cigarette and stared at the exhalation of smoke across the room.

You could almost see her start to get up and come over. If you knew her face, you could see that she was about to—Edge said softly to himself, 'Oh, Jesus Christ, this is awful—' He looked up as there was a faint knock on the door and Barbara Ling came into the room in one of his old dressing gowns.

He looked down at the photographs.

'I came to thank you for taking me in.'

'That's—that's fine.'

'I had another bath.' She paused.

Edge nodded.

'I used all your hot water.'

'Well that's—' Edge said, 'That's perfectly fine.'

'I'm very grateful to you.'

'Would you like a watch?' He took up his mother's silver watch and held it out, 'I haven't really got anyone to give it to and so if you'd like to have a watch—' He said, embarrassed, 'So you can tell what time it is.'

'Did it belong to the girl in the photographs?' She came a little closer and looked down at the objects on the floor.

'I just wound it and it still works and I thought it'd be a pity to put it back in the box.' He asked softly, 'Would you like it?'

Edge said reassuringly, 'It still works. You can hear it ticking.'

'Yes.'

'I just thought it would be such a damn shame to put it away again when it's obviously of some use to someone, so I thought if you could use it—'

'Thank you.' She had long delicate fingers and fragile thin wrists, 'I'll return it to you when you want it back.'

'All right.' Edge said quietly, 'I've been drinking, you see, and—'

Barbara Ling said, 'I'll put it in my pocket for the moment. The strap's frayed. If you've got a bit of thread later maybe I can—'

'Yes.' Edge said happily, 'Yes, that'd be perfectly fine.' He thought, "That's twice I've said that. I haven't said that since I was a boy."

Barbara Ling looked at him carefully.

'That'd be just fine.' He smiled broadly at her. He remembered, that day on the hill wearing Missy's silly hat, pointing down at something and guffawing like a joyous lunatic donkey.

He said with great, secret pleasure, 'Swell!'

102

24

Across the quarter mile of black, night reflecting water, Singh and Duras, standing at the foreshore of the river could see the night silhouettes of the Japanese occupied suburb of Pootung, desolate and dark. Ice was in the air and a persistent sharp breeze from off the water. Singh indicated a dark configuration across the expanse of water—a misshapen derelict building. 'The old Chinese Eastern Railway. You can't make it out at night, but just below it there's the Yangkadu Wharf they used for loading. The lines have all been torn up now.' He swept his gloved finger a few degrees to the right, 'And that's where one of the big coal wharves used to be—the Nee Tai Ship Company. The colliers used to come down this stretch of the river and unload there. A little farther down is where their great rivals, the Han-Yeh-Ping Company used to moor *their* vessels. There was so much competition and bad feeling between them that half the time the colliers didn't get unloaded at all.' He waved his finger into the darkness, 'So a group of enterprising Europeans formed the Coal Merchants' Company of Shanghai and took up the slack. You could come out here in the afternoons and you couldn't hear the trains for the noise of the Chinese coal merchants flogging their coolies faster than the Europeans could flog theirs. People used to take bets on which would collapse first, the coolies or the competition.' He said quietly, 'Now I suppose all the old magnates and coolie floggers are living in cellars or sewers and coolieing themselves.' He paused and gazed out across the water. He asked solicitously, 'Is your headache any better?'

'I can get some pills from one of the Sisters at the school when I go back.'

Singh said, 'One of the most famous stories from when this city used to be something is the story of the man they couldn't hang.' He asked, 'Did you ever hear about it? It's very famous in Shanghai.'

'No.'

'Well, someone had better tell you before Shanghai and everyone in it ceases to exist. The man they couldn't hang was a policeman convicted of murder. He caught another man with his wife and right there, actually inside the police barracks, he chased him around the parade ground with an enormous Webley revolver shooting him—not shooting *at* him, but literally shooting him.' Singh said, 'Like a children's game, or that dance, the Conga—actually running about in circles shooting him in the back. The man he shot—another policeman—had very tough hide and it took the full six shots to finally put an end to him. The murderer was arrested after a struggle and duly tried and sentenced to death.' He moved his hand and waved it in the direction of the Japanese occupied area to the east, 'The old prison used to be near Ward Road and that was where the gallows were kept. Up there, they tried to hang him, but the trap wouldn't open. They tried it twice more without success and then, in desperation, they sent off for the British hangman in Hong Kong to come up and have a go. So he came up, reset the drop, let fly and the rope broke. Then he tried again and something else went wrong.' Singh said, 'I don't recall all the details, but it had something to do with a pulley jamming. The victim, needless to say, claimed it was divine intervention and, finally, his sentence was commuted to life imprisonment. Armies of newspapermen and travel writers used to go up to the gaol to buy his story. He claimed there was a trick to it that only he knew.'

'And was there?'

'No one knows.' Singh said, 'It was a good twenty years ago now and he's either dead or out by now. I knew him. He was a Sikh, like me, and so was the man he shot, and if anyone deserved to go flying off into eternity via the gallows it was him.' He said in an odd voice, 'The tough, loyal, unkillable Sikhs—' Singh said, 'I knew the bastard personally and he wasn't a real Sikh's arsehole. He was just lucky. With all the suffering and death about these days why should a good God have wasted his intervention on scum like that?' He went on without waiting for Duras to reply, 'No, he was just lucky, that's all.' He shrugged and passed it off lightly, 'It's one of the famous stories you should have heard if you want people to believe you were actually here.' He said quietly, still looking across the river, 'I've been thinking about my family in India.'

'I thought you might have been.'

'I mentioned to Jack Edge that I was concerned about them and he told me to slip across the river one night without telling anyone and go home to them.'

Duras did not reply. The water lapping against the wooden pylons of the jetty sounded thick and torpid, suffocating from lack of oxygen, slowing down. Singh said, 'There are certain of the hill tribes who will side against the British if the Japs invade India. And some of the powerful factions among the maharajahs and princes in the provinces. It's to do with *Swaraj*—Home Rule. They think the Japs might give it to them.' He touched at his thick black beard, 'I don't care what the outcome of it all is, but you can see that my first thought has to be the safety of my family.'

Duras looked across towards Pootung. There were little flashes of light there, and then seconds later, muffled gunshots. Singh said, 'I know my clear duty is to stay here with the Police, but since just about everyone's gone I don't see who it is I'm policing any more. My career hasn't been too satisfactory since Jack Edge and I, a long time ago, took sides against someone—a man called Moffatt—' He said bitterly, 'That's another famous Shanghai story—but I still feel a strong sense of duty. The tough-necked Sikh. But he's right. I have to think of my own people first—my children.' He glanced across the river. 'In the end, what happened was that all the coolies from the coal companies went on strike at once and *everyone* went bust.' He turned back, the eyes beneath the tightly wound turban soft and anxious, 'Do you think Jack and—and David Hooper—do you think Jack will be all right?'

'Yes.'

'And you?'

'Yes.'

Singh nodded. There was a buoy lapping under the jetty and Duras realised that hidden there, out of sight, there was a small boat.

'Olivier—'

'Yes?'

'Olivier, will you please tell them that I slipped into the river and I was drowned.'

25

Edge awoke. There was no light coming through the half-open curtains of his bedroom. There was silence. No sound. He lay in bed listening, but the city was still. Something was different. He looked unconsciously towards the door to the adjoining bedroom and it came back to him that there was someone in there—a woman—asleep. He thought for a luxurious moment of women and the smell of women, homes with women in them, dressing tables with bottles of talcum powder and make-up: all the conglomerate smells of perfumes and softness and disorder, lacquered dressing tables with mirrors and hair brushes with long strands of lustrous hair in them, mysterious cupboards with dresses and—He thought, "Maybe I could buy her a tin of something. Some sort of expensive bath oil, or soap. A little camphorwood box with a selection of soaps and bath oils." He listened and thought he heard the lapping of the river. There was stillness and quiet.

He thought, "I haven't bought anything like that for such a long time." He thought of his mother's watch, ticking away in a woman's bedroom again. Lying on a table ticking away through the night as a woman slept by it again.

It pleased him. The silence in the city seemed as if it might go on and on. He thought he heard lapping—the flowing, warm breezes of the wide river—the way it had once been.

In the darkness he smiled to himself.

He fell asleep with nothing more disturbing than the memories of bath soaps on his mind and slept soundly and still until the morning.

In Pearl Harbour, in the Hawaiian islands, five thousand miles away on the other side of the International Dateline, it was Saturday the 29th of November. On the high seas, ploughing heavily through a rising night swell, the Japanese naval force awaited the opening of their sealed orders.

Aircraft were below decks, unceasingly testing and turning their motors.

26

Standing inside Hooper's Number One warehouse at a little after ten the next morning, Moffatt said evenly, 'Let us get one thing clear, Mr Hooper, you don't like me and I don't like you. If I had my way you wouldn't even be here. You'd be back in New York or wherever it is you came from facing trial for grand larceny, or whatever you Americans call it. I happen to call it theft.' He went on without allowing Hooper to answer, 'And something else I don't like is seeing your tame Chinaman flitting around in the dark in here keeping an eye on me. I've now seen his silhouette twice, and if that weapon he's carrying happens to be what I think it is—a Mauser Schnellfeuer carbine—then I suggest you indicate to him by a word or nod that unless he takes it and himself off somewhere quick smart I shall arrest both of you for possession of prohibited firearms.' He asked, 'Is that clear? You have a right to defend your premises, but stretching the point is quite another matter.'

Hooper, a full head taller than Moffatt, nodded his head in the direction of one of the enormous roof-high stacks of crates.

'I should be in church, Mr Hooper. It's Sunday, as you may know. Instead, I find myself passing my time in what any decent man could only describe as a den of avarice and intrigue.'

Hooper said quietly, 'Then, if I may make a suggestion, why the hell don't you just piss off?'

'I've come to expect vulgarity from Americans.'

'What do you want, Moffatt?'

'The few Americans I've ever had the dubious pleasure of coming into contact with have been almost without exception the most common, ill-bred, self-serving collection of braggarts and curs on the face of the Earth.'

'I'll send you my reflections on the British by return post.' Hooper went over to a crate marked *Heavy Duty Blankets* and leant against it, 'Let me know when you come to the moment in your speech when I'm supposed to realise what it is you want and fall down with astonishment.' He took his pipe from the pocket of his oil-stained overalls and began filling it from a pouch, 'I'd appreciate it if you didn't smoke in here. High fire risk.' He lit the tobacco and began puffing to get it glowing.

'You really are the most impertinent Yankee bastard—!'

'I'm still waiting.'

'Which of this collection of trash is leaving the Settlement?'

'The collection of trash duly noted on the manifest handed in to the Police on Saturday together with a correctly filled out application for a pass. That collection of trash.'

'Your application was brought to my personal attention. You realise, of course, that the movement of strategic goods across international frontiers in time of war can be construed as provocation if the shipper is purportedly neutral?'

'Do tell.'

'I am telling you. I am telling you that in my opinion—in the opinion of the police—that such a shipment at the present time would not serve the interests of the neutral community of which you are a member and whose protection you claim.'

'So now you've told me. So now you can go to the church with a clear conscience.'

Moffatt said, 'I know you are supplying the Nationalist guerillas with arms.'

'I am supplying Chinese commercial agents with items specifically ordered, none of which is arms or ammunition.'

'You deny that blankets, machine parts and medical supplies are destined for military use?'

'They could be destined for old ladies' bedsores for all I know.'

'But they are not destined for old ladies' bedsores, are they, Mr Hooper?'

'I have no idea.' Hooper said suddenly, 'Mr Moffatt, let me tell you something: in New York when I was in private practice I used to use words and expressions exactly the same way you do. I used to write quasi-legal letters threatening court action where no court had jurisdiction or where I knew my client had no case. Sometimes, when the people I wrote to knew the law they realised I was trying to bluff them and some of them took it very poorly.' He pointed the stem of the pipe accusingly, 'Now *you* are trying to bluff *me* and *I* take it very poorly.'

'I am telling you what is in the best interests of the community.'

'If it was in the best interests of the community then there would be a legal procedure you could adopt to enforce it. Like refusing to issue me a pass. The Inspector at the Central Police Station could have done it on the spot without calling for you. He didn't. And nor can you. Mr Moffatt, you are trying to put the fear of God into me.' Hooper said, 'And as everyone knows,

God is busy today at the Scottish Presbyterian Church in Soochow Road, quite probably wondering why the hell you aren't there.'

'Hooper, you have the instincts of a—'

'I do. And a thief, which, as you have already said, I am. As a matter of fact I happen to have been innocent.'

'I find that extremely hard to believe.'

'So do I, at times.' Hooper said, 'We both know that when I call for it Monday morning that the pass'll be ready so why don't we spare each other any more mutual disgust and sit at home and listen to the Japanese executing the Chinese just across the wire?'

'I didn't realise that your excursions to arm the Orientals were in the name of humanity and Chinese national salvation—'

'They're in the name of the group of merchants whose goods these legally are, and in the name of their equally legal right to sell them to their fellow countrymen.'

'And do they think you're a thief?'

There was a pause.

'Or is a thief exactly the man suited to their purposes?'

Hooper glanced down at his pipe and turned it over and tapped it on the heel of his shoe.

'Oh, don't tell me you're motivated by some convoluted American sense of trust and honour?'

Hooper examined the ash on the floor and tapped the last smouldering cinders out with the toe of his shoe. 'Is that all?'

Moffatt said slowly and accusingly, 'We know about you, Hooper. We know all about you. We know you've made arrangements to get out the minute all your goods are well and truly sold off to the highest bidder, and we even know that your merchant friends—all of whom deserted their country at the first gunshot—have set you up with a bag full of industrial diamonds to pay your way. We even know how you're getting out. We know all about it. We know you're dealing in arms and smuggling and we even know who your contacts are.' Moffatt said, 'And flying that ridiculous little plane about with the engine turned off doesn't convince anyone that you aren't stealing your merchants blind.'

Hooper said with difficulty, 'Is that all?'

'I'm asking you to do something to help safeguard the continued neutrality of the International Settlement—'

'By not selling goods to the Chinks?'

'Yes!'

Hooper said suddenly, 'You ridiculous prick, the International Settlement was *built* on selling goods to the Chinks! How the fuck do you think the place came to be here? Because you bastards—the British—sold *opium* to the fucking Chinks! Never mind goddamned blankets and medicines—fucking *opium*! And then you sent in a couple of gunboats to mow the protestors down so you could sell them even more opium!' Hooper said vehemently, 'So let me tell you something, you Scottish bloody second-rate pain-in-the-ass, this town was, is, and forever will be, a fucking *plutocracy*—ruled by the goddamned rich! And the goddamned rich as sure as hell don't get rich by building granite churches and dressing up people like you in shiny uniforms—they get rich by selling things! These goods represent the capital of men who have had to *work* for a living—and by God, I'm going to sell them for them! Of course they left at the first fucking gunshot! What the hell do you expect them to do? They're not in the gunshot business, they're in commerce! *You're* in the gunshot business and they're the people who fucking pay you! So you do your bloody job and fend off the nasty Japs and I'll do mine to men who trust me and sell off their goods!' He shouted at Moffatt, 'And Mr bloody Moffatt, the flatfoot next to God, I trust I make *myself* clear!'

'You try and take that unregistered military aircraft up in the air just one more morning—'

'It happens to be a civilian airplane—registered—legally!'

'You just try to put a bloody automatic weapon on it—a bloody Lewis gun or—'

Hooper said patiently, 'I don't have a Lewis gun. If I had a Lewis gun you, my friend, as you and your psalm-singing cronies left their little church—you might well be the first to know.'

'Well, I've put the situation to you in the fairest way I could and I can't do any more in the face of your continued refusal to face realities.'

Hooper glanced skywards.

'I'm sorry to say, Mr Hooper, that the one great drawback to a city like Shanghai, with its many advantages, has been that its lack of basic discipline seems to have always attracted men and women of quite the wrong type.'

Hooper said quietly, 'Mr Moffatt, ain't it the truth?'

'When I've gone you can describe my appeals to you to your

little Chinese friend in the most comical way you can interpret them.'

'As a matter of fact, my little Chinese friend and I will resume—in silence—the game of poker we were playing before you came.'

Moffatt glanced around the warehouse. He sensed the armed mechanic's presence behind a pile of crates.

Hooper said pleasantly, 'And just so you won't feel you've gone away empty-handed, I was losing.'

Moffatt said blandly, 'Mr Hooper, in the end, people like you always do.'

He turned on his heel and walked out.

27

There was a rumour that Japanese flags had been seen hanging from the windows of Chinese houses along the perimeter areas, in readiness for the conquerors. And that the ship due on the 8th of December would be the last to leave before they invaded.

People had begun hoarding coal and food. The few Chinese merchants left in the International Settlement were trying to convert their assets into gold or silver.

It was even said the Sikhs had begun to desert and if that rumour was true, it was the worse sign of all.

28

At the end of the jetty, Moffatt regarded the silt and mud building up in whorls around the wooden pylons and mooring posts of boats and sampans long since departed or sunk. He rested his gloved hand against a corner post on a single remaining wooden railing and leaned out to peer down the length of the river. The mud was thick and slow-moving: he could see counter-circumferences of grey and brown silt moving around in it like embryonic whirlpools. The winter wind off the river was sharp and bitterly cold; he leaned back and turned up the collar of his British Warm with both hands, stamped to restore some warmth to his ankles and made a sighing noise. There was a group of refugees at the end of the wharf with tattered blankets over their heads and shoulders. He surveyed the remnants of the river—grey and lifeless, the few ships and boats still anchored in it rotting and swinging in extinct slow arcs—and sighed again. He touched at his collar to keep the chill out. 'I came to offer my condolences.' He gazed into Edge's face expectantly, 'You'll accept them from me, I trust?'

Edge said nothing.

'He was a good officer. Singh. Even if I hadn't known him personally, one glance at his record of service would have shown he was always conscientious.' Moffatt said, 'And he was a good friend to you. I can't say—to be honest—that I agreed with the interpretation he put on a certain occurrence—best forgotten at a time like this—but nevertheless I had to respect him for his sense of loyalty.' He said, 'I had to look into my office this morning on other business and heard the news. Everyone there had a lot of respect for him.' He gazed out at a moored and decaying collier in the mud, 'A writer once observed that the Sikhs and Gurkhas were the twin forces that really conquered and held the British Empire—I forget the writer's name, but we who know them, Jack, would find that very hard to disagree with.' He made a clucking noise of disapproval at part of the collier's hull, 'In normal circumstances the river would be dragged immediately, but I'm afraid these aren't normal circumstances. Any undue police or naval activity on the Whangpo at this stage might be—The Japanese across the river might construe it as offensive—laying mines or such like. Poor fellow, he must have lost his footing in the dark and struck his head as he fell.'

Edge said, 'I appreciate that you bothered to see the place for yourself.'

'Your houseboy told me where you were. I came to see you. We've had our differences, but the loss of a colleague transcends all that.' Moffatt asked, 'Is there anything in particular you'd like done? I'll write to his family of course, and have the letter translated into his own language, but since you were his best friend so far as I can make out I thought there might be something particular he would have wanted done.'

Edge said quietly, 'I'll tell you something, sir—'

' "Alec" is just fine at a time like this, Jack.'

Edge looked at him for a moment.

'Go on, Jack.'

'Nothing.'

'No, tell me what you were going to say.'

'It's not important.' Edge said, 'Do you know, I have never met anyone whose notion of duty was so over-riding to every other facet of his character as yours—'

'Thank you, Jack.'

Edge said, 'If you want my honest opinion, I think the conniving sod rowed across the river and he's halfway to the Punjab by now.'

'I hope you're right.'

'What?'

'I said, I hope you're right. I'm sorry to say I believe it's only wishful thinking on your part, but if it lessens the pain of the loss then I say go on thinking like that.'

'But you don't think so, do you? You think he perished gallantly and well in the service of the Empire, don't you?'

'I do, yes. He was a good and decent clean-living man and I intend to write to his widow and maximize every one of his good points—of which, as you know, there were many.'

Edge said, 'He was drunk! We'd been out boozing and he came wandering aimlessly down here in a stupor, tripped over, and ended up in the mud!'

'I don't think we need burden his family with that theory, do you?'

'In my considered opinion—'

'All right.' Moffatt said patiently, 'All right. Then at least he's had the decency to fake a good death. At least his final thoughts were to the community he served—to keep up their morale. Consider the situation if he'd just deserted—if our Sikhs and Gurkhas simply took it into their heads to run away. If he has gone over then he's had the British decency to make a good and convincing job of it. People are upset that someone like him has died—it's strengthened their resolve. I think if he did nothing else of merit in his life, that, at least, should earn him our thanks as a man of consideration and honour.' He said definitely, 'I intend to write to his family in the most laudatory terms. I think we can assume he struck his head and was unconscious when he went into the river. I seem to recall reading somewhere that the Sikhs look on drowning as a particularly offensive way to die.'

'That happens to be the Chinese.'

'Well, in any event, it helps the family if they think there was no awareness of death. I think we can also say he was on duty at the time. I can suggest in a subtle way that he died in the line of duty. Without actually going into details of an actual crime, I think the hint can be given that he died bravely. The Sikhs have a reputation as a very fierce and courageous race—his family will appreciate it.' The subject concluded, he asked abruptly, 'I see your name on an application for a transit pass put in by a rather questionable character. I refer to Mr David Hooper. The pass is for Tuesday night. I assume you're going as a private citizen.'

'I'm going upcountry to talk to some of Hooper's Nationalists.'

'May I ask why?'

'I thought they might be pleased to accept responsibility for eliminating two of their country's mortal enemies.'

'The two Japanese?'

'The two Japanese.' Edge said, 'I was going to make out a report in the morning and pass it on to you for official approval—'

'Working on the assumption that such a confession of responsibility would lessen the pressure you imagine the Settlement is under from this Japanese second-in-command fellow?'

'That's about it.'

'You take his ten day limit nonsense seriously?'

Edge said, 'I thought it wouldn't do any harm to cover all the bets.'

'No, quite right. All right. I think you'll find that the senior Japanese officer, Commander Nobata, has the situation well in hand, but why not? It fulfils our obligations if nothing else. I think in the long run you'll find—or at least, I will—that Commander Nobata is letting this young pup have his head solely in order to force him to make a fool of himself, but in the meantime we may as well seem to be carrying out our agreement to the letter. And apart from that, you can keep an eye on our friend of the full warehouse and let me know just exactly who his customers are. Yes. Put it in your report in the morning and go ahead on the assumption that it has my official blessing.' He made a musing noise in his throat and gazed out thoughtfully across the dying grey river. 'Yes, that will suit admirably. Well done.'

Edge said nothing.

Moffatt said quietly, 'You know the official feeling about this alleged invasion. It's all window dressing. The Japanese aren't going to risk going to war with us, but by all means, let's show them we understand their position and find them someone they can channel their anger off into more fruitfully. The Japanese and the Chinese have been at war now for years. The Nationalists would be delighted to swagger about claiming they were such supermen they could kill two Japs under the noses of the Europeans and get away with it.' He said, 'Yes, I'm sure you're right. Someone up there will be only too pleased to add the scalps to his belt.'

'It may not have been them. Quite possibly it could have been—'

'No, stick with the Nationalists. It'll go down better with the Japanese. The Commander will send his fire-eater—Isogai, or whatever his name is—out on some interminable mopping up operation and be rid of him for a while.' He said, 'On reflection, it saves face all round.' He said again, 'Well done.' He paused for a moment and leaned a little closer, 'I would have written to Constable Singh's family in the terms I've described whatever my personal feelings about him or you might have been, but now it makes the task so much more one I can square with my conscience to know that his friends, like him, really do have the best interests of Shanghai at heart.' He said proudly, 'A man like Singh, like you, at the final trump, would never desert his obligations. He died tragically and unnecessarily, but morally, certainly still on the right track. I'm sorry, Jack—but in the fullness of time you'll appreciate what I'm about to say—but I have to tell you there's no possibility on earth that Constable Singh got away to India. He fell into the river and, tragically, died there.' Moffatt said very quietly and sympathetically, 'I'm sorry for you, Jack, but I know it for a fact.' He dropped his voice to a conspiratorial level, 'Jack—' he glanced back quickly to make sure he was out of earshot of the refugees and even the police driver, 'Jack, what you don't know is that the whole thing was witnessed and attested to by a *priest*.' He said finally, with a look of genuine pain in his eyes, 'I'm sorry, my old friend, but there it is.'

He looked away with acute embarrassment, climbed back into his car and quickly went to church.

29

Edge said in astonishment, 'You must be crazy!' It was Tuesday evening, just growing dark and he looked into Hooper's warehouse at the massive outline of the largest road vehicle he had ever seen in his life. 'That's a furniture truck!' It filled almost the entire front section of the building. 'Where are your other trucks?'

'Gone to Heaven.' Hooper said with pride of ownership, 'This is my own.'

'This thing'll be spotted three miles off! Why don't you just paint a luminous target on it and have done with it?' He said very seriously and carefully as if humouring someone obviously demented, 'David, I can't drive this. Can you?'

'Sure I can.'

'Where are the other trucks?'

'They ran over a Jap minefield on the way in. They didn't make it to the wire.'

'And the delivery drivers?'

Hooper shrugged. He shouted out, 'All fixee, Henry?'

Henry's voice came from somewhere at the rear of the monster, 'Apple-pie fixee, David.' There was a series of rattling noises as he secured the tail gate chains. Hooper said reassuringly to Edge, 'There's no problem. I've got all the right papers: border pass, manifest showing U.S. ownership of vehicle and cargo, a document certifying the truck was searched by the Marines—one Lieutenant Dubrinski—and that the goods inside are non-strategic civilian blankets and paraffin heaters, and a perfectly watertight delivery notice to an American warehouse upcountry.' He looked again at the truck with an odd smile on his face. 'In a way, the more conspicuous we are the less likely the Japs are to think we're a Nationalist or Communist convoy and the more likely they are not to take pot-shots at us.' He added good humouredly, 'I must admit that aspect only occurred to me just now while we were talking, but it does make sense.'

Edge looked out through the open doors, 'It'll be pitch black by the time we're across the wire.'

'Silhouette.'

'All I want to do is talk quietly to one of your Nationalists. I hadn't envisaged making it a triumphal night parade through the streets of Imperial Rome—'

'You worry too much.' Hooper said cheerfully, 'By now a Jap patrol has found what's left of the trucks and reported to their bosses that they inadvertently minced up American property and have been ordered to keep their heads down for the rest of the night. It all works in our favour.'

'You should have been a lawyer.'

'All you have to do is ride along in the cab to keep me company.'

'What about Henry?'

'Henry stays with the plane.'

'With the size of that bloody truck I thought for a moment we might be carrying it along with us?' He asked, 'Just what are we carrying? Unofficially.'

'A few truck tyres.'

'How many?'

'Just a couple, and a few assorted bits and pieces.' He glanced at Edge's face, 'Seven hundred Firestone truck tyres and fifteen hundred valves for military radios. And a few heavy duty spark plugs.' He cleared his throat, 'Five thousand spark plugs. And a hundred Colt revolvers.' Hooper asked quickly, 'How is your Chinese lady? I hear from my informed sources that you were seen yesterday blushing your way through Sun Sun's department store searching out frankincense and myrrh.'

'I bought her some talcum powder. She didn't have any.'

'No?' Hooper said, 'I've noticed that too. In the middle of a war the first thing people seem to misplace is their talcum powder.' He grinned widely.

'All right.'

'I could have let you have some. There's a crate of it somewhere in back.'

117

'Knowing you, it probably would have turned out to be lethal.'

Hooper said, 'Look, this job is just in and out. We drive the truck up to an old railway station near Tsang Ka Zah near the intersection of the Shanghai-Nanking-Hankow lines, meet Chan and his cohorts, offload the stuff, and then beat it straight back. It's less than an hour away and, all going well, we can be back home to mother before midnight. All right?' He asked, 'Did you bring your pistol?'

'Of course I didn't.'

Hooper asked, 'What's her name, by the way?' He went forward to the van and opened the cab door, 'Your Chinese lady's name?'

'Barbara Ling.'

'Oh?'

'Her husband was a Nationalist officer, a Major, in Intelligence.'

'I've heard of him. Where is he now?' There was a soft hissing sound as he slid something wrapped in cloth across the leather seat and pulled it free.

'How have you heard of him?'

'Here, take this.' Hooper passed the cloth encased object over. It was obviously some sort of gun. 'Oh, I met most of them at one time or another—the people in Chinese Intelligence in this area. He was one of the people who arranged with my bosses to buy all this stuff. I haven't heard from him for six months.'

'His wife thinks he's dead.'

'Oh? Are you thinking of asking Chan about him?'

Edge hesitated. 'How long have you known this man Chan?'

'Six months. He came along when Ling and his friends dropped out. I think he's an honorary Colonel or Field Marshal or Generalissimo or something. He's in it for the commission. In his own way he's patriotic.'

'You never met Ling's wife?'

'No. Is she pretty?'

'What was he like?'

'Ling? He was all right. Very good English as I recall. Whampao Military College type. He was all right.' He said quietly, 'I really didn't have much to do with him. If his wife thinks he's dead then he probably is. Are you and she—as they say. . .?'

'No.' Edge said abruptly, 'The strangest thing is—this

118

morning—at breakfast, I noticed she wears something around her neck. A little pair of scissors. She's got long nails. I suppose she uses the scissors to look after them.' He said very quickly, 'I suppose she's just from a good family or that they have some sort of sentimental attachment to her, but it's—' He asked, 'You'd have thought most people would have sold everything they had, wouldn't you? To—Stupid, isn't it?'

Hooper made no reply.

'It is, though, isn't it? For a man my age to be thinking about manicure scissors and talcum powder—I gave her my mother's old watch. I must be getting senile.' He ripped open the wrapping on the gun and turned it over in his hands, 'What's this thing supposed to be?' He glanced disapprovingly at Hooper's face, 'This is a riot gun.'

'Do you know how to use it?' He watched as Edge snapped the catch to Safe and tested the weight of it in his hands.

'I know how to use it. Am I going to have to?'

'I hope not.' He called out to Henry, 'All finishee up now, Henry! Go guardee Bert Hall time!' He and Edge climbed up into the cab of the giant vehicle. There was a metal clip just under the dashboard and Edge snapped the gun into it; 'All set, Jack?'

Edge nodded.

'O.K., Henry?'

Edge saw Henry's face appear to one side of the truck. He had what looked like a Mauser Schnellfeuer carbine in his hand. He stood back as Hooper pressed the self-starter and the mammoth engine roared into life. 'Special Number One Apple-pie order truck!'

'Go findee Bert Hall!'

'O.K., David!'

'O.K., pal.' Hooper put the gear lever into first, let the hand brake off and the giant truck moved forward out of the huge doorway. He snapped the masked lights on and they lit up the cold canyon between the warehouses. He glanced across at Edge as the engine roared to negotiate the sharp turn out the doors, 'O.K.?'

Edge touched his ear, 'I can't hear you!'

The truck turned out of the warehouse complex towards the border where Dubrinski was waiting to pass it.

'Forget it.' He reached into his pocket and stuck his empty pipe in his mouth and glanced down quickly at the visible wooden stock of the riot gun. He shouted to Edge above the engine, 'He's a good man is old Henry!'

They drove steadily to the border and passed through the Japanese guards into a wasteland of blackness.

There were constant rattles and banging noises from the frame and engine of the overloaded vehicle—it swayed about dangerously on pot-holed and broken roads. The temperature warning light flashed red and then went out, then as the unwieldy truck crashed wheel-first into a pot-hole and then righted itself the light came on again. Everything loose or movable in the cab banged and jumped as the wheels went into another hole and then fell back onto the seats and floor like old junk. Edge could just make out Hooper's hands and wrists gripping the giant wheel. A series of warning lights flickered on as the front tyres rode over a rock and brought the truck down with a bone-shaking crack. Somewhere up in the mountains there was shelling going on—there were bright flashes and light in ravines and crevices, and to the left, as they travelled north west past the silent and torn up railways lines, the pop-pop of small arms fire as searchlights gunners swept the area for infiltrators. The light was being directed from a weapons carrier somewhere up on a hill. There was a burst of medium machine gun fire as the shooters on the vehicle sprayed another area free of phantoms.

The truck passed a single hut to one side of the road, still burning. Edge touched at the shotgun, but there was no sign of life.

Somewhere up ahead on a spur of the dead and twisted railway line there was a brief exchange of gun fire—heavy automatic weapons and the shallow crack of Japanese rifles, then a series of brittle bangs as grenades were thrown. The slits of light from the masked headlights passed across a section of line close to the track. There was a pile of black wooden sleepers in disorder by the hacked-out line. Edge thought he saw a shadow flit by them back into hiding and a little farther down the line, still smoking holes where high explosive shells had disintegrated a gang of refugees or looters. Briefly, he saw a shoe lying against the rail and then a little farther on, rattan baskets, burnt and frozen.

The sound of the searchlight-directed machine gun came momentarily closer and Hooper turned the truck off onto a side road and speeded up.

There seemed to be no visible signs of life anywhere. The truck struck an old frozen puddle in the track and sharded it into splinters as it passed over it. A long way off, there were dimmed lights moving—tanks—and behind them, although there was nothing to delineate them in the dark, Edge had the feeling there were long lines of heavily-laden troops, moving south.

Hooper gripped the wheel and dared to take his attention from the road and glance over to Edge. 'Village coming up!' He looked back quickly to the windscreen and pressed his foot down on the accelerator.

Edge nodded vigorously to show he had heard. Hooper's finger stabbed ahead into the glow of the headlights to show they were close. He pointed anxiously as the truck rumbled, swaying and gashing its gears, past the first house. There was a single light burning in the house: as they passed Edge saw the side wall had been blown away. A fire flickered in one corner of what had once been the main room (rotted rattan mats smouldered and burned like rush light candles) and then they were into the market square. A dead water buffalo was crushed up against the masonry of a burned house, and, all round it, little points of yellow metallic light: fired cartridge cases. Across from the animal there was a good strong wall still standing. The cartridge cases seemed to indicate it. It was where a firing squad had been.

There was still no sign of life whatsoever—in the mountains the flashes of gunfire twinkled and went out like bright stars. The truck passed over something with a thump and Edge caught a momentary wince on Hooper's part. Hooper said, 'A body.' Up on the mountains the guns stopped and then there was a display of flashes like fireworks and then a pencil-thin line of shimmering light as the flamethrowers set to work. A monstrous explosion echoed down in the midst of a cascade of vari-coloured lights as an ammunition cache went up and then, from the flat land on the other side of the track, an interminable raking burst of sustained fire as the machine gunners on the searchlight truck located a target and shot it and the land around it to ribbons.

An aircraft roared overhead coming from an empty night sky in an instant hammering of high speed machinery and howled into a tight turn. Hooper said, 'Nightfighter—Jap Zero.' The noise disappeared as quickly as it had come and then returned

121

in a screech as the plane changed course to service one of the mountains with its guns.

They saw a single strong light coming up on the road: a level crossing with one warning lamp still intact and burning on the gate. The glow lit Edge's features. He looked down at his hands. They were black gloved, hanging on to the passenger grip on the dashboard—they looked shiny and malevolent—then the truck passed the light and his hands were fragile cold flesh again. He felt the fingers aching with the strain of hanging on. They turned at the top of a hill and for a moment he thought he saw the reflection of the river, glistening white light—he craned out the window and tried to see the lights of the International Settlement. He heard Hooper's voice saying something above the engine.

'In and out, Jack. We can't wait!' He heard Hooper say something else—they seemed to have speeded up; the noise from the engine was shattering— '—and anyone who bothers us—' Hooper pointed down at the shotgun, '—shoot them!'

Edge thought, "What are all these people doing to this country?" He thought, "My country. What are all these people doing to this country?"

A white magnesium flare illuminated them in a brilliant box of stark light. All around them there were men with rifles—and the railway line—they were standing on either side of the shining railway line caught in frozen poses of readiness, aiming their weapons. The truck shuddered to a halt.

Hooper said, 'The good guys.' He glanced at Edge's ceramic white face in the harsh light—his own blue eyes were washed out to opaque windows in the glare—'Chan's men.' He said again, 'The good guys. We're here.'

The flare went out and returned a continent to brutal, simian night.

30

Isogai, his face blackened, a dark, eye-glittering outline hunched over the radio in the commander's section of his medium tank, flicked a switch and pressed the bakelite earphones to his head with gloved hands. A folding machine carbine was clipped to the bare armour plate by his head and below, in rows, magazines of ammunition and concussion grenades.

He listened. His hunched outline in the metal womb moved slightly.

'*Hai*—' he listened. He said again quickly, '*Hai*—yes.' He flicked the switch back to continue the lightning transmission, 'Confirm: Nationalist personnel.' He glanced up through the open hatch—the night was black and starless. 'Acknowledged. Civilian truck.' He listened again, glancing at the radium hands of his chronometer. 'Leader confirms. Enemy personnel in area of civilian vehicle. Responding.' He reached up and clanged the hatch shut as the tank burst into sudden life.

He reopened the radio frequency and began issuing battle orders.

31

Hooper glanced around anxiously. Standing in the glow of storm lanterns hung above the open tail gate of the truck with the riot gun crooked over his elbow, he clapped his hands at the loaders to encourage them. He called to a group of loaders pausing a moment by the growing pyramid of tyres by the railway line, 'Quick time! *Auso! Auso!* Quick time!' He snicked the safety catch forward on the gun and looked back over his shoulder into the darkness. He shouted, 'Careful!' as one of the loaders, like all the others, middle-aged and dressed in unmarked quilted jackets, staggered with a heavy wooden box of valves. He heard the heavy thumping of the shelling still going on up in the mountains. It seemed to be getting nearer. It was a moonless night—he rubbed his gloved hands together and glanced across to Edge and Moses Chan talking quietly on the periphery of the circle of light cast by the lanterns. They were speaking Mandarin: Hooper heard the sibilant rising and falling tones of the language and watched as Chan nodded and turned his head to check that the unloading was continuing. Edge touched his arm and asked him something and Chan turned back, replied to the question, and then shook his head. Hooper moved forward and peered up and down the shattered rail tracks for intruders. He glanced back to the truck and then up into the mountains. He looked at his watch and went forward again clapping his hands to speed up the work.

Moses Chan said firmly, 'No, it's not a responsibility I would care to take, Mr Edge.' He reached up with both gloved hands and reset his fur hat firmly on his head, 'No. I'm sorry. No'.

There was a single very loud explosion up in the mountains as a shell struck home and then, in rapid succession, two more. 'Are you saying then that the Nationalists are not responsible for the murders?'

' "Murders" is perhaps—'

'For the action then—or are you saying that if they were responsible, you, on their behalf, are not prepared to admit it?'

'I am saying that it is not in my power to say anything.'

'On their behalf? Or on your own?'

'What does it matter?' Chan cast a quick eye to the unloading, 'There is nothing I *can* say, Mr Edge. That is what I am saying: that there is nothing I *can* say.'

'You don't deny that the killings were done by—'

'They could have been done by anyone.'

'But, in the event—'

'In the event it would suit your purposes to say they were done by the Nationalists.' He smiled knowingly.

'I fail to see how eliminating two sworn enemies of the Chinese people under the very noses of the International authorities and—'

'The Nationalist Army is not susceptible to flattery. If the Nationalists had a reason to kill the two Japanese then they killed them. They—'

'Surely you mean "we"?'

'I am not concerned with the military aspect of things.'

'I cannot believe you do not have some rank and status—'

'Perhaps I do. I am merely concerned with supplying needed goods.'

'To the Nationalists.'

124

'Mr Hooper would hardly agree if it was to any other group of persons. My sole concern is to retrieve the goods in his warehouse before circumstances pass them by force into the hands of another party.'

'Your predecessor was a Major in Intelligence.'

'Was he?'

'Ling.'

'Oh, yes.'

Edge said, 'I am rather loath to believe that a man in the same position—a man like yourself—would be left totally ignorant of what was happening in this area.'

Moses Chan smiled benevolently, 'I am complimented that you think so.'

'There is a possibility that the threatened invasion of the International Settlement could be averted if we were able to place the responsibility for the deaths of the two Japanese squarely onto the shoulders of your Army. It would then become the job of the Japanese to—'

Moses Chan raised his hand. 'Mr Edge, I have been aware of the line of your reasoning for some time. Admitting however that a Nationalist patrol shot the two unfortunate Japanese infiltrators within the Settlement is simply not within the compass of my—'

'The Settlement is full of refugees.'

'So I believe.'

'Chinese refugees.'

'They are expendable.'

'And the goods still stored there?'

'Being gathered up, as you can see.' Chan said evenly, 'What you may not have realised is that almost all the goods I am purchasing belonged to the Nationalists in the first place. Those tyres for example. They were sold to merchants by the very Army Quartermasters they were entrusted to. I am only buying back what is legally already Nationalist property. The tyres, for example, came from America—and were paid for in American dollars. They were resold illegally to civilians by middlemen and corrupt officers, and now, in order to retrieve them, more American dollars are being paid. Agents less scrupulous than Mr Hooper would not have even sold them back to the Nationalists at all, but rather to the Communists or to bandits and cut-throats for larger profits.' Chan glanced at Hooper by the truck and then, quickly, up to the sound of the shelling in the mountains, 'I fail to see how I can assist you on my own authority and there is no one else in this sector I could suggest you speak to.'

'What about Major Ling?'

'He is dead.'

'Are you sure?'

'I am sure.' Chan said slowly, 'Could you not say you have information that the Japanese met their ends at the hands of elements of the Nationalist forces—without quoting the source of that information? Might that suffice?'

'Are you certain Ling is dead?'

'I am certain.'

'Why aren't your trucks here? Why not have them ready in order to get away quickly?'

'That is my affair.'

'How many trucks do you have?' Edge asked, 'Is Ling in command of the trucks?'

'Ling is dead.'

'He was taken by the Japanese. How can you know he is dead?'

'How do you know he was taken?'

'I was told on impeccable authority.'

'Then that is, similarly, how I know he is dead.' Moses Chan said, 'I see the position you Europeans are in, but to be coarse, the situation of the Europeans is not one that greatly concerns me. Asia is for the Asians.' He said abruptly, his eyes blazing, 'I don't give a damn about the invincible white skinned supermen! We are the masters now!'

'Not according to the Japanese. Surely it is in the interests of everybody if—'

'Edge—' Moses Chan said vehemently, 'Why don't you go home?'

'This is my home.'

'No.' There was a metallic noise from somewhere out in the darkness. Hooper's truck was almost empty. Chan said viciously, 'I will tell you about people like you—'

Hooper heard the sound. He looked up. There were three or four loaders coming back from the tyre dump. They stopped. Hooper saw their faces, then there was a whooshing sound that parted the air between them and a flash. He saw their faces disappear into the flash and then, a millisecond later, the earth around them began to rise. Yellow earth began to rise into the glow of the lanterns. He saw the outlines of the loaders go deeper into the earth as it rose. He felt the concussion coming, coming. . . He screamed at Edge, 'Mortar bombs!' as the explosion hit him with a deafening roar and hurled him against the side of the truck and then the area was lit in a series of fiery lights as the bombs arced over from emplacements and detonated in barrages. He saw one of the loaders run into an instant explosion. His arms lifted off. He saw fountains of blood rise up with the earth and then the white hot shrapnel showered into the pyramid of tyres and hurled them down and away. A machine gun began firing through the dirt and smoke: the unyielding line of tracer bullets went through men and equipment like knives. He saw Chan go running for cover somewhere into the darkness as showers of sparks glanced off the hard earth and rocks. A group of loaders stood helpless in panic in the exact centre of the lighted area. The tracer bullets came racing down to meet them and picked them up like rag dolls. He heard people screaming, then the mortars started again and covered the area in sudden stepping stones of light and catastrophe. He shouted at Edge, but he couldn't see where he was.

It must have all taken less than a moment. Hooper saw the muzzle flash of the machine gun in the darkness as it worked like berserk clockwork. He threw his riot gun to his shoulder and fired at it as fast as he could work the action. The flashes from the machine gun paused for an instant then, enraged, turned themselves on him. He heard someone shouting at him as the tracers whipped through the bodywork of the truck and he managed to reload the gun and get two more shots off from the hip.

A loader had a rifle in his hands. He was running with it towards the machine gun. He raised it to fire as the scythe of tracers raced at him faster than he could think.

The machine gun caught the loader across the stomach and cut him in two. Edge's voice shouted at Hooper, 'Get in! Get in!' Edge was shouting at him. He found himself pulled and wrenched into the passenger's seat as the truck lurched into life. Hooper got the riot gun out the window and pumped off the rest of the magazine. He heard the explosions getting farther away. They were away, on the road. He heard loose objects in the back of the truck jolting and crashing about in the vast emptiness.

Trucks were coming, and tanks. Hooper heard their engine sounds. They came to a wide section in the road and Edge pulled the truck off to one side and turned the lights off.

Edge said, 'Japs.' Hooper heard him saying something else, and then he heard him say, 'Some of the trucks are empty.' He sounded surprised. Hooper saw an officer on one of the tanks. He waved to him and after a moment, looking puzzled, the Japanese officer waved back and then gave the order through his microphone for the convoy to accelerate towards the sound of the firing.

On the driver's door of Hooper's truck there was an American Stars and Stripes flag painted in full colour. It was the first time Edge had seen it. He reached forward to the ignition key and paused for a moment before he turned it.

Hooper said in a whisper as the firing from the area intensified with heavy weapons 'So nice to be neutral. Jesus—no profit tonight.' He looked at Edge for a long moment as if he was about to say something. He looked down at his charred gloves.

'O.K.?'

'Yeah.' Hooper said, 'Home, James,' and leant back in the bullet riddled seat as Edge started the engine and moved the vehicle back onto the road. Two or three times on the journey back he seemed about to say something, but each time he changed his mind and stayed silent.

32

CONFIDENTIAL

For distribution CONFIDENTIALLY to British members of the Force only.

As a British member of the Force you may be worried as to your duty at the present crisis; not necessarily to the Council but to the British Empire in its hour of trial.

I can assure you that until the war against Germany is over our duty lies in Shanghai.

Not only have we the strongest official support for this view but if you will give the matter careful thought the answer is obvious.

I need not lay stress on the risks and hardships endured by our Fighting Forces at home, nor on the local conditions, dangers and difficulties all of you are called upon to face here. The greater the danger and the more trying the conditions to be faced *where we are needed* the greater the obligation to stick it out until Britain is victorious.

I feel many of you may be influenced by the newspapers' laudatory articles on those going home and feel you also would like to take part. You must remember that such praise is very ill deserved in the case of men leaving jobs which His Majesty's Government wishes them to retain.

There have been exceptions and a few of those leaving us, valued men I am sorry to lose, have genuine urgent reasons necessitating resignation at this time. Every case is considered on its special merits where such exist.

I fully realise the urge to go home and help and I shall be pleased to see and discuss things with you if it will be helpful.

In any case I hope this note will give you that substantial assurance many of you may need that every good British subject in the Police Service is needed in the Service and that personal and family reasons, at normal times worthy of every consideration, should at this time of crisis be regarded as secondary.

To some of you this means more sacrifice, but I am confident, in realising the situation, you will without further hesitation continue to carry your full share of our local burden.

You are requested to keep this note locked with your private papers and not to discuss it in public places such as canteens and so on.

(Signed)

Commissioner of Police.

Moffatt said quietly as she turned the paper over to see if there was anything additional written on the back, 'All right, Katherine?' He came forward across their bedroom and took the paper from her and put it back carefully into a manilla envelope, 'But you mustn't tell anyone I showed it to you.' He placed it carefully in a metal deed box on the bed with his framed notice of appointment to staff rank and a leather box containing his service medals from the Great War and turned the lock with a tiny key on his keychain, 'It was issued less than six weeks ago and since I had no hand in drafting it you can take it as a genuine un-biased expression of the current political situation. The danger of invasion by the Japs wasn't even thought worthy of mention. The only difficulty the European community is in is from patriotism.' He took the box in both hands and returned it to a small cupboard set into the wall and left the door open. (For a moment his wife saw his holstered pistol hanging in there from a hook.) 'I've broken the rules so you can settle your mind as to the truth of the situation.' He glanced back towards the bathroom. His bath was running, 'All right?'

There was a pause. His wife looked at the reflection of her face in her dressing table mirror. She gazed carefully at a strand of her hair that had fallen out of place, pushed it back with her hand, and then took up an ivory-backed hairbrush.

'Katherine—?'

'Yes.' The voice came out as sudden and brittle. She brushed her finger across her eyelid, 'Yes.'

'Good. Then I feel that in this instance, we can—'

'You could still get me on the ship, Alec. In your position you could get me on the ship whatever the cost.' She began brushing her hair with long hard strokes, 'You could. You could pull rank and get me on board. I know you could—you shouldn't deny it—I know you could!'

'Doesn't seeing that official statement make you see that it's—'

'It's all just words! I don't understand what it's about!'

'It's about the—'

'It's all just about people going home to fight the Germans! For all I know, there's another paper you're not even showing me that was written later that says that people should get out—and you wouldn't even show me that one! I don't know what this one's about—it's all just about men wanting to fight!'

'You stupid, bloody woman, there is no other statement!'

'I don't want to fight! I don't know anything about fighting! I want to get home!' She turned on him, her eyes blazing, 'Well, I don't need you—I've got my own way of getting home and you can't stop me! I know someone who can get me on the ship on the eighth and there's nothing you can do about it! I know someone!'

'Who? Who do you know? Have any notion of what passage on a ship *costs* by now?'

'And why should it? Why should it cost a lot?'

130

'You're not making sense—'

'If there's no danger: if there's no danger why should it cost a lot? Why shouldn't it just be the normal fare to Hong Kong or Macao or wherever it's going?'

Moffatt said, 'Because the ship you're talking about isn't going to Hong Kong or Macao, it's going all the way to Australia!'

'Why? Why should it?'

'Why? Because people like you have lost their nerve! People like you—it's getting out of China because people like you have got hysterical and started believing rumours and they haven't got the simple grit to see out their responsibilities—*that's why!*'

'You just want to hang on so that when the rich come back they'll make you a *taipan* and I can be a taipan's wife—a tai tai! I don't want to be a tai-tai—I'm just an ordinary woman and I—'

'Who the hell do you know who could get you on the ship without me?'

'No one.' She shut her mouth hard.

'Who do you claim you know?'

'No one!'

Moffatt said evenly, 'Listen, Katherine, I'm asking you to tell me what mad scheme you think you're cooking up—'

'I won't make a fool of you. You don't have to worry about that!'

'Katherine, who do you claim you know?'

'Mr Hooper! I claim to know Mr Hooper! Mr Hooper can get me out!'

'How the hell do you know—'

'I know *of* him then. I don't know him, but I know *of* him! He's got diamonds and gold and—Mr Hooper could get me out!'

'*Why?*'

'Because he's got money and—'

'*Why should he?*'

'Because he—because—' Her eyes filled with tears, 'I just want to go on the ship, Alec.' She covered her face with her hand, 'I just want to go on the ship. Please. . .'

Moffatt came over and rested his hands on her shoulders. He looked down at her hair, bright and glistening. It was grey in places and getting old. He glanced up for a moment and saw his own face. He said softly, 'Katherine, there'll be other ships next year. Next year things will all be different. People will come back—we'll get the river dredged—we'll get things back to normal. It's just now, with these peace negotiations going on in America—but they'll turn out all right in the end too. Why, in the Great War, the Japanese were our allies. The commander of the Japanese here is almost as Western in his thinking as you or I—I ask you, why would he want to do anything as silly as starting a war with Britain? It's just the Chinese they're against, not us. You've been such a good girl all these years—you just have to keep your chin up until things get back to normal. Your friends will all come back and you'll sit around playing bridge and meeting for tea the way you used to and all this will just be another story you can tell when we go back home on leave again.' He said tenderly, 'Katherine, I need your support. You and I have to try and make a fresh start with each other—' He paused.

'What if they come?'

'No, dear, they won't come.' He pressed a little harder on her shoulders to show she had his strength to bear her up.

Her voice was very quiet. He thought she wavered, 'But if they—'

'They won't come, dear.' Moffatt said, 'If anything like that ever happened I'd be here to protect you.'

'But if they—if you couldn't—if they came in through the door to do—what they—and you were hurt and you just couldn't—' Her face suddenly looked up into his, 'What would you do, Alec?'

'We don't have to talk about this, dear.'

'What would you do?'

'Let's go to bed now, Katherine.' He said on a sudden impulse of affection, 'We could talk in the dark.' He smiled at her, 'It's a long time since we've done that.' He grinned at something, 'Do you remember when we were first married and we had those quarters over in Bubbling Well Road and the walls to the next apartment were so thin that we—'

'Alec, what would you do?'

'Let it go, Katherine.'

'Please tell me!'

'I'd protect you, of course!'

'How?'

'How what?'

'How? How would you protect me? If they came through the door and they—if you were hurt and they were—'

'I'd spare you any suffering—'

132

'I—' Her face was confused. The sound of the water running constantly into the bath confused her. She glanced across the room and saw the open cupboard. The service pistol was hanging up in its leather holster. She saw its butt protruding: black and hard and—she knew the magazine held squat, huge calibre—She looked at him.

Moffatt said quietly, 'I swear to you, dear, I'd bring myself to do it. I give you my word of honour that before I let anyone—' He said softly, 'Katherine, I'm not the man everyone thinks I am. I promise you I'd—' He said quickly, 'Katherine, can't we—' He saw her mouth begin to tremble. She stared at him. 'Katherine, I know it's—'

'Oh dear God.'

'Katherine, please—'

'Oh dear God, you're planning to kill me.'

'No, dear, I—'

'Oh dear God, you're planning to kill me!' Her entire body shook at the sight of him, *'OH DEAR GOD!!'*

As the water suddenly overflowed from the bath and ran out into the bedroom, he had to hold her down on the floor with his hand over her mouth to stop her screaming.

33

Bent forward over the desk in his book lined study on the third floor of the Shanghai Catholic Mission for Chinese Children, Duras pondered methods of escape. All about him on the floor were unrolled maps and charts of China and its provinces crisscrossed with routes in black ink going from one Mission station to another—the impossibility was to know how many of the stations were still open. Several sheets of paper on the floor were covered in neatly-written arithmetic and multiplication where he had estimated the cost of shipping his artifacts out on the coming ship—but seventeen tea chests were obviously prohibitive in terms of space and finance and he had abandoned the idea. He had even considered Hooper, but whatever the arrangements the American had made to get his aircraft out certainly didn't include boxes of fragile treasures and again there was the question of cost. It was well-known Hooper had diamonds hidden to pay his way out and anyone reckoning passage in those terms was buying transport by the square inch and would have no room for anything but his own possessions.

He thought, "When the Japs smash their way into the school they'll reach for the first thing that takes their fancy. They're peasants: they'll see beautiful objects and know they're valuable and then, because they won't know what to do with them, they'll smash them. To get even with their betters." He thought with a smile, "Ingrained French class snobbery." But it was true he had seen it happen. He thought of his own church upcountry and remembered what they had done to the single pane of stained glass in the altar window. It hadn't been much: a nineteenth century copy of a portion of one of the Notre Dame nave scenes done in Chinese style, but wantonly and totally without purpose they had ripped it down from the window and crunched it into splinters with their rifle butts before getting on with the routine work of shooting his congregation.

He thought, "At least the artifacts weren't there. Thank God I had the foresight to hide them in the hills in anticipation." He paused and for the thousandth time since it had happened re-assured himself that even if he had told them that there were treasures for the taking nothing would have stopped the shooting. "All that would have happened is that they would have smashed the treasures in front of me before they killed me too—for not telling them sooner."

He thought, "I did the right thing getting them out safely." He listened for a moment to the silence in the school and thought abruptly, "Did I?" Upstairs, in the long dormitories there were children asleep. He thought about his dead congregation, "I did all I could. What more could I have done or said? The treasures were important. They are all the world has of thousands of years of Chinese civilisation and culture. What good could I have done by giving them to the Japs?" He said aloud in the book filled room, 'I'm wrong. I know I am. I should forget about escape and stay here with the children.' He thought, "They'll smash all my treasures to pieces." He said aloud, 'God in Heaven, what should I do?'

He thought, "If only I had the courage to open one of the boxes and deny the things inside it." He thought, "I'm a man

134

with an awful, single obsession." He thought of the children upstairs asleep, and of his dead congregation, of the stained glass window and of—

He thought of rifle butts and destruction and the unceasing firing and firing of guns.

He closed his eyes and tried unsuccessfully to think about God.

34

Still wearing overcoat and gloves, Edge stood wordlessly at the open door and surveyed the chaos of his bedroom. Cupboard doors had been torn off their hinges and the contents strewn on the floor, all the drawers in the dressing table had been upended and hurled against the walls, the mattress slashed into ribbons with a knife, the tin cabin trunk broken into and all the books, papers and photographs pulled out and torn into scraps. The shutter on the oak roll-top desk had been forced open and all the fitted compartments rifled. There were papers and letters ripped to shreds around it. Bottles of blue and black ink had been poured over the walls. Only the curtains were intact: the thief, at night, had been careful to work in secrecy. There was a heap of books on the floor next to the desk—each of the spines pulled apart and the pages scattered like fuel for a fire. A bedside clock lay drunkenly by the legs of the desk, its face carefully smashed and stopped a little before ten.

Edge looked at Barbara Ling. He asked, 'Lee?'

She said, 'I told him I wanted to examine his housekeeping books. He was stealing you blind on the squeeze.'

'Yes.'

'He defecated on your carpet.' There was a bucket half full of disinfectant by the open door. She nodded at the smashed box, 'He waited until I was in the kitchen. He took everything you had out the other night, the shotgun and anything valuable, and he tore up all the photographs. I've glued one or two of them together. They're on the kitchen table.'

'Thank you.'

'They're not very good. I couldn't find all the pieces.'

'That's all right.'

'I shouldn't have asked to see his books. It's not up to me. He probably thought I—he said something about talcum powder.'

'There was a tin of it on the table by the bed. It was for you. Has he taken that too?'

'It was poured out over—over what he did on the floor.'

He noticed for the first time that she was still wearing the dressing gown—one of his old ones, too big for her, wound almost twice around her waist. It was silk—it came down to her ankles. Momentarily, he saw the silver scissors on a chain around her neck. 'Did he take the watch?'

'No.' She held out her wrist to show him. 'You can have it back if you want it.'

'No.'

'Are you going to try to find him?'

'No, he won't still be in the International Settlement. He'll have gone across the wire into the Chinese city to try to get away to Canton or Chungking. He'll be long gone by now.'

'I didn't hear a thing. The telephone was ringing and I called him to answer it. I found this when I came in to look for him.'

'Who was it on the phone?' Edge hadn't moved from the doorway. He touched at his gloves but it seemed the wrong place to take them off.

'Someone from the police. He said he was the Duty Officer and you were to see the Deputy Assistant Commissioner for instructions.'

'O.K.' Edge felt a heavy tiredness in the muscles below his eyes. He put his hand to his cheek. 'I spoke to someone tonight who knew your husband. I asked him if he'd heard anything, but he hadn't. He believed he was killed by the Japanese.' He moved forward, looking down at the debris, picked up a single tan shoe, and put it carefully back in one of the cupboards. 'I thought maybe he might have got away and been looking for you.' He asked, 'Is it true that a lot of the goods held in warehouses here were illegally sold by the Nationalists?'

'It's true, yes. They were American aid delivered to the Army through Chinese agents who bought them back from corrupt officers in the same transaction. Then the goods were sold legally to merchants here in the International Settlement. My husband was trying to buy them back. He tried to convince them that they should sell to the Nationalists at a lower price out of patriotism.' She smiled at something, 'He also pointed out that if they didn't, and the Nationalists were victorious, then the merchants shouldn't make too many plans for their old age when peace comes.' She smiled again, 'He was very persuasive about it.'

'In every case?'

'Sometimes the merchants found more lucrative markets: the Communists or bandits—why are you asking me all this?'

'Did your husband believe the Nationalists would win?'

'Over the Japanese, yes. My husband had been in battle against the Japanese. He thought they were efficient soldiers, but he thought they could be beaten. Even though Chiang Kai Shek seemed more interested in using his Army to fight the Communists.' She offered, 'If you want to go to bed in the other room I can stay here and clean up.'

'What was he like?'

'My husband?'

'Yes.'

'It was a long time ago.'

'According to the men I spoke to, he disappeared—'

'He was captured.'

'—he was captured about six months ago. I wondered what he was like.'

Barbara Ling said, 'The photographs I've repaired are on the kitchen table. If you tell me which pieces belong to which picture I can glue them together for you.' She heard Edge draw a long weary sigh, 'Why don't you get some sleep?'

Edge paused. 'What will you do if the Japanese get into the Settlement? I was outside tonight and you can't go back.'

'Can you get me out?'

'No.'

Barbara Ling shrugged. 'Then I don't have any choice.'

'There's a ship coming at the end of the week. Do you know anyone who might be able to help you get a passage on it? Someone in the Nationalist Army? One of their people here in the Settlement?'

'My husband was only a Major. Generals can't even get out.'

'Then what will you do?' Edge said quickly, 'You can stay here—' he glanced around '—such as it is, but if they do come there's nothing much I can do to help you. As the wife of a Nationalist officer, you—'

'As the wife of a Nationalist officer—' She paused, 'As the

wife of a Nationalist officer, I won't give them the satisfaction.'

'I see.'

'If you could let me have a revolver I know where to aim.'

'What are the scissors for?'

'I'd prefer a revolver if you could spare one.'

'Don't you know *anyone* who could help you?'

'I'm sorry.'

'Maybe they won't come.'

'Yes.'

Edge said suddenly, 'God, they bloody will though, won't they?' He said quietly, 'They always do, don't they? The Japs, the Boxers, the—People like that always come.' He said abruptly, 'I'm glad he didn't get your watch.' He told her slowly, 'If there was some way I could get you out I would.'

'I believe you.'

'Do you?'

'Yes.'

Edge looked around the room. He felt an immense tiredness come upon him. He said intensely as she came forward to him, 'If only there was something I could do. . .'

He felt the swell of her breasts against him as he took her in his arms.

In Tokyo, the War Cabinet met for a late night sitting. All the military members of the Cabinet wore their uniforms and decorations. Their black leather boots made a clanging noise as they went in concert down the long empty corridors.

They carried maps.

35

Commander Nobata sat in his bedroom thinking of rivers and oceans and of the flurries of wheeling and crying sea birds that followed and circled behind the white foaming propeller wakes of metal ships. He was in his shirtsleeves and trousers, he looked down at his polished leather shoes and thought of decking and the warmth of officers' messes with starched white tablecloths and framed photographs on the walls.

He took a cigar from a small humidor on his bedside table, rolled it between his fingers to test the quality of the leaf and then snipped it off neatly with his silver cutter. There was a bedside clock by the humidor, a gift from the *corps diplomatique* in London on the occasion of his recall in 1928: its ticking went on uninterruptedly, the alarm hand set for five a.m. He lit his cigar with his gold Dunhill and watched the smoke curl up to the ceiling. He touched at the corners of his eyes with his other hand and thought of the seabirds again and of steam-driven ships firing black powder from their guns. He remembered old battle standards, long dead faces, charts and orders for places changed, out of date and forgotten.

Sounds came back to him: the throbbing of engines, bugle calls to general quarters, the squeaking sound the lanyard made as battle standards rose, the clattering of boots on metal companionways, orders and shouts of excitement, the smell of brass and linen, the catastrophe of smoke from broadsides, the sudden ship-length recoil. He remembered the clattering of anchors and the tranquility of strange harbours at night and the water lapping against plates: the hushed voices of men meeting in lamplit corridors and smoking quietly on closed down flying bridges—the gentle rolling of a great ship at her harbour moorings.

He remembered the old Japan. The colour of cherry blossoms in parks, the clicking of wooden *geta* on women's feet, rich kimonos starched clean and fresh, families walking in parks and gardens.

He remembered London, the sound of laughter and glasses made from fine crystal, the babble of conversation in gracious elegant rooms, The Great Western Railway leaving from Paddington Station amid a cascade of steam and strapped bags and promises to enjoy the countryside, old friends with Purdey and Holland and Holland shotguns in soft leather cases—the smell of fresh mornings on estates, the yapping of dogs and the banging of the guns as the birds came over on the glorious first day of shooting. He smelled the damp greenness of woods and the anticipation of dogs, voices a long way off along the line cursing their luck and laughing—the smell of brandy and claret in front of broad fireplaces.

He thought of this forsaken place and of the river—the boats and ships all rotted and rusting, infected with insects and decay, filling and wallowing in brackish silt-slow ponds of still filth. He thought of laughter: there was none left. Ships that turned at speed in calm water, their bows cleaving waves of foam and froth, the smoke from funnels finding the wind and arcing away behind clean lines and grace—he thought of his youth and having cigarettes clamped in his mouth against the breeze and feeling strength and speed in his muscles. He looked across the room at his peaked cap: fit for nothing now but a dead uncle's unclaimed cabin trunk in a dusty attic. He thought of compasses and wheels and rigid-backed alert ratings in immaculate uniforms turning them by fractions across the great and familiar abysses of oceans; he remembered the sound of ships' clocks chiming in darkened corridors as he lay tired and awake on his bunk listening to the throbbing of the engines.

He thought of cursing ship repairers in cable fouled dockyards and the shattering noise of rivet hammers and the smell of tar and paint and smiled at the remembrance of the faces of the chargehands. He thought of them swearing at him and explaining engineering problems, blueprints covered in abstruse technical drawings, the wind whipping the paper backwards and forwards as he shouted above the din that the Navy too had a schedule to meet; ducking down as some piece of machinery from the refitting sailed dangerously close on a crane, the chargehand continuing to put his point of view on his haunches.

He thought of the open sea and great warships sailing in majesty through it. He thought of sailor's stories swapped at cocktail parties and crawling through Nelson's *Victory* at Portsmouth with a British Naval officer intent on showing him how the old cannon below decks were served in the midst of battle. He thought of bumping his head and the officer saying 'My dear fellow—' and coming to his aid solicitously and then banging his own. The talk of modern men in modern ships.

His mind came back to the present and he rejected it.

He puffed his cigar and recalled an Oxford-Cambridge boat race. He looked across to his desk at the silver swivel calendar. Wednesday, December the third, 1941. He tried to recall what year the boat race had been—sometime in the late twenties—and who won. Or had it been a draw. He smiled and couldn't remember.

He thought of colours and noise and laughter, of the sound of the British officer bumping his head and measuring his length on the gun deck of Nelson's ship, rubbing his head and bursting into happy laughter—he remembered the smell of the seasons and warm days. He remembered his youth. He went to his desk and telephoned his old friend from London, the Dutch Consul in the International Settlement.

Then, after a short, wonderful conversation about old times, he went smiling into his locked room at the end of the corridor, and in total silence, not crying out once, using the fine Umetada Miojiu short sword that had been in the possession of his family for over three hundred years, firmly and without hesitation, acting not from desperation, he killed himself.

36

Isogai said reflectively, 'Your city is dying.' It was the next morning, bitterly cold and he stood a little forward of Edge on the roadway of a small hill overlooking the river. The decay and silence of the Settlement seemed to be in another country, just across a perimeter of rusting black barbed wire. 'It has all the signs.' He nodded towards the foreshore along the Bund, 'All the windows in your great buildings are broken or boarded-up.' The streets appeared lifeless and frozen in the morning chill, 'The river is finished.' He said almost to himself, at the picture of desolation, 'Not so long ago—a few months—the city was still alive. Barely alive, but alive.' He turned to face Edge, 'Now it is nothing but prey.'

'The city is full of refugees.'

Isogai grunted.

'Captain Isogai, as much as I appreciate this informal tour of the Japanese perimeter, it is Commander Nobata I expected to—'

Isogai asked abruptly, 'Are you what they call an Old China Hand, Mr Edge?'

'No.'

'What is an Old China Hand? Is it someone whose family was involved in the Opium Wars?'

'It is someone familiar with China.'

'Oh? I am familiar with China.'

'It is normally—'

'—associated with Europeans?'

'That is the usual association, yes.'

'The Japanese have been engaged in combat with the Chinese for many more years than some of your "Old China Hands" have been in China. Does that not make us Japanese "Old China Hands"?'

'I have no idea.' He began, 'Captain, in regard to—'

'You are a European yourself, are you not?'

'Not all Europeans are familiar with the current expressions.'

'I had thought it was a very old expression.' Isogai said, 'I had thought it was *current* in the middle of the last century.'

'Then you are probably better qualified to answer your own question than I am. Or perhaps Commander Nobata, when I see him—'

'He is indisposed.'

Edge glanced at the waiting Japanese staff car on the roadway, 'Then if you would have your driver take me to—'

Isogai said quietly, 'I come here every day.' He glanced down at the city, 'It is like a museum to me. A shrine.' He pointed his hand in the direction of the Bund, 'I know every building along the foreshore and the name of every street, the names of the famous Europeans who lived there—the Sassoons, Dents, Jardine, Matheson—all of them and indeed, what each of them was famous *for*. I have read books about it in English—about the warships that came up the river, the warehouses of the successful merchants, the races of sailing ships to return to Europe with their cargoes of silks and spices, the famous nightclubs and the stories of notable eccentrics and adventurers: I know everything about it.' He shook his head at something, 'I have never once been inside its confines, never once even walked along the Bund or past the great commercial houses but I know more about Shanghai than any other man alive.' He said forcefully, 'It has been my study—my life's interest. I should like to walk in it once before it dies, but it is impossible.' He glanced at Edge's face, 'Oh, it will die, Mr Edge.' He made an odd smile, 'And so will I. It is my duty to die, and, like the death of Shanghai, it is a death that is ordained at a certain time.' He said, 'I talk to you as one man to another because this is my special place—' There was a sudden sharpness to his voice, 'In ordinary circumstances you would have been punished for speaking directly to a Japanese officer without first asking permission.'

'I have certain questions to put to your Commanding Officer concerning the murders of the two Japanese soldiers.'

'He is indisposed.'

'Then may I put my questions to you?'

'You may not. Your questions will not be answered.'

'An agreement was made between the authorities in the International Settlement and Commander—'

'I am aware of the agreement. You were given ten days. You have less than six of them left.' Isogai glanced down towards the river, 'There is nothing more to be said.'

'You cannot believe you are capable of fighting the entire world! The Chinese and the—' Edge said peremptorily, 'I wish to register an official request to speak to the Commanding Officer of this sector.'

'The acting Commanding Officer for this sector is myself.' He said abruptly, 'The Chinese are a corrupt race. Their forces of the spirit have been weakened by centuries of obese self-satisfaction and culture. They have forgotten how to be lean. They wallow in corruption and indecision and they are propped up by profit-mad American businessmen who are also fat and well-fed and wear black top hats and carry useless canes with diamond tops.' He waved an accusing finger in the direction of a border emplacement across the wire manned by American Marines, 'And our potential great enemies, the Americans— their soldiers on parade are covered from head to foot in gold and silver braid and badges and lanyards. They wear laundered uniforms, with chocolate bars and chewing gum in their pockets and they call their officers by their first names.' There was a long burst of machine gun fire a long way off, 'And the British go into battle playing music. And they *surrender*. The Japanese do not surrender.'

'That does not interest me.'

'We in Japan have no need of such braid and badges and comforts. A soldier's task is to infect and kill—the Japanese Army has poisonous fangs and they are always bared.' He looked down at the city and said simply, 'The International Settlement will feel them.' He said suddenly, 'I will die down there. It will be my grave.'

'Is that why you—'

'Why I come to contemplate it? Yes. It will be where I fall for Japan. I am prepared to die in whatever region of battle the Emperor commands me, but it is fitting that it should be in Shanghai. It accords with my personal wishes.' He turned to face Edge, his eyes bright and intense, 'I have prayed for it—for

143

Shanghai to be my death-place—and the Emperor has answered my prayers.' He swept his hand down towards the city, 'It will be the grave of Isogai Masonobu and I shall kill many of the Emperor's enemies to consecrate it and to show myself worthy of his special consideration.' He said, 'You were given ten days. Then there will be a great battle and perhaps you and I will meet as enemies.'

'I do not find that such an appealing thought.'

'I embrace it!'

'We are still attempting to find the people who killed your soldiers. A bargain was struck.'

'I do you a great honour! I accept the Europeans who built the International Settlement as men of worth—of giants fit to strive against the Japanese warrior caste and give and receive glorious death in the flames of combat!' Isogai said, 'I will tell you how bargains are struck by the Japanese Army—no, I will *show* you— I will have my driver *show* you—I will walk back down the hill and you may ride—go! Go to the car!' He shouted out a series of orders in Japanese and the driver—a uniformed Corporal— stepped out of the driver's seat and opened the rear door, 'Go and see!'

'What? See what?'

'The invincibility of the ultimate Old China Hands—we, the Japanese.' He took Edge by the coat sleeve and held him for an instant, 'Shanghai will fall.' He stared intensely into Edge's eyes, 'Your city will die. Your city will die because I, Isogai Masonobu, will kill it! It will be my memorial!' He said with enormous anger, *'Go!'*

37

Their destination was a heavily guarded quartermaster's compound set off to one side of a giant tank park filled with light and medium fighting vehicles. The driver motioned to Edge to stay in the car and then himself got out, showed a pass to the sentry on the gate and exchanged a few words with him. The sentry nodded and indicated a mound of stores near the centre of the compound. Satisfied, the driver came back and got into the front seat of the car, grinning.

Edge took out his notebook and wrote a single Chinese character on a clean page and added a Japanese interrogation mark to it. The driver looked down at it and shook his head.

The character read, *Captured?* The driver took out his own pen and crossed it out. He jerked his head in the direction of the Firestone tyres and spark plugs in the centre of the compound, all in perfect condition and ready for immediate Japanese use, and wrote instead, *Bought.*

The driver looked at the European's face for a moment, then said sarcastically in English, 'Old China Hand.'

It was an expression he had heard his officer say over and over on his many trips to the hill overlooking the International Settlement and the driver had picked it up in order to curry favour.

He said it to the European again and grinned at the, to him, meaningless words with the happiness of a half-educated man who thinks he has mastered a great and important concept.

38

Hooper shouted, 'But Goddammit, Jack, Chan *paid* me! He sent his boy around first thing this morning and he *paid* me—I've wired it off through Hong Kong to America!' He clenched his fist and stared out of the window of Edge's apartment into the approaching darkness of night, 'His boy said they'd fought off the Japs and gotten the stuff away and then, in goddamned American dollars, he *paid* me!' He stared at the reflection in the window of his own face, 'That dirty son of a bitch—' he swung around to face Edge and Barbara Ling, 'Goddammit, he *paid* me! That's why there were no trucks waiting! He was going to use Japanese trucks! He lost most of his original trucks in that mine-field and he was going to use Japanese trucks—Then who the hell was that firing on us? Christ! It was the Nationalists—the *real* Nationalists—' He looked at Barbara Ling for confirmation, 'It was, wasn't it?'

Edge said quietly, 'Evidently Major Ling had been after Moses Chan for some time. When he caught up with him Chan had him taken by the Japanese.'

'You're certain it was the same stuff? The Firestones and the —'

'It was the same stuff. It was all there.'

'Yeah!' He looked at Barbara Ling, 'And the people I work for—the ones in the States—the great Chinese patriotic merchants —'

'They employed Chan as their go-between to the Japanese.' Barbara Ling looked away.

'And your husband, did he think I was in it too?'

Edge said, 'What does it matter?'

'He did, didn't he? He knew who the merchants had hired. What did he refer to me as? As their goddamned little—'

'He thought you were an American gangster they'd found in —' She added quickly, 'I didn't know Jack knew you —'

'Jack, I thought they believed me! I told them about the embezzlement and I thought they believed me! I thought they were fair men who—' he said bitterly, 'I was just what they wanted, wasn't I?' He asked Edge abruptly, 'What about Chan?'

'I don't know.'

'That bastard's outlived his usefulness too, hasn't he? By now.'

'I would have thought so.'

'This character Isogai—the one who's taken over—'

'He probably had Chan shot. David, you weren't to know you were being used.'

'And who's going to believe that?'

'*I* believe it.'

'Yeah.' Hooper nodded. 'How are you two getting along anyway?' He said evenly to Edge, 'You look happy enough.' He smiled at Barbara Ling, 'The love of a good woman—' He looked away. 'Well, that's the end of it then, isn't it?'

'You can still get out.'

'Sure. And go where? No.' Hooper said slowly, 'War's coming. We all know that. And what does that make me: selling American goods to the Japanese? And worse, American goods given by the American people to the Chinese. They execute traitors at home these days, Jack. They strap them into the electric chair and then they juice them until their hair catches fire. They'd already like to get me back there on the fraud charge. They tried to extradite me once—for this they'd send in J. Edgar Hoover to drag me back by the fucking heels!' He said, 'No, I can forget going back anywhere. I've been conned by experts and you can lay odds they've got iron clad proof showing they only dealt with the Nationalists and that selling to the Japs for profit was entirely my idea.' He said suddenly quietly, 'Well, the warehouses aren't quite empty yet and by Christ, they're going to find the rest of their profits badly cropped!' He paused. 'One thing: Henry had nothing to do with all this. You know that, don't you?'

'Yes.'

'And when you make your report—'

'I didn't mention anything about the goods—'

'But you will. If this character Isogai feels safe enough to spill the beans then it's sure he's safe enough to set up the invasion. So you have to report it—but Henry doesn't figure in all this and I want to leave him out. I swear to you, Jack, he had no part in any of it and I want you to take my word for it and just leave him out. All right?'

'And what about you?'

'Tell them the truth about me.' He paused, 'But if you could —' He halted awkwardly, 'You remember that idiot Dubrinski?'

Edge nodded.

'Well. Clarence kind of thought I was some sort of—he's the American type, he looks up to people, you know. . . ' He said with an embarrassed shrug, 'And I wouldn't like him to think of me as—he's a good fellow, Jack. He believes all that stuff about the good old U.S. of A. and, well, I wouldn't like him to think that I've been laughing at him—'

Barbara Ling said with concern, 'But you haven't.'

'You know how stories get—' He asked Edge, 'Would you do that for me, Jack. Tell Dubrinski the truth? I seem to be asking all manner of favours, and I can't think of one damn reason on earth why you should do any of them. I always thought I was an independent type—the rugged American individualist who didn't give a shit about the Old Spirit of '76, but the truth is—' There seemed to be tears in his eyes, 'The truth is, I—I really—I really liked living in the fucking place and the trouble is I believe all that horseshit about—' He forced a grin, 'When they play the goddamned Star Spangled Arsehole I have to hold onto my seat just to stop leaping up and saluting and that's—that's really disgusting. It even disgusts me—' He said angrily, 'And they've conned me out of everything—everything! Well, Christ, they've just taken a sudden nose dive on Wall Street, those bastards!'

Barbara Ling said, 'I'm sorry.' She touched him on the arm, 'If my husband had known you better he could have—'

'I wouldn't have listened.' He patted her on the hand and stepped back a pace, 'No, you stick with the good guy in the white hat.' He said to Edge, 'It puts paid to what Moffatt called my unregistered little warplane.'

'Bert Hall?'

'Bert Hall.' He looked at Barbara Ling, 'It's a long story.' He paused for a moment, 'I told Moffatt to stuff it, Jack, I told him that he could stuff it, that it was a duly registered non-military, safe little civilian plane . . .' He paused again, 'But it was a warplane once.'

'I know that,'

'It flew in battle over Europe with the American volunteers in France.' He looked at Barbara Ling, 'With the *Lafayette Escadrille*. It was a warplane.'

'Yes.'

'I saved it from the scrapheap. I believed in those bastards so much I didn't even use their petrol! Jesus, they must be laughing!' He said to fix it in Edge's mind, 'That was all Henry did: he helped me with the plane—he had nothing to do with anything else except the plane. I want you to believe that.'

Edge nodded.

'The poor bastard is going to be heartbroken when he hears that Bert Hall isn't getting out and that he isn't going with it. I don't think he gives a damn about me, but Jesus, that plane is his life! By Christ, if those lying bastards safe in their big houses in the States think they're going to get another cent's profit then they'd better sell out now to the highest bidder!' He glanced out the window at the dark expanse of the river, 'Thanks anyway for not giving me a load of crap about how I can explain it all away to people like Moffatt and start off again with a clean slate.' He said suddenly, 'There aren't too many of us left now, Jack, are there?'

'Not too many.'

'Are you getting out? You and Barbara?'

'I can't.'

'Did you tell Singh to go?'

'Yes.'

'I thought so. I thought Olivier would lie for him.'

'He won't say if he did or not.'

'Yeah.' Hooper said, 'That was a hell of a good club we had going in Jean-Claude's for a while, wasn't it? It was a hell of a good club. Christ, Jack, we had some funny nights there!' He went on without warning of what he was about to say, 'I killed those two Japs, by the way. In case you were wondering.'

'What?'

'Yeah. It was me. I don't think it makes any real difference to the situation, but if it's of any use to you then you might as well know. They came to the warehouse and got in and I killed them both. I thought they were thieves. Obviously now, they'd been sent around by the Japs to check that Chan had given them a complete list of what to expect to come their way on the shipments. They saw the plane and I thought they were trying to—so I killed them and dragged their bodies away from the warehouse.'

'By yourself?'

'Yeah, by myself. I came in suddenly from outside and there they were in the dark and I killed them.'

'Just like that?'

'Yeah, just like that.'

'You came into a darkened room and you made them out straight away. And then you drew your little revolver and you shot them both dead. With one shot each. At medium range. Is that what happened?'

Hooper nodded.

'You couldn't even hit that goddamned Hot Pot at medium range with one shot!'

'Well, that's what happened—'

Edge said, 'And furthermore, they were both killed by high velocity bullets. It was in the report. They were killed with a rifle. You don't happen to carry a rifle.'

Hooper said nothing.

'But Henry does. He carries a Mauser carbine. I've seen it.'

'You leave him out of this! I've told you what happened and you can put it in your report and that's all there is! Why the hell don't you and your woman get on board the ship and just get the fuck out of here? Where's the percentage of staying on and getting your goddamned throats cut?'

'It's not a question of percentages!'

'Of course it's a question of percentages! Do you really think the entire Japanese Army is hanging about waiting to see whether or not you find out who knocked off two goddamned *Privates*? O.K., now you know and so what? No one around here is going to hand over a European to them! Don't waste your time telling them it was the Nationalists—they're not going to bother about that either! They're coming in when they want to and if they haven't got one damned excuse then they'll sure as hell find another!' Hooper said, 'Listen, it's all up with us here in China—get out while you can—both of you.' He glanced at Barbara Ling, 'What about you? Would you go?'

'Yes.' She glanced at Edge, 'I'd go if I could.'

'Goddammit, Jack, what else do you need?'

'It isn't as easy at that! Where the hell would I go?'

'Somewhere with *her*! That's what you want, isn't it?'

'Dammit, David—'

'All right.' Hooper raised his hand, 'All right. Just so long as you remember what I said about Henry.'

'And what about you, blast it?'

Hooper looked away.

'What about you, David?'

Hooper said softly, 'Back there, at the railhead that night, while I was standing about like Pecos Charlie shooting from the hip—He hesitated for a moment. 'You saved my life back there, Jack.' He came forward and put out his hand. Edge took it. 'I won't forget it. Whatever else people can say about me—' He paused again. 'I won't forget it, Jack. You can be sure of that.' He released Edge's hand and grinned at Barbara Ling, 'You take my advice, lady, and get this grizzled old flatfoot out of here—O.K.? Quick smart. All right?'

Barbara Ling looked at him sadly.

He said as he went to the door, 'Jack, those nights at the Gindrinkers' Club—' he paused to collect himself. He said, blinking, to Barbara Ling, 'Jesus, you don't know what you missed!'

He looked at them both for a long moment then opened the door quickly and was gone.

39

Seated at his desk, Moffatt glanced quickly over his shoulder. The door was closed and he was alone in his bedroom. He said into the telephone, 'No, sir, no one can overhear me.' He listened intently, looking down at the whorls and striations of polished grain on the desk top.

The Police Commissioner's voice said slowly, 'I'm sorry to ring you in the evening like this, Alec.' He paused for a moment. There was no sound behind his voice and Moffatt visualised him at the double sized mahogany desk in his carpet lined office, 'Earlier today I received a telephone call from the Dutch Consul here, Mr Meyer. It was a disturbing call and it seemed only right to me that my senior officers should be appraised of its import immediately after I had fully considered it.' He stopped again. 'I have only just now come to a final decision about it.'

Moffatt said, 'Yes, sir. . .'

The pause continued. 'I believe you were personally acquainted with the sector officer, Commander Nobata? In the course of your duties.'

'Yes, that's right. What about him?'

'He's dead, Alec. We haven't any official confirmation from the Japanese, nor in the nature of things do we expect any, but it is the opinion of the Dutch Consul, who knew this man personally over a number of years, that for reasons best known to himself, he decided to take the easy way out and commit suicide.' He added quickly, 'I have no understanding of his motives, nor does the Consul—at least, none that make good sense to me—but I am persuaded that the Consul knows what he's talking about. Evidently he had a late night telephone conversation with this man Nobata and it was made pretty clear to him by implication that, politically, he was on the way out. I've looked up a report from your man Edge in which he details a meeting he had this morning with Nobata's obvious successor, a Tank Captain named Isogai, and, if Edge is to be believed, Isogai is a very dangerous man indeed.'

'There is no doubt, sir, that Sergeant Edge knows the Oriental mind.' He looked around quickly, but his wife was still in the sitting room on the other side of the closed door, out of earshot.

'One of the reasons, no doubt, he struck you as the suitable man to deal with these people.'

'One of the reasons, sir.'

The Commissioner's voice said abruptly, 'Alec, notwithstanding the circular issued to our people not so long ago, I feel it may be in the best interests of the British Empire to save what we can now in case—' he paused for a moment, looking for the words, '—in case events overtake us. Alec, to put it into plain words, I'm sending some of our men home.'

'In my opinion, sir, the Japanese would never dare—'

'—to where they can be of more value to the nation. Men who, by virtue of their personalities and experience, would be a great loss to the conflict in Europe if they were to be interned or killed in Shanghai fighting a tin-pot nation like the Japanese. While there appeared to be some possibility that the invasion of the International Settlement might only be the posturing of a few lunatics among the Japanese junior officer class and that it would be held in check by wiser heads, I felt justified in keeping men here. As you know.'

'Yes, sir.'

'—however, the suicide of this man Nobata leads me to believe that there is some sort of power struggle going on amongst the Japanese and that, at least temporarily, the Young Turks have got the upper hand. I've spoken by phone to the Military Attaché at the American Embassy in Chungking and although he was guarded in his comments it is apparently common knowledge that the Washington peace talks have been somewhat less than reassuring.' His voice dropped to a confidential level, 'It is now my opinion, Alec, that the Japanese might chance their arm momentarily and take the Settlement in the hope that they could avoid intervention by claiming it to be part of their conquests in China. How the Americans might react to that I have no idea, but with the war in Europe straining every muscle I don't think we can expect much response from the United Kingdom or the Commonwealth. In that case, I feel it is my duty to make up a list of men and get them away to safety—back home.' He said with forced enthusiasm, 'God knows I had enough applications before the circular, so there's no shortage of patriotism; and our officers are trained men—their value back home would be enormous.'

'Yes, sir.'

'It's a hard decision to make, Alec, to balance apparent duty and real necessity, but I feel it's the right one.'

'Very well, sir.'

'I knew I could count on you.'

Moffatt paused. It was gratifying to hear it said. He asked, 'How do we propose to evacuate such a large number of people?'

'In fact, there aren't that many. Our very first duty is still to our people in the Settlement. I've made a list of the men to go and it only comes down to about sixteen names. They'll be leaving on the ship due this week —' he hesitated for a moment and must have looked at a piece of paper on his desk, 'The *Bocca Tigris*—she's a small freighter with Macao registration, sailing for Australia. From there they can be flown back to England by the Air Force. Naturally, their families will accompany them, although, with one or two exceptions, their wives and children are already safe in England.'

'It should be a great reunion for them, sir.' Moffatt said, 'I appreciate you taking the trouble to let me know personally.' He said encouragingly, 'Maybe we can arrange a send-off at the Shanghai Club.'

'I'd be happy to order the champagne myself out of my own pocket.'

'I know you would, sir.'

The Commissioner said, 'My God, Alec, I wish I were younger. I wish I could find a reason to send myself. To have a go at those Nazi bastards.'

'Yes, sir.'

'Something for your book about your experiences one of these days.' He made a hollow laughing sound, 'The chapter entitled, "How the Old Goat Cried in his Beer at the Sound of Bugles." ' He went on suddenly in an efficient tone of voice. 'We'll have to begin destroying documents and files as soon as possible— anything that might be of use to the Nips—I thought I'd put you in the picture first personally. That's why I took the liberty of telephoning you at home—'

'It was no liberty, sir.'

'Alec, the International Settlement in Shanghai has been in existence exactly ninety-nine years. Next year would have been our centenary—I think the police can say that in that time they have given of their very best. They have something to have been proud of. I think—I would hope—that when all this is over and you begin to enjoy your well-earned retirement and write that book you're always talking about, that that would be the line you would take yourself.'

Moffatt said lightly, 'Unless I accidentally commit some terrible *gaffe* and get myself fired, sir, I have no intention of retiring for some time.'

'You are very, very highly thought of in this office, Deputy Assistant Commissioner.'

'Thank you, sir.'

'I can tell you, Alec, that in the normal course of events, when my own retirement would have fallen due in two or three years, it would have been my very strong recommendation that you should have been the one to fill my chair. As Commissioner.'

'Thank you very much sir!' Moffatt said in a whisper, 'Thank you very much indeed, sir—'

'I know the sort of man you are, Mr Moffatt. Not unlike me—a man who perceives the difference between right and wrong, duty and self-indulgence, and liberty and licence, clearly and cleanly, based on Christian principles that have not changed for two thousand years.'

'I hardly know what to say, sir—I —' Moffatt sought for words, 'You can always rely on me, sir.'

'I do, Alec. I know what the concept of duty and service means to you.'

'Thank you, sir.'

'How is Mrs Moffatt?'

'Very well, sir, thank you.'

'Good.' There was an awkward pause. 'Listen, Alec—'

'Sir?'

'Some people may think that the few men chosen to go are running out. There can't be any hullabaloo about their going. No receptions at the Club, nothing. The danger of alerting the Japanese to our apparent concern would be too great. Officially, I can't appear to rescind my earlier circular. Officially, I have to say I'm releasing these men from duty on strictly compassionate grounds. To the people left behind here I'm sorry to say it might appear that these men were nothing more than craven cowards running out on their responsibilities.' He said, quickly, 'I know they are all officers who would not wear happily what might appear to some to be a slur on their characters, but our country is locked in war for the second time in twenty years and we all have to pull together to finish off the bloody Hun for once and for all.' He said, 'Only they and I will know the real reason for their leaving. Shanghai is doomed, Alec, I have a funny feeling none of us will ever meet again as fellow policemen—' There was a long pause. 'Alec, these sixteen or so people—'

Moffatt waited, running his finger idly across a line of grain in the top of his desk.

'Alec, you're one of them.'

She heard him shouting. From the sitting room she heard his voice shouting the same words over and over. She went to the bedroom and saw him on his feet at the desk. He had the telephone pressed hard against his ear and he was shouting the same thing over and over into the receiver. She saw saliva on his mouth. He shouted the same thing over and over.

She was afraid to go up to him. Something terrible had happened. She was to blame.

She stepped back and waited for him to tell her that something terrible had happened. There were tears of frustration and anger in his eyes.

He screamed at whoever was on the other end of the phone, 'I demand to have it in writing! Damn you to hell, you soft-gutted bastard, do you hear me? *I want it in writing!*'

She thought each night that her penance was endless.

The ship was due in thirteen hours.

40

In the stone walled treasure room beneath the school, Duras sat facing the tea chests and thinking about God. The single light bulb swung in arcs from the wooden supports of the floor above. It was five in the morning: four flights up the children were asleep in long dormitories. He imagined them breathing and turning in their sleep. Somewhere, a long way off, there was the crackle of small arms fire—somewhere across the bitterly cold river in the darkness of silhouetted and silent buildings there was a heavier noise—a thump like a small movement of the earth—an artillery shell fallen somewhere on open ground, followed by a muffled paper bag popping in the same vicinity—a tank or a light field gun firing at masonry or into concrete corridors.

He reached out with his hand and touched the wall of the stone room. It was damp, like a tomb. The light continued to swing in small movements. He stood at one of the plywood tea chests and pushed against it, not too hard. It was open. He reached into it and took out a clay figurine about ten inches high, bent down, and placed it carefully on the ground. The moving yellow light flickered down its length and touched at shadows and folds in its form. It was ancient clay: there was a faint, brittle scraping sound as he drew back the calloused skin of his palms from it.

The object was a sarcophagus figure of a robed attendant clasping its hands together in the enveloping sleeves of its gown—he classified it without thinking: a court attendant found in the evacuated tomb of a minor provincial bureaucrat from the Ch'u period, dateable to three hundred years before Christ. The figurine was impassive and contemplative, its eyes cast down and inward-seeing, averted from the temptations of the world.

Duras thought, "Perhaps the figurine represents a priest sent to turn the bureaucrat's soul towards matters of the perfection of the spirit." He smiled to himself. Perhaps the bureaucrat had been a boozing, happy pisspot with an enormous belly and a jelly-shivering laugh. He grinned at the idea, "And the priest was as thin and hungry as his figurine-image and he had a high, whining voice and the official, belching and farting from good food and wine, kept grinning happily at him and saying, 'Yes, Father, yes, Father,' until finally in the midst of a full paunch and a befuddled cosiness, he dropped off into an eternity of alcoholic mist in his tomb." Duras thought, "And woke up in the next world with the whining priest's voice piercing his happy hangover."

He thought in some verbal connection, "The nature of God is one of constant beautification of the spirit."

The clay figurine spoke to him in its own voice across two thousand years of soundless service and Duras thought, "You had the tranquility to wait." He thought, "Above your stone crypt in the ground men fought and struggled for two thousand years. In instants, civilizations came and went. Unfamiliar voices and accents argued and whispered—men of all races and aspirations came and went. You heard the sounds of war and love, of commerce and thievery. And waited. You had never seen a man with round eyes until I found you." He thought, "And now you endure me as you endured all the others, in silence, inward-seeing, with your gaze cast down into eternity. I came into your broken tomb and took you in my hands and you showed nothing. I might have raised you above my head and dashed you to the ground and still you showed nothing. Destruction is a matter of no interest."

He thought of the children asleep. He gazed at the imperturbable clay. "Would it be a matter of no interest that as I sat here with my hands cupped around you protectively you heard the Japanese running up the stairs killing and slashing? Is that also, over the centuries, a matter of no interest?" He thought, "The bell in the school will not ring to warn the children because the nuns will go to the children first and try to cover them with their own bodies." He thought, "But there will be stragglers and they will get in the way of the men running up the stairs."

He looked at the figurine.

He said to the figurine, 'I will wait by the bell when the time comes and ring it to warn the children and then I will keep the children in the Chapel and this time I will tell the Japanese that there are treasures here.' He said in almost a threatening voice, 'And instead, they will come down here and find you.'

He stood up. He said, 'I wish you well although you would not wish anything for yourself.'

He said, 'I wish you well.'

He paused at the door. The figurine had its back to him. He saw its acceptance of eternity in its simplicity. He asked the effigy, 'What am I to you?'

He grinned at the mute object. He said, all at once, 'You were not perfect either. You are also only a representation of what you wanted to be. You drank the official's wine along with him and ate his rich food. You belched and farted too. You, you are nothing more than I am—you were a man!'

He thought, "The Mass is a joyous wonderful time full of great mysteries and the laughter and happiness of a God with an unending love for the world—" He reviled the figurine, 'Christ was no self-serving mystic seeking the smug knowledge of his own salvation over all other men—he was a carpenter with rough hands who stormed across the world full of laughter and fierce optimism and love!'

He said to the figurine, 'I am not a miser without a god.'

157

He closed his eyes for a moment. He grinned at the figurine. 'But I wish you well.' He thought, "What a poor fool I have become." He felt, for an instant as he went to snap off the light that, in the darkness, from over all those centuries, there might be, barely audible, the soft intake of a sigh.

He turned off the light. He paused for a brief instant.

There was no sound.

He went up the stairs towards the chapel and the school, two at a time.

He heard a single sound, a heartbeat, of great joy.

It was his own.

41

Hooper was flying. It was dawn, Friday the fifth of December, and, for the last time, he was flying. He made a wide, slow sweep out over the river, banked to catch the line of silent grey buildings on the Bund, and then circled over the warehouses, seeing them as long rectangular buildings lying in a giant U shape. He saw the furniture truck parked out in what had been his runway and the roofs of all the buildings, repaired and patched for a hundred years. He pulled the nose of the Nieuport up slightly and found height again, climbed to a little over a thousand feet and began moving in wide, leisurely circles. He heard the throbbing of the Le Rhône engine and nodded to himself. He leaned forward and touched forward of the cockpit with his glove. He could hear the airplane vibrating and the wash of the propeller trembling along it.

He thought the great thing about war was that it was all so clear cut, no issues to complicate flying a little airplane or firing off a gun. A few puffs of white smoke from out-of-range field guns, a salute to an adversary and then home to Mother and— He thought, "I wonder if it was ever really like that." He heard the air currents twanging against the rigging between the biplanes. There was oil on his helmet and goggles. He wiped it away with his leather glove and glanced down at the instruments. They registered he was flying. He thought, "It's all taken for granted, but it constantly amazes me. *Flying*."

He leaned over and examined the side of the fuselage: it was paint flecked and spotted with oil. He smiled sadly to himself and moved the stick into a left bank. He craned out of the cockpit, side slipping, and saw Henry standing between the warehouses: a single black figure in a bleak landscape, and he thought, "What the hell's he doing?" The entire complex of warehouses was wired to the roofs with dynamite and drums of aviation gasoline. He tried to see the electric firing fuse running out to the fence surrounding them. He craned down, rising to avoid the downdrafts of the dawn air, "He won't blow it. He'll leave it all intact and then he'll get in touch with one of his pals and make arrangements to sell it. It was never me. His loyalty stopped at the plane." He thought, "He didn't even shake hands with me. He just stood there with a blank look on his face and watched the plane take off and he hasn't moved from the same spot for almost twenty minutes."

Hooper checked the fuel gauge, "He's just standing there waiting until something happens and then he'll forget it and look after himself." Hooper thought, "He's got his half share of the diamonds clutched in his hand and now he's probably working out how he can capitalise on the stuff in the warehouses as well." He thought, "I don't give a damn any more."

He said violently into the rushing wind, 'You dirty son of a bitch! You lied to me too!'

Moffatt heard the plane a long way off. He lay quietly in bed with his eyes open, staring at the window. Light was coming in between the curtains and he lay still, watching it. On the carpeted floor he could make out the packed and labelled suitcases and he lay still looking out through the window and watching the approach of morning.

He heard his wife's breathing next to him. It was easy and regular. He thought, in her sleep, she might be smiling.

He watched the morning coming, wide awake, hearing the airplane, and thinking of Scotland as a place of many sitting rooms with lace doylies and cups of tea and questions that could not be answered. He listened to the airplane circling over the river. He heard his wife's soft breathing.

Resolutions he kept trying to make kept slipping away incompletely formed.

Hooper shouted into the slipstream, 'Blow it up, you bastard!' The words were whipped away from his mouth. He shouted into the wind, 'You lousy, cheating Chinese bastard, do one thing for me and blow it to hell!' He shouted ferociously, 'Blow it to hell for me!'

He pleaded silently in his head, "Please, please do just this one last thing —" He looked down at the figure on the ground. It was gone. "Oh, please don't dismantle it all. Please." He felt tears of frustration. "Please . . ." He thought, "I'm not going down again." He put the plane into a fast power climb, "Please . . ." 'Just one goddamned thing for me!' He smashed his fist against the vibrating cowling and screamed at it, *God damn you!*' He reached stalling point and dived the aircraft away from the river, scudding across the wire perimeter, and thought, "No one gives a damn."

He thought, "It was all wrong from the start and everything I ever did —" He raised the nose and saw the countryside rushing past below him.

He saw the helmeted figures of the Japanese looking up and running.

He looked back over the rudder at the roofs of the warehouses, receding. He moved the throttle in and heard the engine racing at top pitch. He thought, "You should never believe in anything." He began to raise the aircraft up as two Zeros came down at him from somewhere at five thousand feet. He saw the spinners on their noses shimmering like spinning scythes, saw oil moving back along their nacelles, the twinkling of the cannon as the shells ripped across the closing distance and he thought—

Bert Hall shuddered. There were noises in Hooper's ears, exploding and shattering sounds as the shells smashed and splintered. He felt a tremendous thud behind him and a push in the middle of his back—then the sound of two modern engines shrieking at high performance to turn onto him for a second run. He saw the red circles on the silver metal wings and thought for a moment in an absurd gesture he should draw his revolver and take a chivalrous pot-shot at—he felt something break inside the plane, the heart, and cease to be something that, above the earth, free and clean, *flew*.

He thought, dissolving, "No one ever, ever gave a damn," as, in the main warehouse, standing a few feet from the crates of dynamite and drums of fuel, the diamonds scattered about him on the floor, Henry, with tears streaming down his face, holding the firing box in both hands like an offering, pressed down the plunger.

Shanghai was a place where, in the Winter of an average year, the police picked up 29,000 dead bodies from the streets and lanes.

The cause of death was starvation and the bitter, unrelievedly constant cold.

42

In Tokyo, after an all-night sitting, the Naval Chief of Staff, Admiral Nagano, in company with the Chief of Staff of the Army, General Sugiyama, drove to the Imperial Palace and there, in conference with the Emperor, put forward their planning date for the commencement of hostilities against the forces of the United States of America, Great Britain and the Kingdom of Holland's territories in the Pacific.

The primary operation was to be directed against the Americans and to be code-named Operation Z. The date set for Operation Z was to be, in Asia, December the 8th; at the prime target, Pearl Harbour, taking into account the International Dateline, a little before 8 a.m. on December 7th. They outlined the form of attack to the Emperor in detail. The Emperor, acting on advice from his Court officials and his own estimate of the political situation, gave his approval and made it clear to both officers that it was his wish and international convention that clear warning was to be transmitted to the American government in advance of the attack. He spoke abstractly about the prewar imperial conferences for some little time, evidently reminiscing, and then, after a nod from one of his private secretaries, dismissed both the officers and bade them good fortune.

The two officers then drove back to their Headquarters where Admiral Nagano reported the Imperial sanction to Admiral

Yamamoto, and an hour and a half later, Yamamoto, in charge of operations, opened his office safe and broke the seal on an operations folder containing the code words to be sent to the naval force already at sea. The cypher read *Niitaka yama nobore 1208*—climb Mount Niitaka, eight of the twelfth: *Attack as planned, December 8th.* He despatched to Consul General Kita in Honolulu:

IN VIEW OF THE PRESENT SITUATION THE PRESENCE IN PORT OF WARSHIPS AIRCRAFT CARRIERS AND CRUISERS IS OF UTMOST IMPORTANCE X HEREAFTER TO THE UTMOST OF YOUR ABILITY REPORT DAY BY DAY X CABLE IN CODE WHETHER OR NOT ANY BARRAGE BALLOONS ABOVE PEARL HARBOUR OR ANY INDICATIONS ANY WILL BE SENT UP X ALSO ADVISE WHETHER OR NOT WAR-SHIPS PROVIDED WITH ANTITORPEDO NETS X

Kita replied:

THE FOLLOWING SHIPS IN PORT YESTERDAY AFTER-NOON EIGHT (8) BATTLESHIPS THREE (3) LIGHT CRUISERS SIXTEEN (16) DESTROYERS

He sent the details of defences and then began listing the vessels by name:

ARIZONA NEVADA OKLAHOMA CALIFORNIA . . .

In Honolulu, both messages were intercepted by U.S. Naval Intelligence and passed on to Washington for decoding, but since they dealt not with mainland America, but only the island of Hawaii, the information in them was given a low priority and pigeonholed to be dealt with when time permitted.

In the Pacific, on track for Pearl, the Japanese task force steamed at a steady 14 knots, awaiting final orders. Silent and unseen, three submarines scouted ahead of the force, searching out neutral vessels that might give their position away. They found none—the Pacific that day was vast, still and empty.

The lookouts on their vantage points on the Japanese force kept up a constant sweep for American patrol planes.

None came. The element of surprise was complete.

Simultaneously, all the vessels in the task force received the same message. They executed a sweeping turn and began moving at speed towards their target.

On the aircraft carriers, the pilots went to their torpedo planes

162

and gave them a final complete external check. The armourers began loading the ammunition bays, and in the lifts from the magazine, experts began final procedures toward arming and fusing the torpedoes. The pilots and observers climbed into their cockpits to inspect controls and instruments, to verify their radio transmitters and electrical equipment and to hide little keepsakes and good luck tokens down the sides of their seats.

The pilots heard ships' bells calling them to briefings. They drew anticipatory breaths, said a word to the armourers or patted the cases of the torpedoes and went towards companionways. There was less than sixty hours left, some of that flying time. They went briskly, rubbing at their chins and cheeks anxiously, finding their throats dry, passing sailors carrying battle ensigns up towards the flag deck, weapons and ammunition being checked in open armouries. They heard the sound of the engines increasing, the clanging shut of watertight doors, the chatter of radio telephones as one ship spoke to another.

Climb Mount Niitaka!

Their hands were wet and clammy. They longed to pull on their thick flying gloves. They imagined the sound of aircraft engines, the moment of release, and the great chaos of battle.

They reached the briefing rooms and fell silent. Their commanding officers, flying and non-flying, looked at them with awe.

They bowed their heads for a short religious ceremony of purification.

43

During the night, unheard at first and without its running lights, the ship had made the tortuous fourteen mile journey from the mouth of the Yangtse-kiang. In the light of morning people glanced out their windows at the light and saw it.

It was there, the *Bocca Tigris*, tied up against the last remaining deep channel dock near the Bund, smoke dribbling out from its smoke stack as the engines below decks turned over to provide electricity to its cabins and companionways. It was a little vessel, no more than 7,000 tons, flying a grimy Portuguese flag and its docking and unloading pennants, nothing much, a dirty second-rate little tramp steamer, but people marvelled at it wordlessly.

Up on the top deck, two of the Chinese crew, rugged up against the cold in quilted cotton jackets, were sweeping in a desultory fashion and glancing out across the docks. There was a burning warehouse a little way off and every so often, as they thought a wall might finally give way and crash to the ground, they stopped sweeping and gave it their full attention, then when it did not, shook their heads philosophically and went on sweeping.

On the bridge, the Captain, a middle-aged Portuguese with smooth olive skin, muffled to the chin and ears by his thick uniform coat and winter cap looked down at them with boredom and then, leaning forward over the bridge rail, looked up and down the full length of the hull and gave no obvious reaction to what he saw. He took out a silver pocket watch, considered the time for a moment and then bent his head to the tide tables in his China Coaster's Nautical Manual for 1941. He leaned back and called something into the wheelhouse and his First Officer asked a question and the Captain shook his head. There was no powerline link available from the shore and the engines must continue to turn over to give the ship power.

There was hammering and sawing coming from somewhere near the port deck cabins as the ship's carpenter extended cabins into dormitories and from the stern pipes the steady expulsion of hot and dirty water into the mud. The ratlines were down. The Captain leaned forward again, still carrying on a conversation with the Mate, to inspect them, again made no reaction to what he saw and, leaning back, pointed out across the International Settlement to some feature he had known in better days. He looked at his watch again and seemed anxious about something, indicated the forward hatchcovers and suggested some way they could better be secured or amended.

The Mate nodded his head and shivered at the cold, then evidently returned to the conversation of better days and, pointing it out, asked the Captain about something he saw in the distance.

The Captain had changed his mind about talking about the past. He leaned forward again and inspected the level of the

164

river and how low his ship lay in it. The next suitable high tide would not be until 2 a.m. on Monday morning and he had no figures to suggest at what rate the silt was building up. He said something to the Mate and the Mate shrugged. There was nothing that anyone could do about it. The Captain fell silent and gazed down at the unpainted concrete dock. Off in the distance, he could hear muffled artillery fire and thought he imagined fighter aircraft circling. He looked vaguely at the First Officer and then leaned out again to consider the hull.

The inaudible sound of the mud rising and pushing against the metal plates below the water line continued to niggle at him.

He gave a curt order to raise a second neutral Portuguese flag from an aft halyard and went inside the wheelhouse to look at the charts and smoke a cigar to mask his anxiety.

In the city, sounds and orders and questions between people in bare, cleared-up rooms echoed against walls. Curtains had come down from windows—there were bumpings and crashings as servants and houseboys manoeuvred heavy packing cases and trunks down stairs, shouts and cajolings as they were pushed and shoved onto the backs of wagons or in rickshaws or slid, metal on metal grating, into the open mouthed boots of cars.

There were papers to be collected, filed, finalised, left pinned to doors for landlords or friends, nameplates to be taken down, telephones disconnected, clothes packed, repacked, and then repacked again, decisions concerning small or large useless knicknacks and possessions to be made. Books with blight in their spines, or volumes of nineteenth century Gems of Poetry, old children's toys, the legacy of tenants of the apartment long gone away to be thrown out, little gifts of extreme uselessness, uncompleted collections of Oriental ivory gods and goddesses, broken chess and draughts sets to be distributed or discarded, the wireless, monolithic in its scarred and rubbed mahogany cabinet, the earth wire once arranged and laid out with surgeon-like delicacy and planning along picture frames and around old gas light fixtures all to be ripped out and disconnected.

There were corners to be looked under, bed frames, the rising edges of carpets where once a diamond ring had remained unfound for days: old, known, familiar places with their private nooks and crannies to be investigated—all the secrets of the apartments and houses known only to their occupants to be checked for one last, final time.

There were the gardens or windowboxes: a cutting of a favourite bush, or a pebble, something to be souvenired and taken; there were the cardboard shoeboxes of past souvenirs and treasures from other, long ago, elsewhere homes to be examined—curiously wondering what on earth this tiny piece of coloured glass, or that especial needle or cotton reel meant; and who had once sent an ordinary birthday card, unsigned, that must have meant . . . ?

'Was it from you?'

'I don't know.' Curious, momentary wonder. And then the animals and pets, hard to flush aquarium goldfish down the water closet, but still perhaps they might—better than leaving them. And the cats: a small calibre shot from somewhere down in the garden, a momentary pause and then—

'We can't let the thing run wild. They'll only eat it.' The dogs however, being different, going tongue-panting and happy in the car to the vet's, coming back wrapped up to a special place near the house. 'He would have liked that —' processions of unspeaking neighbours going in and out of buildings no longer their homes, carrying packets and bundles, taking away things to be disposed of.

A long way off, the traffic along the Bund all stilled, the air clear and cold, the end of something. Voices in empty echoing rooms on telephones, making promises, exchanging addresses, asking about Australia, brief half-hearted negotiations for the car, trailing off in silence. Voices saying in the absence of words to say, 'Well . . .'

'No, we're leaving now . . . it sails sometime Sunday night or Monday . . . no, safer on board . . . yes . . .' pauses, then voices saying, 'I shall miss you too—maybe when all this is over—'

Voices from those going to those left behind, 'Maybe when this is all over we could . . .'

Voices saying goodbye.

44

A silence had descended on the city.

On the hill overlooking it, a single figure stood a little way from his staff car taking in the scene.

Isogai watched.

He felt a great moment was almost upon him.

45

Edge sat at the cleared table in his apartment turning the leather sachet of diamonds over in his hand. The news of Hooper's death had been on the radio a few minutes after he had found the sachet pushed through his letterslot. He turned the sachet upside down and the diamonds spilled out onto his palm, uncut and gleaming dully. He put them on the table and spread them out with his finger. His shoulder had a deep early morning arthritic chill in it. He rubbed at it absently with his hand. He said after a moment, 'It just seems so bloody pointless!'

'The way he died?' Barbara Ling stood at the window. Across the roofs she could make out the ship: its smokestack and sections of the derricks on the freight deck. She turned to look at him.

Edge shook his head. 'Going. Going seems so pointless. Just wandering casually down to the ship, producing these, getting a cabin and sailing away—after everything, it just seems so pointless. I've spent my entire life here, and just to pack a bag and—' He saw her turn her back to the window, 'It just doesn't seem—'

'What? Honourable? Righteous?'

'It just doesn't seem *appropriate*.'

'*Why not?*'

'It just doesn't seem right!'

'And what does?' She turned back to face him angrily.

'What do you mean?'

'I mean, what *does* seem right and appropriate? Staying here? For what?'

Edge said, 'They're half yours, you know that, the diamonds. You heard him last night. About leaving. You know he meant you too. You can go.'

'I intend to!'

'Fine.'

'I'll take my charity from anyone prepared to offer it and barter and beg my way on board even if my entire share only buys me space in the rope locker! I don't suffer from your philosophising—I've been out on the streets. I don't have an urge to die gloriously. I have an urge to survive!'

'I'm not talking about dying gloriously!'

'Then what are you talking about? What do you think will happen to you when they come? These people—the Japs—they don't take prisoners. They think that if they take a prisoner he's so ashamed that all he wants is a quick death—and if he isn't ashamed then he should be, and he should be dead—they kill people!'

'I'm not talking about soldiers!'

'Neither am I!'

Edge said softly, 'I'm fifty years old, I've spent all my life here. In China. I don't know anywhere else. I can't just pack up and say goodbye to everything I've ever done!'

'I can! What have you ever done? China doesn't care about you! I'm Chinese—what do I care about China?'

'That's different!'

'Why is it different?'

'It's just different.' Edge said, 'It's just different—it—'

'How is it different?'

'It just is!'

'Look out the window! Anyone who can afford it—anyone with money or position or power who can cajole or plead or buy their way on board that ship is leaving! Everyone! People like you! Your people!'

'What *people*?'

'The Europeans! People like you!' She stopped abruptly and gazed at him, 'Is that it?' Her voice dropped. She looked at him carefully, 'That's it, isn't it? It wasn't enough for you being born here, or speaking the language, or even having a Chinese wife—certainly not having a Chinese mistress—there's just one other thing missing, isn't there?'

Edge said suddenly, 'This is silly!'

'Is it? Is it silly!'

'*Yes!*'

'Good, then why don't you scoop up the diamonds into your pockets and say to yourself, I'm a rich man. I've got the diamonds, I've got a way out, I'm too old for military service, and such as she is, I've got a Chinese mistress to keep me happy in bed and to reminisce about the good old days with?' She shouted at him, 'Because that's what a real Chinese would say! A real Chinese! That's the way their minds work!'

'I don't happen to be a real Chinese! I happen to be me!'

'So because you're you, you intend to stay here and commit suicide just like your friend Hooper!'

'I don't know he committed suicide!'

'Of course he did! He was afraid of obscurity! He could have gotten away with forged papers but he couldn't bear the thought of being anyone but himself either! Fortunately for me, women in China have thought of themselves as the vassals of their husbands and parents so long that any one identity that carries with it food and shelter and a modicum of happiness is just about the same in terms of importance and self esteem as any other!'

'*He wanted to get his airplane out!*'

'He could have bought another!'

Edge shouted at her, 'This is my goddamned country and no one is telling me when and how to leave it! And especially not a dead man! I don't know why the hell he gave me the diamonds. I never said I wanted to go! That was his idea! I never said anything about it!' Edge smashed at the table top with his open hand, 'God *damn* him! You were the one who talked about leaving, not me!'

Barbara Ling said softly, 'Perhaps he thought if I went you might go with me.' She looked at Edge carefully, 'Is that right or wrong?'

'The diamonds are as much yours as mine. That's how he meant them—you take them for whatever reason you like. Take them and go.'

'And what will you do?'

'I don't know.'

'You won't find anything heroic or noble here!'

'I don't want anything heroic or noble!'

'Then come with me on the ship.'

'No.' He looked away.

Barbara Ling said, 'I swear to you, there is no one act that will make all your time in China seem worth while. You Europeans—there has to be some shining moment to cap your lives—like Hooper. The Chinese are happy just to waste away after the end of something. No, they don't even waste away: they start again. To them—'

'I know all about the Chinese and what they—'

'If I was better in bed, would you? Would you come on the ship with me?'

'That's ridiculous!'

'My husband—'

'I don't want to hear about your husband.'

'My husband—'

'I said, I don't want to hear about him!'

'My husband was caught by the Japanese and taken to a spot just near Nantao—to an old killing ground—'

Edge closed his eyes.

'And in the most noble way, in a manner befitting his rank and his position and his view of himself in China's history, in the events of the world, as a thinking sentient being, as a soldier with medals and dignity and honour, he was stood against a post set in the ground—along with fourteen other people all standing against posts in the ground—and then he was shot dead.'

'What do you want me to say?'

'— and that was his glorious important death. A great fulfilment to a life of wonderful and significant complexity. Pinned to his heart there was a piece of paper with numbers on it: millimetres and angles and points of correction. On all the men standing against the poles. I heard all about it from someone who saw it from a distance. The old killing ground is used for something else now. As a rifle range.'

Edge rubbed his forehead with his hand.

'And the firing squad wasn't a firing squad at all. It was a section of untrained young boys from Japan, and there were no drum rolls and they didn't line up ceremonially at point blank range, and there was no officer with a silver sword to tell them when to shoot—they fired when they felt like it. They fired from a hundred and fifty yards. They fired and then, if they missed

170

the man they were aiming at, they stopped to have a cigarette and reset their rifles. And then they tried again—do you understand what I'm saying?'

Edge nodded.

'Do you? Do you comprehend what I'm telling you? Do you? They used him for nothing more important than zero-ing in their rifles! They fired and fired until he was dead and it didn't matter to them in the least!' She broke down and began sobbing, 'He was nothing to them! He was so little to them that they—that they used him for target practice!'

Edge said softly, 'I'm so—'

'So won't you come with me? I've—I've got no one else left—won't you—Jack, I'm so afraid to be alone again!'

'I can't . . .'

The diamonds lay in disordered lines on the table, like the tracks of tiny snails.

'Please, Jack. Please . . .'

Through the window, she could see the ship waiting. There was an abrupt authoritative knock at the front door and she put her hand to her eyes and looked away.

46

Kate Moffatt said at the door, 'Get rid of the Chink for a few minutes and I'll talk to you, Jack.' She stepped inside the room, 'I'll leave my coat on. I shan't be staying long.' She glanced at Barbara Ling.

Edge said, 'What do you want, Kate?'

'The, ah, Chinese woman—'

'What do you want?'

'Very well.' She came to the centre of the room, by-passing Barbara Ling and contriving to have her back to her. She glanced out the window at the roofs and the smudge of smoke from the funnel of the *Bocca Tigris*, 'I—' she set her voice at an even, formal tone, 'I came to tell you, Jack, that any . . . misunderstandings that might have existed between us . . . at any time are now all so much water off the duck's back. I wanted to speak to you alone about it, but—since you appear to insist on having—' she flicked her eyes to Ling's reflection behind her in the window glass, 'I wanted you to feel at the end that there was no animosity between us—just the same . . . friendly relationship.' She closed the collar of her topcoat around her throat. 'Just so long as you know. It's the right thing to do and it was up to me to make the first move. Well—' she glanced back towards the window uncomfortably, 'Well, I've made my little speech and there's no more to say other than that I've always—'

Edge smiled at her.

'Why are you smiling?'

Edge said, 'You're going home, aren't you?'

'Well—yes—' Her eyes moved to the reflection of the Chinese woman in the window, 'As a matter of fact, I do happen to have a passage on the ship—as a matter of fact—the, ah, Deputy Assistant Commissioner and I—'

'He's going too?

'Yes. Yes, he is, actually.' She saw Barbara Ling's reflection in the window. The blasted Chinese was making herself comfortable in a chair and sitting down to watch! 'I'd stay for tea, Jack, and tell you all about it, but you'll appreciate that the arrangements and packing have taken up quite a lot of my time and as you'll appreciate, Jack, I merely stopped by to see if there was anything I could do for you—' The Chinese woman watched blandly. 'Anything in the way of—'

'I'm very glad for you, Kate.' Edge moved forward to take her hand, but she brushed him away.

'Well, I'm glad there's no animosity, Jack. Friends should part happily. Naturally, the Commissioner himself wanted to give us a farewell party—under normal circumstances, of course, it would have been unforgivable had he not, but, well, this time, Alec and I, we've agreed to forgo the pleasure and leave him to get on with his more pressing duties. He's farewelling other officers, but in Alec's case—being of such senior rank—well, we've agreed to forgo the pleasure and let him—' She said suddenly, 'If you'd care to come too I'm sure I can arrange it for you.'

'Come? Where?'

Her voice was even and unemotional, 'On the ship of course.'

'Do you mean to *Australia*?'

'Yes. To Australia. I gather it's a very pleasant country. They

172

speak English there, you know. I gather there are some people there who are reasonably civilized. And there are friends of mine—from here—who have settled there. Of course, we wouldn't be staying long. We'd be going home to Britain because of the war, but still—'

'I can't do that.'

'Alec has been given an important job back home. I can't say what it is: secrecy, you know, but it's very important and influential and I'm sure when he gets back home and everything's all right again, that—'

Edge asked, 'Have you packed everything?'

'Of course I've packed everything! Don't try to change the subject! I'm offering you a chance people would give their right arms for—I don't want a whole lot of silly questions about packing! Do you want to come? Yes or no?'

'It's totally ridiculous—'

'If you're worried about a job, Alec can always get you—I'm not saying you'd have to be some sort of menial. Quite a good job. Maybe even something to do with China if that's what you want. Translating or—You'd have to talk to him of course, but he'd get you in somewhere. You could be his assistant or something—'

'Kate, listen—'

'No. I want to do something for you and you're trying to make me look silly, but I don't care. You only debase yourself, not me.' She glanced over at the Chink, 'Could we talk alone?' She saw Barbara Ling light a cigarette, still looking at her, 'You: savvy pidgin? You go quicktime kitchen. You—'

Barbara Ling said softly, 'Unfortunately for you, I don't happen to belong in the kitchen.'

'Don't you be so impertinent!' She turned to Edge, 'Jack, tell this person—'

Barbara Ling said, 'I'm just vaguely curious about one of my fellow passengers.'

'You cheeky little—' She looked at Edge, 'Mr Hooper's diamonds.'

Edge nodded.

'I see.'

Barbara Ling said, 'I hear there's no First or Second class on the ship so maybe we'll have to—'

'There is a First Class.'

'Oh, good. Then I'll take it. Which class will you be taking?'

Katherine Moffatt ignored her. She looked at Edge thought-fully, 'I know quite a lot of fine ladies in Britain, Jack. I've just been trying to think, and I think that some of my friends who have settled in Australia—in the capital city, Sydney—were unfortunate enough to lose their dear husbands and I'm certain that, given the right approach, that a gentleman like yourself, a friend of the Deputy Assistant Commissioner—'

Barbara Ling said quietly, 'The local lunatic asylum seems to have forgotten to lock its doors.'

'You be quiet! I'm talking to Mr Edge, and when Europeans talk you Chinks have to shut up and be respectful!'

Edge said, 'That's enough, Kate.'

'Why are you taking her side?'

'You're making yourself look foolish, Kate.'

'In front of *her*?'

'In front of everyone. I appreciate your motives in coming to see me—'

'To tell you I forgive you, yes.'

'What?'

'That's why I came. To tell you I forgive you.'

'For what?'

'You know for what.' She said conspiratorially, wagging her finger, '*Pas devant.*'

'Don't be absurd!'

'You can come with your own people if you want to. That's the offer I'm making you. I don't think that's absurd at all. I think it's very lucky for you. Alec has mellowed towards you, and now that everything between us is all right, I'm prepared to use my good offices with him to persuade him to let you get home with your own people—with the English.'

'I don't happen to be English.'

'Well. American. Whatever. Home.'

'This is my home, Kate.'

'Not if all your people have gone. Who have you got left?' She glanced at Ling and curled her mouth, 'The Chinks? They only want what they can get.' She demanded from Barbara Ling, 'Isn't that right?'

'Oh completely. Thousands of years of Chinese culture and civilization have geared my thinking to only one thing: to be a silly little European lady wearing a funny hat.' She drew in on her cigarette and looked at her watch, touching it with the fingers of her other hand for a moment, 'Jack and I want to say

174

goodbye in bed sometime today if you won't be too much longer—'

Edge said roughly, 'For God's sake!'

'Mrs . . . Moffatt, is it? All Chinese women are basically whores at heart—isn't that what they tell you?'

'The one or two Chinese ladies I used to know—'

'Servants, Mrs Moffatt? Or ladies?'

'Servants are never ladies, my dear. Surely you would know that?'

Barbara Ling smiled at her.

'And wipe that silly grin off your face!'

'You stupid woman!' .

Kate Moffatt's voice dropped. She said very calmly, 'Jack, do you think you could ask her to go into another room while we have a private conversation?'

'No, Kate.'

'Very well.' She sighed. 'This of course doesn't make any difference to what I was saying. I appreciate that a man isn't like a woman, that he has certain bodily needs that—'

Edge said, 'She's very important to me, Kate.'

'I'm sorry, but my offer doesn't include your—whatever she represents to you.'

'I'm not leaving.' He said it to both of them. He said formally to Kate, 'I'm too old to start somewhere else.'

Kate nodded. 'I see.' She turned to Barbara Ling. 'You, as you may know, there are some things that people can't take with them. For example, our neighbour: a gentleman from the Hong Kong-Shanghai Bank had to have his pet dog put down this morning, and—well—' she drew a breath to strengthen herself, 'Well, I had planned to give something equally precious to me to a dear South African friend of mine—someone you don't know, Jack, but if it's a case of—' She turned to Barbara Ling, 'I appeal to you to forget your own petty wants and let this poor man go back to his own people. I'm sure he'll let you keep the diamonds and things and quite probably even this apartment—' She raised her finger to keep Edge out of the conversation. Barbara Ling had stood up. 'And just to help the arrangement, I've got a lovely little blue motor car—a Fiat Topolino—' she said quickly, like a salesman, 'It's in very good condition, it's bright blue, and it looks very impressive on the roads and people turn around to look at it—'

Barbara Ling said with a strange look on her face, 'Yes?'

'—and I'm prepared to throw that in as well.' She turned quickly to Edge, 'You'll go and see Alec sometime later today at the dock, will you? The ship doesn't leave until Sunday night—' She asked Barbara Ling, 'Well, what do you say?'

47

Edge had come back from seeing Kate out. He said embarrassed, 'I apologise to you for her.' He glanced down at Barbara Ling in the chair, still smoking, and said awkwardly, 'You have to try to make allowances.'

She looked up at him wordlessly.

'Women like her never wanted to come to places like this in the first place. They build up a picture of themselves that's a hundred years out of date as a defence so they can fit into some ready-made furrow and—There are lots of people like that, not only here, but in India and—'

Barbara Ling smiled at him.

'—so you have to—'

'I'm not a frail blossom. I don't wilt and cringe because some ridiculous woman—'

'I know that. I was just—'

'You were just defending me.'

'I wasn't defending you.'

'Yes, you were. And thank you.' Barbara Ling said, 'It's nice to be defended. Nevertheless, as a piece of commercial advice I don't think a merger between you and one of her genteel Australian ladies would be quite—'

Edge laughed in relief. '—in the best interests of the shareholders.' They grinned at each other. 'I once saw someone drinking out of a little teacup with a butterfly handle on it, painted yellow—do you suppose that's what her friends use?'

'I shouldn't be surprised.'

'I'd have to do my manly duty once every three months under

176

a framed picture postcard of Edinburgh or a water coloured photograph of dear George, her first husband, as he was in life.'

Edge said, 'Fine decent man, George, let me tell you about his varicose veins—'

'Let me tell you about mine first. And what the doctor said about poor George's glands and his erection problem.'

Edge said, 'She'll be happier when she's with her friends again. They can play rubbers of bridge and complain about the servant problem.' He said quickly, 'She was—worried—for a long time.'

'I won't hold you to what you said to her to win a point.' She glanced up and stubbed out the cigarette. 'I've told you why you should come on the ship. I won't try to use her against you. Nevertheless, I'm very flattered that you told her that I was important to you.'

Edge nodded.

'As a recently bathed and scented ex-gutter refugee it's very good for my image of myself as a woman.'

'I'm sorry if I've embarrassed you.'

'You haven't embarrassed me.' Barbara Ling said with a trace of bitterness, 'If you'd prefer, we can go back to the banter about Mrs Moffatt's friends in Australia. You were enjoying that part of the conversation.' She stood up and walked to the window, 'I'm not nineteen years old so what can I say? That if you came with me we could live on love? Or "It's best if you stay here and we'll have the memory of our few hours together"? All that? No, I've suffered the sentimental disadvantage of having been brought up as a dutiful Chinese daughter and wife. What I need to suggest to you is a compromise.'

Edge said, 'Stay here. That's a compromise.'

'That's a compromise for you.' Barbara Ling said, 'You are a very attractive man. You attract me. You are good and generous in bed and—' she paused and looked first at the window and then to Edge, 'And generally, you are a good and generous man, but—'

'But you have to get out of China.'

'Yes! I have to get out of China: the Middle Kingdom about which—so far as you're concerned—the entire world revolves. It's your country, not mine—you've invented it, not me—' She held up her hand to silence him, 'And you may be right. The China you've invented may be just, exactly one hundred percent the way China is. You may be right.'

'What could I do in Australia?'

'I don't know what you could do!'

'Grow a moustache and go about on the lecture circuit telling people about my exotic experiences in the mysterious East? Sexual customs and beheadings ten cents a coloured slide—just how much do menopausal Women's Clubs pay these days? And what happens when—'

'I know all that!'

'I know you do!'

'Jack, I can't stay! You have to understand that! *I don't happen to want to be killed!* Do you? Oh, yes, yes, you do, don't you? Just exactly like your friend Hooper—'

Edge said, 'I'm just too old! I should be thinking of *going* home at my age, not leaving it—'

'*This isn't your home!*'

'Isn't it?'

'Is it? *China?* What about America? Your father was an American—Or England—What about England? Your mother must have—'

'I've never been to either place. Never.' He rubbed at his shoulder, 'I know China. That's all.'

'I can't stay, Jack. And I won't. Not for you.'

'I understand that.'

'*Why?* Why do you understand that? Why the hell don't you plead with me to stay with you? Why don't you make me feel sorry for you and tell me you'll make sure everything is all right?'

'Do you want me to?'

'No, of course I don't want you to! But why do you have to stand out in the open in the middle of a broad street with your arms open shouting, "I'm a target—kill me!" '

'I don't do that.'

'You do, damn it! You can't even get angry at that stupid woman! You have to tell people to try and make allowances—why doesn't *she* make allowances? Why don't you say to hell with the stinking place, nothing's more important than my own skin—why don't you say that?' Her voice dropped, 'Why don't you say that?' She asked quietly, 'Aren't you afraid?'

'Of course I'm afraid.'

'You're not though, are you? You're the archetypal Confucian good man: you look down on your enemies with understanding and compassion and according to the theory they're so humiliated by their own baseness that they slink away in shame. That's what you are!'

'Rubbish!'

'It isn't rubbish!'

Edge said dismissively, 'I have to go and change if I'm seeing Moffatt at the docks.'

'You won't even save your own little bit of China. China is too big for that, even your own little bit of it.'

'Maybe—maybe this man Isogai—'

'No.'

'God damn and blast it, what the hell's the point? What am I supposed to do?' He shouted at her, 'Blast it all to fucking hell, was I supposed to just stand by and let the poor bastard die in agony?'

'What poor—?'

'Forget it! Nothing!'

'What are you—'

'I said forget it! It was a long time ago. Just forget it.' Edge said, 'All right, I agree with you: I'm being a fool—O.K.? I'm being a damn fool and I'm very sorry that I can't come with you and I'm sorry if that makes me seem to you to be some sort of self-serving plaster saint, but that's how I am. And I'm not going to say that after all this is over and things are back to normal we can meet up and start again, because, if you're right, it'll never be all over and since I'm such a bloody fool, I'm sure you are right!'

'Come with me, Jack.'

'No!' Edge calmed abruptly, 'No.' He said quietly, 'I'll get you your passage on the ship if you like. I have to go down there anyway.'

'I'll get my own.'

'As you like.' He paused. He said softly, 'I'm being a damn fool, aren't I? I should come, shouldn't I?'

'That's up to you.'

'I am. I'm being a fool.'

Barbara Ling said nothing.

'Will you still be here when I get back?'

She closed her eyes for a moment, 'Will you be back tonight?'

'Yes.'

'Then I'll still be here.' She shrugged. 'Yes, why not? I suppose tonight is something—' She shrugged again casually, 'Why not? What time will you be back? Early?'

'Early.'

'Good.' She went to the window, 'Fine.' She said off-handedly, 'Good. See you then.'

With her back to him, at the reflective glass of the window, she thought he couldn't see her face.

48

On the dock, the Marines had strung out coils of barbed wire. The wire was held in place at either end by wooden stanchions and the Marines stood in line abreast, rifles at port, a few feet behind it near the ship's rudder and half-visible propeller. The fire behind the dock, in the giant warehouses, had intensified. Little pieces of mouldering tarpaper floated down in the slight wind like ticker tape and swirled before passing over the superstructure of the ship and falling somewhere out of sight in the river. From time to time there were snapping sounds as wood in the fire fractured with the heat.

The line was steady and wordless. It faced the refugees across the black wire stolidly. Dubrinski moved his rifle—a bolt action Springfield—and looked along the line. Next to him, his Sergeant caught his eye and made a non-committal raise of his eyebrows. Dubrinski returned his gaze to the refugees. They were still, huddled in groups against the cold, and he considered there was no necessity to warn them off. He moved his eyes through the groups looking for weapons and then back to the smoke and tarpaper from the warehouses. He heard someone at the end of the line, against a stone building (he thought he knew who it was) say in an undertone, 'It's just like another fugging parade—' and he hissed down at the man, 'No talking!'

He looked at the refugees. The fire in the warehouses had caught hold of something that burned freely and the high flames made the hollows in their faces flicker with a yellow light. He thought, "America will never go to war." He thought of all the faces in Manhattan, the brightness of shop windows, steam rising from the wide, open thoroughfares and squares, "It's all happening too far away." He thought, "This hasn't got anything to do with prairies or mountains or deserts, or New York or—" he thought, "This is something taking place in the newspapers." He thought of his Polish-Russian parents trying to make sense of the radio. *Amos 'n' Andy*—trying to explain to them slowly and carefully what made him and his brothers laugh. He thought, "In the real world of America none of this is really happening."

He thought of his father and his goddamn Cossacks. He thought, "Why the hell every time he didn't understand something in America did he start talking about the Cossacks and how they'd cut down his father and uncle." He thought, "Who the hell in America wants to hear about Russian Cossacks and the Tsar and troubles on the Polish border?" He remembered saying, 'We're Americans now, not Poles,' and his father looking at him for a moment before muttering some curse at him in Slav and leaving the room.

There was a sudden ball of flame from the warehouses and the refugees moved back. He heard his father say, 'They charged the poor people laughing and swinging their swords.' He described the jingling sound the horses' harness made, 'The swords came out with a ringing sound you could hear up and down the street and then the jingling got louder and you could hear the hooves on the snow and then they came in a line like—' and Dubrinski thought, "This is ridiculous. The entire United States of America—" he thought, "The United States of America doesn't care about what happens in China."

He thought, "These people, the refugees, the ship's got nothing to do with them." He thought, "We're just protecting overseas American interests." He thought, "The last of the businessmen and bankers will all sail away and then the Marines will be taken out and that'll be the end of it." He thought, "It's all good experience for a young officer, but there isn't really any possibility of being *killed* here. That's ridiculous. It's too final and pointless and it's got nothing to do with America."

He glanced down the line of Marines. *Czesław Dubrinski*. That was a name from somewhere else. *Clarence*. He thought, "Dubrinski is okay out of deference to my father and it's too late to change it now, but 'Czesław' is insulting. That wasn't fair to

181

me and if he had any gratitude for the country that took him in he wouldn't keep addressing letters to me as *Czesław*.

The refugees came closer to the wire and he heard the man at the end of the line click something on his rifle. He caught his eye and the man clicked it back.

The Europeans were coming. He heard the cars turning off from one of the main roads. He felt sorry for the refugees. The throbbing from the ship seemed to be growing louder. Little flecks of burning tarpaper from the warehouses billowed overhead. The refugees surged a few feet closer. He heard the click again from the end of the line. The refugees came nearer and rested on the wire.

He thought, "America was good to him. Why the hell doesn't he forget all this Polish stuff about massacres and Cossacks and the old country?"

There was an enormous bang from the warehouses as something exploded. He saw the refugees begin to push against the wire. One of the stanchions toppled and then collapsed. The refugees came forward. He heard the Europeans' cars coming. He ordered, 'Hold your fire. Hold the line—nothing's going to happen—' The refugees were dispersing. He said, 'Nothing. Nothing's going to happen, boys. Just hold the line.' He looked quickly to the man against the stone building and said to him soothingly, 'It's O.K. Nothing's going to happen. Just hold the line. All right?'

They came, the convoy of cars. They were coming: the Europeans. Dubrinski thought desperately to himself, "America will never—" He saw the flames from the warehouses. He thought of Hooper for a moment. He saw the relief guard coming, British infantry. They had their bayonets fixed on their rifles, like Cossacks' swords, glittering in the light. He prayed in Polish, "Oh God, don't let America get involved in all this!"

The warehouses, following the explosion, were burning with terrible ferocity. He could feel the heat on his face.

49

Moffatt tapped at the stern railing of the ship with his open palm, 'Well, Jack, you're on your own now.' He forced a thin smile and gazed across the river towards Pootung. Passengers and loaders still milled around the dock. He glanced down at them for a moment and then looked away with distaste, 'You and your bloody little city, you're both on your own now.' A wind whipped at his hair and he brushed it back past his ear, 'You know what's happened, I expect. I expect you've heard all about it?'

'Katherine came to say goodbye. She said you were—'

'She would.' He nodded to himself in bitter disappointment, 'I expect absolutely everybody knows that I've been chucked out by now.' He looked at Edge's face quickly, 'You didn't know?'

'No, I didn't.'

'Oh, yes. They've chucked me out. Got rid of me. Given me the old royal heave-ho straight out onto the arse.' He said quietly, 'So now you and your bloody little Shanghai—'

'I'm sorry to hear it.'

'Are you? I doubt that. Have you noticed what's happening across the river? The Japs are setting up their batteries of guns. So why should you be sorry to hear I'm getting out before the shooting starts?' He said querulously, 'Oh, yeah, the shooting is going to start all right. You were right about that, the same way you were right about everything else. It'll start all right, and when it's all over and the smoke has cleared, the White Man who gave of his best all his life will just be a dirty memory to be spat on and vilified. You were right. So why the hell should you be sorry I'm getting out?'

'I'm sorry you feel you're going so ignominiously.'

'Oh, I am. That's the word all right. And I feel bloody sorry for myself.' He swallowed and looked down at the tips of the half-visible propeller in the river, 'Katherine's very happy about it—I suppose that's something.'

Edge did not reply.

'She's down below in the cabin organising the stewards. She keeps asking them when the band's coming. She keeps telling them there'll be a band waiting for us at the other end—in

Australia—and then another one when we get home to Scotland. I thought she knew I'd been thrown out.' He asked softly, 'Doesn't she?'

'Evidently not.'

Moffatt paused for a moment. 'So what are you going to do about the Japs?'

'Is it up to me to do anything?'

'Oh, yes, it's up to you. You're on your own.' He shrugged. 'I did my best, but it just wasn't good enough. Nobata's dead—I picked the wrong horse—so that only leaves you and your little yellow friend Isogai. So what are you going to do about him?'

'I'll do what I'm told to do.'

'By whom, Jack? By whom? Who do you think *knows*? No, those bastards are going to shoot the place to pieces and then march in as if they own it and then the slaughter is going to start.'

'If you're right, I don't see what I can do.'

'No. Much more sensible to get yourself chucked out like your old friend Moffatt the bloody Disgraced. Clever bloke, Moffatt, knows just when to test the wind and get himself cashiered. Knows just when to abuse his superiors and let the side down. Clever bastard, Moffatt. Very sly. That's what they'll say. Anybody who's left. Or if they ever come back—' He said suddenly, 'And they won't. No one'll ever live here now except a whole pile of your little yellow brothers.' He looked down at his palms on the railing, 'And the irony of it all is that anybody who spent his life here keeping his record clean will have wasted every moment of a totally wasted life because the first thing those Nip buggers are going to do is take out all the records, stick them up in a pile in the middle of the street, and set fire to them.' He blinked back tears, 'So I've been chucked out—and everything I ever did for the record is just a pile of dirty ashes blown in the faces of grimy, helmeted Nips.' He said, 'That's my life and a hell of a lot of people are going to get a good laugh out of it.'

'If you say so.'

'I do. A hell of a good bloody laugh.' He said abruptly, 'I was wrong that day on the hill—at that execution. I want you to know that. I was wrong.'

'It doesn't matter.'

'It does. It does matter. It may not matter to you, but it matters to me. I want at least to do one thing with a bit of

184

honour before I go and I want to say for the record—' he paused for a moment and smiled at himself bitterly, '—for the record that you did the right thing and I was wrong to persecute you for it.'

'It was too long ago now.'

'For God's sake, allow me the grace to apologize, will you? That's not too much to ask, is it? I was wrong. I admit it.'

'All right.'

'I was bloody wrong! And you were right to do what you did. Did she ever tell you about—did Katherine ever tell you about—' He said quickly, 'I was tortured by it. By what happened. By that man at the grave and the rifle shot—by what you—' He fell silent for a moment.

'Forget it.'

Moffatt said, 'It should have been me. I should have been the one—to put the poor bastard out of his—it should have been me but I was too afraid of what people might think! God, that's a confession to make to someone whose life you've ruined—'

Edge said evenly, 'You didn't ruin my life.'

'Didn't I?'

'No.'

'Didn't I, Jack?'

'No.' Edge said, 'There was always more to my life than being a man in uniform—'

'But not to mine, is that what you're saying? I treated you badly—shabbily. I was so bloody afraid of what the bloody Shanghai Club might say and I let you go downhill without lifting a finger to help. And then, when there were other chances for you later, I stopped them too. Me. Because I was still afraid of what people might—'

'*Who the hell do you think you are?*'

'It's bloody true and I know it!'

'All you know is that you're thumping your breast thrashing about in a swamp of maudlin self-pity at my bloody expense! So what if they've sacked you? So bloody what? Don't you ever take your goddam brass buttons and your braid off? Isn't there some sort of *man* under all your serge and medals and God knows what else? I didn't ask your permission to kill that poor sod on the hill: I did it because I thought it was the right thing to do. You had nothing to do with it. You talk as if were I given the chance to do it over again I'd ask you to take over so you could be the martyr to the bloody Shanghai Club instead of me!'

'You'd do it again?'

'I'd see that it didn't have to happen! Christ, you're a pious little bastard, aren't you?'

'Am I?'

'Yes, you bloody are!'

Moffatt said quietly, 'Then it's all been a waste, hasn't it? Everything I've ever tried to do . . .'

'What have you ever tried to do?'

Moffatt's lip was trembling. 'I don't know.' He looked at Edge curiously, 'I don't know, Jack, and that's the truth. I've been standing here wondering and I don't really know. What do you think? Have I ever done anything?'

Edge did not reply.

'I've been here in China for God knows how long and when I get home they're going to think I'm a real old Colonial Administrator, but I'm not, am I? I don't know a thing more about it than I did the day I arrived. Oh, I know all about picturesque native customs and picturesque native beliefs and philosophies, but as for the bloody picturesque natives themselves, the Chinese, I don't know a damn thing, do I? Twenty years and I don't even speak the language. What sort of Colonial Administrator is that?'

'That's the usual sort of Colonial Administrator!'

'And what about you? You don't know anything about my bloody society! About England or Scotland or America or Australia so why the hell are you better than me? Why the hell are you—'

'I wouldn't presume to live in your society in a position of power I never earned.'

'Wouldn't you if you were given the chance?'

'No, I bloody wouldn't!'

'I was nothing back home—nothing! I would have ended up as a bank clerk or a—and Katherine, she isn't the Old English Aristocrat she pretends to be—*her father was a bloody farm labourer*! Why shouldn't we have had the right to improve ourselves? Other people do it so why shouldn't we? I was the Deputy Assistant Commissioner—even if it was under false pretences, it was worth it, wasn't it? Even if it was under false pretences—'

'If it was under false pretences you shouldn't mind being chucked out when—'

'When what?'

'When the bloody picturesque natives finally saw through you!'

'God, you really love those rotten people, don't you? You shot that poor sod dead that day because he was one of your own!'

'I would have done the same for a dog in the street!'

Moffatt looked at him, 'Maybe you would. You missed your vocation. You should have been a missionary like your father and mother.'

'Maybe I should have.'

'There's nothing back in England or America for you, is there? Nothing at all. After this, God knows there's nothing there for me, but there never was for you, was there? We—the Europeans—we always did things with one eye on the people back home. We—but there wasn't ever anything like that for you, was there? What did the Chinks think about what you did that day?'

'I never asked any of them.'

Moffatt hesitated. 'What are you going to do?'

'I'm going to see Isogai again.'

'And do what?' Moffatt asked, 'Is there anything I can do to help?'

'No.'

'I see.' He paused. 'Well . . .' He said abruptly, 'It's a good thing she's going back at least—Katherine—don't you think?'

'Yes.'

'I mean, it'll be better for her there. I suppose they'll give me some sort of job and we can get a home and—' He rubbed at his face, 'She used to be—Well, you know what she was like—before.'

Edge nodded.

'They—the feeling is that—why I was chucked out was . . . it was felt that I was thinking of myself before the good of the Police and the Empire. How do you like that? It's probably true. Is it?'

'I have no idea at all.'

Moffatt forced a smile, 'You're not a very sympathetic bastard, are you?'

'Do you want sympathy?'

'No—no.' He shook his head. 'No. Thanks for that anyway.' He said thoughtfully, 'I was going to say that you could come too. On the ship. That I could arrange it. But I owe you the same courtesy at least, don't I?' He said softly, 'Is your city worth saving—for the Chinese?'

'I think so.'

'And are you going to save it?'

'Are you staying on board now? You and Katherine?'

'It's safer, yes.'

'When does it sail?'

'Monday—about 2 a.m. On the tide. Katherine—Katherine wanted to go to church on Sunday, for the last time, but I think, all things considered, we'll stay on board. There's a chapel on board. There always is on Portuguese ships. I suppose we can . . .'

'Sure.'

'I—I was sorry to hear about your friend Hooper—he, ah—he once said a very humorous thing to me about the Presbyterian Church in Soochow Road—' he blinked, 'But, ah—I—I really can't quite remember—I didn't think it was funny at the time, but I—'

Edge said, 'He was a very funny man sometimes.'

'He was a friend of yours, wasn't he?'

'He was all right.' Edge looked at his watch. It was 2 p.m. 'I have to go.'

'About that day, I—about the execution. I—'

Edge nodded.

'I suppose I wanted your forgiveness.' He smiled self-consciously, 'That's a bit effeminate, isn't it? To ask for forgiveness? But if there's anything I can ever do, you—you only have to ask.' He moved forward and for a moment Edge thought he was going to put his hand on his shoulder, 'Jack . . . anything.' His eyes stared at Edge desperately, 'Anything . . . anything at all . . .' He looked away across the river, and put his hand across his eyes, 'All right?'

He said with a tremble in his voice, 'Anything at all.'

50

In Pearl Harbour, on the U.S.S. Nevada, the Navy Chaplain made an alteration to the list of Sunday religious services for the various denominations on board. It was dark, the only illumination a lamp at the foot of the stairs to the bridge, and he wrote the parade date and time in with infinite ecumenical care: *0755 hrs, Sunday, December the 7th, 1941.*

It was a calm, quiet night. The Chaplain glanced across the dark water of the anchorage to the other ships. They were silhouetted, tranquil, majestic. He looked up at the clear night sky and thought for a moment of his home in Kansas.

He squinted at the writing on the notice and went below, smiling.

51

On Isogai's hill, artillerymen and three squads from the Transport Corps were using mules to site heavy field howitzers into firing positions overlooking the city. It was early Saturday morning, bitterly cold, and the struggling beasts shivered and strained in clouds of expelled vapour as the Transport men cajoled and whipped them to drag the masses of camouflage-painted metal across the flinty ground. One of the creatures let out a braying honk of protest and slipped back onto its forelegs, a Transport man pulling at its bit. A human chain of artillerymen passed boxes of shells hand-to-hand from a truck parked on the road down past the mule to the firing points. The mule brayed a second time, rose briefly, bucking, and then was dragged into submission by the handler. The lines between it and the howitzer tightened, its hindquarter muscles stood out and it took the load, and then, under the persistent urgings of its master, it began moving again.

From the hill, the International Settlement shimmered in a faint river mist, the darker smoke from the burning warehouses momentarily obscuring and then revealing the outline of the ship with the arbitrary shifts of the wind. Edge glanced at one of the naked shells. There was a red conical tip at its point: the fuse, and behind it, snug in its machined solid casing of steel, a tightly packed compound of chemicals of frightful power. There was a faint smile playing about Isogai's face.

'And who, Mr Edge—may one ask—has sent you on this mission of begging?' He glanced at the shells and guns and smiled again, 'May one ask? Or is it simply a notion you have formed entirely on your own account?'

'I have come to apply for an extension of time. So far, the killer of your two soldiers has not been apprehended—' Edge watched the guns and the mules, the cases of shells being passed efficiently from one gloved hand to the next, 'Enquiries are still—'

Isogai said, 'Enquiries are still proceeding.'

'Yes.'

'And the Police expect an early arrest. I read your newspapers. I am familiar with the form.'

'Then you will also be familiar with the fact that investigations take time. There is no need for all this—and there are tanks massing along the border—'

'And other artillery pieces on the foreshore of the river at Pootung. Yes.' Isogai said conversationally, 'You were given a limited number of days in which to apprehend the murderers of the two Japanese soldiers. You were informed that should you fail to do this, the Japanese Imperial Army would consider that the forces of law and order within the International Settlement had broken down and, in order to restore continuity, the Japanese Imperial Army would cross the borders of the Settlement to impose a regime of government and justice to replace your own. That is what you were told. The Japanese Imperial Army has been very fair. You were granted adequate time, first by the previous officer in charge of this sector, Commander Nobata of the Imperial Navy, and then, as a token of continuing trust, by me, but you have not justified that trust. To be scrupulous, my report will say that in my opinion your efforts were hampered continually and mercilessly by gangs of traitorous mercenaries and profiteers working undercover for the defeated armies of Chiang Kai Shek, but that will be only marks on a piece of paper.' He smiled again and looked at the guns.

'The International Settlement is made up of the citizens of nations who are not at war with Japan!'

Isogai looked at his watch. 'The deadline will run out at

190

midnight tomorrow night. The task set was not an impossible one and any deceit has all been on your side. As always the Japanese Imperial Army has conducted itself honourably. There is still time to locate the perpetrators of the murders and hand them over for punishment.'

'That cannot be done.'

'Then the future of the Settlement is clear.'

'That cannot be done because you are not recognised as having legal jurisdiction in the Settlement—to hand anyone over to certain death—' he paused for a reply.

'Oh, yes, assuredly to certain death.'

'—to certain death, would be tantamount to surrendering the Settlement. As well as being a party to an illegal murder.'

'In China, Japan represents the legal forces of the state.'

'They do not represent them in the Settlement.'

'Thus far. In China—'

'The International Settlement is not China!'

'I will not argue history with you.'

'What will you argue?'

'I will argue nothing. There is no dissenting voice. The future is inevitable.' Isogai said casually, 'And that vessel—the *Bocca Tigris*, is it called?—carrying away the Old China Hands, that will not leave.'

'That is a Portuguese ship—not at war with Japan—carrying families to Australia, which is also not at war with Japan!'

'It is a vessel moored in unfriendly waters containing important people who will be required for the future administration of—'

'It is full of women!'

'Traitors and the wives of traitors. Should it show resistance to the Japanese Imperial Forces by attempting to contact guerilla forces farther down the river it will be considered a legitimate target of war.' He glanced down at the clearing mist towards the smoke stack, 'It is possible the perpetrators of incidents are on board and there will be the question of punishments.' He smiled again.

Edge said slowly, 'And of course, there is no glory in conquering Rome when Caesar is no longer there.'

'I am not impressed with European analogies.' He said quickly, 'Nor should there be any attempt to destroy the city. Such vandalism would be met with the sternest retribution. The city and its people—the people who built it—the inheritors of the

191

founders of the city will be left intact.' He narrowed his eyes. 'Those are my orders. The ship will not leave.'

'Is that the policy of the Emperor of Japan—to slaughter women and fire on unarmed vessels?'

'That is *my* policy! Unlike the late Nobata, officers of the Army do not have to ask permission for every sneeze or fart from Tokyo.'

'The city is a ghost town! Everything has gone or stopped or fallen into decay. It's over, finished— What in God's name does Japan want it for?'

'*I* want it!' He lowered his voice as an artilleryman looked around, 'And, Mr Edge, if I do nothing else in my life, I intend to have it.'

'And are your troops prepared to die for it in order to satisfy your personal vanity? Are they prepared to go into battle against the British and the Americans?'

Isogai made a dismissive chuckle, 'The Americans—and a few British sentries—'

'Are they, damn it?'

'The Japanese soldier does what he is told!' He touched at the thousand stitches obi under his tunic, 'Unlike you, we are not afraid of death.'

'Commander Nobata—'

'I have defeated Commander Nobata!' Isogai's eyes blazed. 'That old man! That—that *cobweb*!'

Edge said exploratorily, 'What if the International Settlement was to surrender peacefully?'

'To me?'

'Yes. If they were to surrender?'

Isogai said evenly, 'Then it would be a triumph of the will, not unexpected.'

'I see.'

'Is it being considered?' His mask dropped. He was eager. 'Is—' He said abruptly, 'You are attempting to bait me.'

'I am attempting to consider all the possibilities.'

'Who has suggested the notion?' He looked at Edge with contempt. 'Not you. Not a lowly—'

'People you would consider to be the inheritors of the old Shanghai. The descendants of the men who founded the Settlement in the nineteenth century. The men of the great *hongs* and the clipper ships, the men who—'

'I am familiar with history!'

'Those people. People like—'

'Your man, Moffatt?' He saw Edge looked surprised that he knew the name, 'The arrogant man who returned the bodies to an inferior race? Him? Is he one of the men who have suggested it?'

'I am merely—'

'Where?'

'What do you mean?'

'I mean, *where*? Where was it discussed? *Where*? In what place? Where? In the—' Isogai paused. He said reflectively, 'Of course. Where else? It would have been discussed in leather armchairs with white-coated servants bringing drinks and little silver trays of food. Where the Bund could be seen through wide windows.' He smiled to himself, 'Where the great clipper ships carrying tea and opium once moored. Where the—' He said abruptly, 'And they have sent you to me in order to—'

'I have only suggested it as a possibility—'

'Yes, yes!'

Edge said, 'You could still be the conqueror of Shanghai without a shot being fired.'

'I do not need the situation explained to me! Is this notion a serious political move or is it merely some invention of your own?' He answered his own question, 'No. It is theirs. They would choose a person of lowly station in life. A Sergeant. They would choose a man who would echo their words exactly.' He said with an effort to appear casual, 'This idea was discussed in the Shanghai Club at Number Three, the Bund, was it not?'

Edge glanced at the guns.

Isogai said, 'It is seven stories high. The plinths and columns are of Ningpo granite. I have read that the Grand Hall is paved in white marble. Is that true?'

Edge did not reply.

'It has one hundred and eighty rooms. It has been the pulse and heartbeat of the International Settlement for over—' Isogai said suddenly, 'You are not a member?'

'No.'

'No, you would not be.' He paused and gazed down at the city.

'It is only a—'

'You may tell them that you have put the idea to me.' He paused again, gathering his thoughts, 'You may tell them that my purpose is unswayed by their words.' He went on more quickly, 'You may tell them that the Japanese Imperial Army's thrust is irresistible. That—that nothing will alter its historic destiny. You may tell them that.'

'I will say what you have said.'

'The city must remain intact.' He stood very still, looking at Edge, not seeing him, 'Tell them that it must remain as it has always been.' His eyes glistened for a moment, 'Tell them that I am not a barbarian, that I know their city and their endeavours through long history, and their—that my entry there would be merely a passing over from one hand to another—that I understand about dishonour and that . . .' He touched unconsciously at his sword. Edge saw him clench his fist to wipe the perspiration from his palm, 'The International Settlement of Shanghai . . .' His eyes moved irresistibly down the hill towards the city in the mist, *'Tell them I am worthy of it!'*

His hands were shaking in anticipation. He hesitated for an instant and then, quickly, turned away to his guns.

52

In Tokyo, a cable was received from General Tsutomu Sakai commanding the 23rd Army near Canton. The contents of the cable were passed on urgently to The Imperial Naval General Staff and an emergency Joint Services Meeting was convened. The cable stated that an Army transport plane carrying a courier from Tokyo to the Southern Japanese Army in China had crashed in a mountainous region of Kwantung province controlled by the Nationalists and that the fate of the courier, a Major Sukisaka, and the leather briefcase he carried was not known.

The documents contained full details of the surprise attack on Pearl Harbour and co-incidental assaults to be launched by Army forces in China and Singapore. A cable was sent immediately to Sakai asking for more information.

There was no more information. The aircraft had fallen into enemy hands. Spotter planes sent to the area had seen no evidence of casualties from the air and it was assumed that the surviving crew and passengers of the crashed aircraft, stunned or rendered unconscious by the impact, had been captured by the Nationalists without a fight.

There were known to be direct communications between Chiang Kai Shek and Roosevelt. If Major Sukisaka had not had time to destroy the papers in his briefcase before the Nationalists came, the Joint Services Meeting knew it would only be a matter of hours until Washington was informed fully of their contents. Not only the attacking aircraft would be in jeopardy from a prepared resistance, but later reports from Hawaii suggested that elements of the American Navy were still at sea and could well be placed within range of the Japanese Naval attack force within a matter of hours. The Prime Minister, General Tojo, was apprised of the situation. He in turn contacted the Emperor and members of his Cabinet.

At eleven a.m. Tokyo time, when the Joint Services Meeting finally broke up, a coded cable was sent first, to General Terauchi, the Commander of the Southern Army in China, the intended recipient of the briefcase, and then, fifteen minutes later, to General Sakai outside Canton.

It was a gamble, but the Meeting reasoned that so far luck had been on their side. There were only a few more hours to go. Surely, the chances that the courier, as a trained man, would have had the presence of mind to—

The decision was made. Both cables read HINODE YAMA-GATA—"commence operations as planned."

No word was sent to the Japanese forces surrounding the International Settlement in Shanghai concerning the coming hostilities. The understanding was that it was for General Sakai to contact them personally when the time came.

Sakai had the dossier on Major Isogai Masonobu, the officer in temporary charge of the Army ringing the city, and following the exchange of cables with Tokyo, he looked through it again to verify that Isogai was the type of officer he could rely on to execute his duty at short notice.

He glanced at the map of the International Settlement—a single piece of a jigsaw pattern in an enormously wide and complex world picture—and thought a few tanks alone would do the job.

He glanced at his watch. He had his own preparations to make.

He decided to leave informing Shanghai until the very last moment.

53

Edge kneaded at his shoulder with his hand. He stood in the main room of his apartment looking out the window and smoking. Outside, it was 5 a.m. and black night: he could hear Barbara Ling packing in the bedroom. His shoulder hurt arthritically. He moved the muscles back and forth in a rolling motion, then went on kneading it absently and thought of bright warm daylight and Wu Chang. Wu Chang when he had been a boy, and hard yellow earth and the warmth of Summer, of trees, and the smell of starched clothes and flowers, the polished deep shine on varnished church wood: trees and grass and light and hills. His cigarette went out and he relit it and thought of Hooper and Singh and Duras and Missy and Katherine Moffatt. He thought, "She asked if I heard the secret harmonies, but there are no secret harmonies. There are only people." He thought, "Whatever harmony they have is for historians long after they've all gone." He closed his eyes and all the sights and movements of his parents' mission in Wu Chang came back, flickering like figures and places in an old silent film. He thought, *God, such a long time ago.*

He thought, "I ran away." He had a picture in his mind—a sepia photograph of his parents standing outside the Mission with smiles on their faces for posterity, half a dozen of their Chinese converts in their best Sunday silk sitting on carved-back dining chairs behind them, also smiling and looking determinedly into the lens, and he thought, "They wouldn't leave. When the Boxers threatened to burn their church down, my parents smiled graciously to the messenger who had come to warn them, gave him a bowl of tea and a Bible and went on about their business secure in the protection of Christ."

The smell of his father's old black powder shotgun came back to him: giant plumes of billowing white smoke erupting from the yellow fire-flash of one of the barrels. He remembered his father's canvas duck hat, stuck with a feather, unburned expelled grains of gunpowder rolling about on the brim, the dog chasing through grass and brush to retrieve, the smell of the gun like the smouldering case of an exploded skyrocket, his mother playing English music hall songs on the harmonium in the Church. *Down at the Old Bull and Bush.* Such a long time ago. Old picture postcards of America and England side by side on a

196

bookcase in the sitting room, his father's books in Chinese, and his mother trying to get her tongue around the tone changes of Mandarin and laughing. Their faith rock hard.

The night outside was cold. There was condensation on the window panes from a mist coming in from the river. He heard Barbara Ling moving about in the other room.

The whistling and exploding of firecrackers to frighten away evil spirits. The Society of Harmonious Fists—the Boxers. Flags and pennants and decorated swords—they came over the hill in the middle of the day like a street procession, the duck-hunting dog padding up to meet them.

He thought, "I know that somewhere between the hill and the Mission there was a sudden silence. The dog sensed it and stopped. I know there was a silence and then the screaming started and they ran. I know they killed the dog with a slash from a sword or an axe, but I have no memory of it at all. And I ran. My father, in his braces and shirtsleeves, his collar detached, went out to meet them like an untidy gardener going forward to nod to the landowner of his garden, but I wasn't there to be with him. He raised his hands in greeting. The procession swallowed him, and then they passed by and after a moment they halted outside the house and another figure appeared at the door and the procession went inside. Then they emerged again and the two figures were lying down—and the house and the Church simply burned to the ground without any violence."

So easy and soundless. Passing over. He thought, "That was one of the expressions the Missionary Society used when they took me in. *Passing over*. The procession passed over and the two little figures lay down on the ground and they passed— And they forgave me. The Missionary Society forgave me, and my parents, gone to God, in Heaven, they forgave me too. The secret harmony. China moved over them and brushed them aside and they fell onto the ground and lay there while their lives' work burned properly and appropriately back to ashes. And the Boxers went away into history. And from where I hid it was peaceful and orderly and celebratory with only the spots of colour on white to suggest that there might have been gasps and anger and the movement of steel through the air. Brief movements of people and steel in time like the seasons of leaves on trees." Edge thought, "I ran away and hid."

He touched at his shoulder.

He put his face against the window pane and closed his eyes.

'I have to go now, Jack.' She looked away from him and down to the watch on her wrist. 'I telephoned for a rickshaw. It's downstairs. With the cold, there won't be anyone on the streets. It's safer. I'd rather you didn't come with me.'

'All right.'

'The ship leaves very early tomorrow morning on the tide—it's safer if I—' She said softly, 'I bought two tickets if you want to change your mind.'

'No.'

'Then there's nothing more to be said, is there?' She said suddenly, 'Maybe the ship won't leave. Maybe the Japanese'll stop it and you'll find me back in your bath wallowing in bath salts and you'll think, "That bloody woman's back again!" and you'll have to make excuses to your new mistress at the door until you can get into the bathroom and bundle the old one outside. Maybe—maybe, Jack, I—' She went to the door quickly and opened it, carrying a suitcase, 'Maybe you and I—' She paused, waiting.

Edge said, 'Goodbye. God speed.' He turned away from her.

'Jack, I—'

He touched at his shoulder. He felt her presence at the door. He heard the door shut, and then, in the great silence of the city he heard her footsteps on the stairs. He heard the rickshaw move off along the deserted, black night road below.

Movements in time, flickering images of times long past. He had a picture of the ship, silent, its engines turning, waiting.

Over the city there was the silence of still night. He thought of the river, of harmonies and people, uniforms and the smell of starched clothes, and of the dog that had stopped half way up the hill. Nameless. The nameless dog that had stopped half way up the hill.

He looked out of the window at all the empty buildings and the mist in the streets, at the outline of the ship's masts and the light from burning warehouses, at a city run down and decayed and dying. He watched night clouds and the silhouettes of birds moving across grey light and darkness.

In the morning, for the first time in many years, in a leather belt holster under his civilian clothes, he carried his pistol.

In China it was 10 a.m. Sunday, December the seventh, nineteen forty one—in Pearl Harbour, seventeen hours behind—immaterial.

In the movements of the leaves on trees and the halting of nameless dogs on nameless hills, it was all immaterial.

It was a date and a time and a place of no particular significance.

He went quickly through the city towards the American Marines' post at the border.

Thy rod and thy staff—

He touched at the pistol under his coat.

54

At sea, the Japanese fleet was less than nine hours from its destination: a little over two hours' flying time from the islands of Hawaii. It was still night and the waters of the Pacific were calm with a faint wind blowing down the decks from the port side. At the prearranged point, the aircraft carriers would turn into the wind for the rising aircraft and the two submarines and destroyers flanking and running ahead of the convoy would take up station around them to provide protection from surprise attack.

Below decks, the torpedo and fighter aircraft were fuelled and armed in readiness, the armourers and elevator personnel sitting under the wings talking in whispers.

On the bridges there were maps out held down by little tokens of luck and good fortune. Battle flags hung limply at the bases of staffs and riggings ready to be run up, and gun crews touched at their calibration knobs and plugged and unplugged wires from microphones and headsets into the communications consuls by loaded ammunition holders.

Helmeted faces in shadows looked up at the sky. There were glows from the luminous hands of wristwatches and, here and there, yellow pin-points of light from unlawful cigarettes held protectively in cupped hands.

The great ocean was grey and deep steady as the fleet moved unstoppably near and nearer to its ultimate destination.

55

Moffatt stood at the end of the dock and said in a whisper, 'My God, Jack, you can't be serious!'

'I've spoken to an American officer at the border and he's agreed to co-operate in supplying transport.'

'He agreed?'

'Unofficially, yes.'

'The whole *thing's* unofficial!' Moffatt glanced back to the ship and lowered his voice yet again, 'You want me to simply ring this man Isogai up on the telephone and invite him into the Settlement like some sort of welcome guest—I can't believe you mean it. If you've apprehended the person who killed the two Japs then there are courts and procedures—What am I supposed to say if he asks me why we're handing him over without even—he wouldn't come. Why should he? And alone? Why should he come alone? Anything could happen to him.'

'You went alone when you delivered the bodies to Nobata.'

'At least I had a driver and some *semblance* of protection—if we're prepared to waive jurisdiction it's tantamount to telling the Japanese we can't control our own city. We might as well just open the border to them and be done with it!' He glanced back to the ship. There were families on the decks carrying luggage into cabins. 'Who is this killer you've caught anyway?'

'I didn't say I'd caught him. His name's Henry Chu.' He saw Moffatt shake his head. 'David Hooper's mechanic. He's in what's left of the warehouses over there.'

Moffatt said incredulously, 'And the Americans have agreed to—' He hesitated. 'But, it is so damned *unofficial*!'

'So are you now, Alec.'

'But I've still got a responsibility to—' his voice trailed off, '—to . . .' He demanded abruptly, 'Why me?'

'Why not?'

'That doesn't answer my question. Why me?'

'Because Isogai will listen to you.'

'*Why?*'

'Because you represent something to him.'

Moffatt said nothing.

'You represent—'

Moffatt said, 'I don't want to know.'

'All right.' Edge said quietly, 'You said no one knew what to do any more. Officially. You said it was up to me. You said if there was ever anything you could do to help—well, now there is. I know it's a hard thing to do but I'm asking you to take it on trust. If you ask he'll come.'

'But how do you *know*?'

'I know.'

'The secret harmonies?' Moffatt said, 'Oh, I've heard Katherine talk about you and the Asians—'

'There are no secret harmonies.'

'But you know that what you're doing is right? You're sure? I have to be certain.' He paused for a moment, 'Do I?' He asked Edge, 'Why do I have to be certain? I was certain that—There are no certainties, are there? Not here, not at the killing ground all those years ago, not anywhere. I—I thought talking to you on the ship that I'd changed, that I could see all the sham in—but I'm still the same, aren't I? I still have to be certain. I just won't admit that the book of rules could be wrong. I've been disgraced and sent packing and I still want to do the right thing. But by whom? If I ring this man won't I be admitting that after—after all the history of the International—won't I be admitting we've just thrown in the towel? What could I put that down to?'

'You could always put it down to political compromise.'

Moffatt looked away to the ship, 'You don't leave a man much, do you? If he comes how do you know he won't bring his army with him?'

'He'll come alone.'

'Or at least have them standing by?'

'He won't. He won't tell anyone. It'll be a private arrangement.'

'Between him—and me? And what do we get in return?'

Edge looked at the ship.

'The ship? The city? What?'

'That remains to be seen.'

'But we will get *something*?' Moffatt said, 'To deal with that—I haven't even met him, why should I mean anything to him? Personally? And where does this meeting take place?'

'The American Marine Officer knows.'

'Who is he? Is he a friend of yours?'

'His name's Lieutenant Dubrinski. He was a friend of David Hooper's.'

'You just said Hooper's man killed the two Japs! These people you're talking about are the scum of the Settlement! Hooper and—is that what all our years here have been reduced to?

Hooper? My God, was he right? Was everything we ever did here built on nothing but avarice and—is everything we ever did in the Settlement reduced to—'

'There is almost no Settlement left!' Edge said roughly, 'Will you do it or not?'

'—but what do I tell him?'

'Tell him you're prepared to meet him to hand over the man responsible for the murder of his men!'

'And what if he doesn't believe it's the right man? What if he thinks it's just some scapegoat we've rounded up for the express purpose of—'

'He'll know it's the right man.'

'*How?*'

Edge said evenly, 'Because he's known from the start. Or at least, if he didn't, Nobata did. And now, with Nobata out of the way, he knows.'

'But how?'

'Because the two Japanese soldiers didn't accidentally stray into the Settlement at all. They were *sent* down here to check up on something and if Nobata didn't know exactly who killed them—personally—then he at least knew why they were killed and where.'

'What were they sent to—' Moffatt said abruptly, 'Something to do with the warehouses and Hooper—correct?'

'Something like that.'

'So he was running guns to both sides. I thought so.'

Edge said again, 'Will you do it or not? Telephone him and—'

'And he'll come?'

'Yes.'

'If I ask him.'

'Yes.'

'And then what?'

'That's all you have to do.'

'But, *and then what?*'

Edge said calmly, 'That doesn't matter to you. Your physical presence won't be required. You'll have done your part. You can just forget it and—'

Moffatt said bitterly, 'And sail away.'

'Yes.'

'Like you did? Just sail away the way you sailed away after—'

'Forget that bloody execution, will you?'

'I can't forget it! I can't forget it should have been me! There was a chance there to—to prove myself—and I just—even my own wife—I missed my one, single chance to—'

'To be human?'

'Yes! To be bloody human!'

'Well, now you've got another!'

'This?'

'Yes!'

'This? Tell him we've caught some little Chink who—' He halted abruptly, 'My God, is this man Chu—the mechanic—is he alive or dead?'

Edge said nothing.

'He's dead, isn't he? Jesus Christ, *what the hell are you going to do when he finds out it's all a trick?*'

'He isn't going to find out.'

Moffatt paused. There was a strange expression on his face. He said slowly, 'You don't strike bargains with people. I know you too well. So what are you going to do? What do you know that I don't? About the bloody Asians? What do you know that I never knew?'

'I don't know anything that you don't know.'

'Oh, yes. You know something all right. You know he'll come. Against all reasonable objections and cautions, you know that if I ask him he'll come. People like me, we prance about and give orders and write letters home and we're the great authorities on China over tea and biscuits and cream cakes, and we pontificate on this and that—and everyone says, *Oo, ah* . . . but we don't know a damn thing, do we? Not when it comes down to it. It's people like you: the people who are fixtures. They're the ones who know. The fixtures like—like—'

Edge said, 'Like the bloody Shanghai Club?'

'No, not like the bloody Shanghai Club! Like the river and the land—like the goddamned pores in the earth! You people know things that—the secret harmonies that—'

'All I ever did was look further than the uniforms and the colour of a man's skin. If that's the secret harmony then it isn't very much of a secret.' Edge said again, 'He'll come if you ask him.'

'When?'

'Tonight. At midnight. Before the ship sails.'

Moffatt nodded.

'It'll cost, Alec. He won't make it easy for you. There's a telephone in the docks office. I'm sure you've got enough authority to use it.' He made a strange smile, 'After all, you're still a bloody White Man, aren't you?'

Moffatt glanced at his watch. It was four thirty five in the afternoon. He said in a very soft voice, 'Then I'd better get on with it, hadn't I, Jack?' He said suddenly, 'But my God, at the final trump, at the very end, it really isn't bloody much at all, is it?'

'What?'

Moffatt said tightly over his shoulder, 'Being a fucking White Man!' They reached the docks office and he pushed open the paint-peeling wooden door.

56

The docks office had been cleared of people. Edge stood at the half open door looking out at the black curved bow of the ship and the hull. There were a few passengers moving about on the deck staring out across the city. He knew none of them. Behind him, he heard a heavy click from the telephone inside the docks office and then, after a moment, a muted burble of words as a connection was opened. He imagined Moffatt standing very straight and erect at the telephone. There was a brief silence and then another audible click. Edge waited. The throbbing of the ship's engines was constant. There was a cold wind blowing down the dock, worrying at tarpaper and wood fibres blown over from the warehouses. Moffatt said clearly, as an announcement, 'Captain Isogai?'—there was evidently a pause—'This is Deputy Assistant Commissioner Moffatt of the Shanghai International Settlement Police'—there must have been a momentary silence at the other end of the line—'Did you understand what I said?' Edge stepped out onto the dock and closed the door. He heard Moffatt's voice say a moment before the sound of the engines overtook it, with an effort at control, 'I believe, Captain, that you and I have something to discuss . . .'

He looked, but she was not there on the deck.

He glanced at his watch.

57

In Washington it was 2 a.m. Sunday morning.

An official communication had been received from the Japanese Embassy during the night and an informal conference had been called in the State Department to puzzle out its meaning. It asked in the most urgent tones for a meeting with Secretary of State Cordell Hull at precisely 1 p.m. that afternoon, Sunday December the seventh and gave no suggestion, as it should, the conference thought, that at that time a reply to President Roosevelt's note to the Emperor would be forthcoming. Both Ambassadors Nomura and Kurusu of the Embassy Peace Conference delegation had applied to be present at the meeting and, surprising in a race as formally polite as the Japanese, the note contained no apology for disturbing Secretary Hull on the weekend.

Intelligence sources reported that recently intercepted messages from Tokyo to the Embassy had spoken of a long transmission due during the night and the desirability of an accurate translation of each of the transmission's fourteen parts. So far, cryptographers in Washington had broken down two of the parts, but they reported that they appeared to be merely a reiteration of previous Japanese diplomatic positions vis-à-vis the Peace Conference and hinted at no new information. With the weekend, the same Intelligence sources pointed out, their staff was well below strength and translations and evaluations could only be arrived at slowly. A report from the FBI stated that there appeared to be no undue activity at the Embassy nor any sign that anything out of the ordinary was taking place.

The request for the meeting had already been granted as a matter of course and the conference, deciding finally that the lateness of the hour and the well-known awkwardness of the Japanese when expressing themselves in English had caused them to over-react to what was otherwise nothing more than a revised set of negotiating demands, broke up at 3:30 a.m.

At 3:45 a.m. Washington time, the Japanese battle fleet in the Pacific came to a state of secondary readiness. Weather reports from the Hawaiian Consul-General Kita had been coming in during the night and it was clear from meteorological projection charts set up in the pilots' briefing rooms that there would be good calm air all the way across the Pacific and maximum visibility over the target.

In Honolulu where the reports were intercepted, American Intelligence graded them under Routine and the fact that a new word appeared at the end of the final transmission: *Banzai!*—ten thousand years—nothing more than loyal greetings from a patriot to his country and Emperor five thousand miles away.

On the fleet, wind directions were calculated and the first of the aircraft moved towards their launching stations.

Five and a half hours' steaming time and two hours by aircraft to the target—the men on the bridges glanced at each other silently.

The moment was almost in sight.

58

Moffatt came out of the docks office and looked around. He looked up at the ship. Briefly, he saw his wife bustle out of a cabin, pause as if she had forgotten something, and then go back out of sight again. Behind him, the warehouses were still partially on fire: tarpaper and flecks of wood fibre and paint chips fell about him like snow. He paused for a moment. 'We're square now, Jack. Now we're square, you and I. For everything.' He glanced up at the hull of the ship, 'I want you to know that. Now we're square. You and I were never friends and we never will be now, but I want you to understand that as one man to another, we're all paid up. Do I make myself clear? Do you agree? Nothing owing on either side.'

Edge nodded.

'I've done what you asked. It was my choice and I did it, and now you and I are square. And now I'm not just sailing away, I'm going because those are the orders I was given and one of the things my conscience tells me to do is to try to obey orders. I want you to understand that. I want you to understand that where I could, I always tried to obey orders.'

'I'm sorry it was hard for you.'

'He made it hard for me.' He paused again, 'But I did what you asked. I won't see you again. Maybe I'll come back to Shanghai one day, but I doubt you and I will ever meet again.'

He hesitated for a moment. 'I believe I can still be useful back home. I intend to try my best, in any event—' He looked away. 'I'm sorry if I've made life difficult for you, but that's the way I was.'

'I know that.'

'I—' Moffatt said, 'I don't know what to say to you. I'd like to say something—' He paused, lost for words. 'But I don't know what to say to you.'

On Battleship Row in Pearl, it was a little after midnight, Sunday morning.

Bored peacetime sailors readied themselves for the change of watch. In Washington, the light in the conference room of the State Department had been extinguished.

'You were right about him—about Isogai. He said I represented—to him at least—the old Shanghai—' He forced a smile, 'The old Shanghai of the Shanghai Club at Number Three, the Bund, were his exact words.'

Edge smiled at him.

'Well, goodbye, Jack.' He held out his hand stiffly. He said slowly, finally, 'God help you, Jack—he said he'd come.'

59

What if this present were the world's last night . . . ? Edge thought, "Poetry." He thought, "Strange to remember that."

Four hurricane lanterns had been placed in position in the centre of the ruined number one warehouse: they formed a corridor of light on either side of a clear section of floor looking out through girders and a fallen wall towards the road outside. Above him, the roof had gone and he could see stars in the cleared night sky and the moon in its final quarter. A wind from the river and the flattened desolation of Pootung across the river hammered at sections of loose corrugated iron on the walls. There was the smell of burning. Erratic faint columns of grey smoke rose from the piles of debris behind the lanterns like will-o'-the-wisps and there were cracking and breaking noises as lengths of hardwood or glass or bakelite beneath the compressed debris heated up and split.

The throbbing of the ship's engines was steady, like a pulse. He heard a clattering and banging from somewhere in the direction of the docks, then silence and then the continuing throbbing again. He glanced up through the black supports and framework of the open roof and saw a night bird pass by on silent wings.

It was midnight. He moved a little back from the rectangle of yellow light and stood near the charred and seized-up hulk of a giant agricultural engine, holding his cigarette in his cupped hand and looking at its glow against his palm. The steady throbbing of the *Bocca Tigris'* engines was the only sound left in Shanghai—Shanghai had culminated there. He drew in on the cigarette and wondered why he had never taken the time to learn the names of all the stars. The wind rattled at the empty warehouse and then died away momentarily.

Far away, across the city, over the wind-whipped roofs and empty gaping windows, through the ghost streets, there was Duras' school and church. He could imagine the square bell-tower looking out across the still river and, in the river itself, the hulks of dead ships, the mud seeping and suffocating the water like lava flow, and, farther away, to the north west, the street lights of Chapei shining in pools on ruined buildings, the lights finally running down and going out, exploding in splintering pops as their filaments gave out. The wind from the river blew across the dying land and rattled at the warehouse.

He thought, "All the clipper ships are long gone and rotted on islands and atolls somewhere, or broken up in shipyards long closed down." The wind was not a wind for clipper ships. He thought, "All that finished a long time ago." He thought of Hooper gliding over the city in the bright buoyant daylight air. This wind was the wind of night. He remembered colours, but the wind and the night were black and colourless.

He moved his cigarette to his left hand and pulled his leather gloves up higher around his wrists. He looked over at the lanterns and then out towards the road: there was a faint twitching feeling in his stomach and he thought, "I could walk out along that road and be free of this place forever." (He thought, "But there's nowhere to go. Not this night anyway.") He wondered what Australia must be like: hot, with flowers and palm trees, harbours with sailing boats and ferries—coming into a new place, sailing into harbour on a ship, seeing the skyline for the first time, the smells of the sea and trees from the foreshore, people waving. He looked at his watch and saw it was five minutes after midnight. Thy rod and Thy staff—he heard a rattling noise of chains and an electric motor as the ship took up its gangplank, then a single clang as deck gates were closed and he thought, "They're leaving." He heard the engines pause for a moment and then restart, then build up, a sudden splashing as the giant propeller bit into the river experimentally, then a rush of high pressure steam as the boilers came to life and he thought, "It's happening. They're getting up steam to leave. Full tide. It's almost over." He heard a swishing sound as the propeller revolved heavily and sent foam and debris scudding away in a flurry of dredged up water, an order given: they were readying the ship to cast off. He looked at his watch. An hour and a half and the great steel bulk would move under its own power—he heard the engines building up steam. There was, momentarily, a reflected glow in the sky as the lights came on under the power of the ship's generators. Things were being made ready. The steady throbbing came back as the engine shafts turned easily and free out of gear, working themselves up to the moment of release.

Edge exhaled smoke from his cigarette. His hand was shaking and he dropped the cigarette onto the charred cement floor and crushed it with the toe of his shoe. He heard his own breathing come in time to the pounding of the engines of the ship. He thought, "I never learned all the names of the stars." A night bird went quickly across the black sky, going away. Cold, final night. The gangplank up and bolted and lashed down tight. His hands were shaking with the cold.

What if this present were the world's last night . . .?

He rubbed his knuckles across his mouth. He smelled the leather of his gloves and the smell of burning and cremation in the warehouse. He looked at his watch. Twenty minutes after midnight. His mouth was dry. He felt his hands shaking. The cold wind bit at him—his chest trembled with it.

Thy rod and thy—

His hands shook.

Alone, on the world's last night, he waited.

At the border, alone, Isogai climbed into Dubrinski's jeep. There was a Springfield rifle on the back seat and a spare clip of ammunition. Isogai glanced at it and smiled to himself. Across the wire the Japanese tanks waited in single column. Isogai looked at them significantly and then back to the rifle. He glanced at Dubrinski waiting to start the engine. He was aware of his family sword, sheathed, lethal sharp in its scabbard. He tapped its end against the high polish of his leather boots to make a soft clicking sound. He lit a cigarette from a silver case and put the case casually back in his tunic pocket.

Dubrinski said softly under his breath, 'You son of a bitch . . !' and leaned forward to turn the ignition key.

The jeep swept away from the border at high speed.

At sea, all the propellers on all the planes were turning. Signal lamps were flickering from the bridges of one ship to another. The Pacific had become wild and white foam flecked. The slipstream of the aero engines fluttered and tore at the clothing of men on the flight decks. Cockpit cabins were being winched closed by the pilots. They held their hands together over their instruments and clenched them to contain their impatience.

Battle flags began rising on the masts and riggings. They caught the wind and streamed out. Men in wheelhouses and at their battle stations heard the drumming of the aircraft pistons in their ears. The great fleet began turning slowly through the waves and foam of the ocean towards morning.

On all the ships, men shook hands solemnly. The sound of the revving aircraft reverberated across the ocean.

In Japanese Headquarters, Shanghai, the fat Sergeant Clerk's phone rang. 'Captain Isogai's office—' He heard the voice of General Sakai say, 'Officer Commanding. Hurry.'

'Not here, General.' He heard the General curse. The General's voice said urgently, 'Combat alert. Do you understand?'

'Yes, sir.'

'In readiness.' The General's voice was clipped and impatient, 'Inform the Captain's forces—'

'Yes, sir.' The Sergeant hesitated. 'May I fight, sir?'

'What?'

The Sergeant bit his lip.

'What did you say?'

'I request permission to fight, sir.'

'Where the devil is your officer?'

'I can tell them, sir.' The Sergeant said through gritted teeth, 'I request permission to give my life for the Emperor.' He said anxiously, '—sir.'

The General paused for a fraction of a second, 'Stand by for a final instruction—' He paused again, '—very soon—'

'Yes, sir! Sir, my request, sir—'

'—Granted.'

'Thank you, sir!'

There was a momentary silence on the line.

'Sir—?'

He heard the General draw a breath. There was a hard silence.

'General Sakai, sir—'

He heard Sakai say a single word.

'. . . *Banzai!*'

There were tears of joy flowing down the Sergeant's face.

Edge saw him. He saw the jeep stop and he saw him, alone, in full uniform. He saw the jeep pause for a moment and then drive quickly away and he saw Isogai standing there.

His trembling stopped. He heard the ship's engines throbbing steadily as they built up power.

The wind dropped. He saw him hesitate for a moment. He saw him look across towards the ship and then down at the ground of the International Settlement. Edge saw him look at the lights in the warehouse. He saw him take a step forward. Edge moved back out of the light.

He saw him. He saw Isogai come.

The propellers were turning. Their circles of clear light moved faster and faster. Men ran across the flight decks, out of the way. They saw the battle standards streaming as they went—the noise of the engines roared in their ears. In Pearl Harbour, less than two hours' flying time away, it was 6 a.m. on the seventh of December, 1941, a new day. The engines reached a crescendo and as the ships completed their turn and the wind rushed down the flight decks, the aircraft attained their last, ultimate moment. Their sound roared louder and louder and became shattering as the engines reached their pitch of power. The command went through all the ships simultaneously—it was screamed and shouted through microphones to the pilots, through loudspeakers to the men on deck and at their battle

211

stations. It rose above the engines and echoed across the waters of the ocean. It was like a great cheer:

'LAUNCH. . . AIRCRAFT!!'

Isogai. He was coming. Coming . . .

60

Inside the warehouse, Isogai put his hand to the hilt of his sword, glancing cautiously at the lanterns flickering around him, then back over his shoulder for a moment to where the jeep had gone. He stood tight and immobile like a statue, moving his finger minutely on the sword hilt. He seemed to tense his neck muscles, draw his neck down protectively and listen. The throbbing of the ship was everywhere: he listened for other sounds in it. He moved his head to one side and looked across into the darkness of one side of the warehouse. His body was turned slightly to one side, tensed. His fingers moved on the sword and found a hard purchase. There was a metallic grating from the ship—a steel door being crashed shut, or chain dropped onto a deck—but Isogai did not hear it. He listened for sounds inside the warehouse. He said abruptly, 'Moffatt?'

He waited. There was no reply.

'Moffatt—' His eyes narrowed. 'Moffatt!'

Edge stepped forward into the light.

'Where is your superior officer?'

Edge's hands rested by his sides. He stood still. Isogai looked past him. 'What is the purpose of these lights?'

Edge's eyes stayed on his face.

'This place is not altogether satisfactory.' Isogai heard a sound—a rat scuttling through the warm ashes of a pile of burned silk, 'It has the advantage to your people of privacy, but it is not altogether satisfactory to me.' Edge saw him smile to himself, 'Your people have chosen this place to save face for themselves, and I, in turn, must say—in order to meet them at

212

their game—that it is not satisfactory.' He paused. 'And now I have done so. I am magnanimous in victory. Further, I should complain to you—as the junior emissary of the enemy vanquished—that it is also not satisfactory to be kept waiting. This I also do.' His voice changed and gave an order, 'Now the preliminaries are over. They may make the journey from their Shanghai Club to surrender to me. It is an old game. I know the rules. Now, where are your people?'

Through the sound of the ship, Edge could hear the hissing of the hurricane lanterns on the floor. He looked at one: the little yellow flame burned hard and bright inside its glass cage. He looked back to Isogai and found nothing to say. They stood facing each other like duellists at either end of a corridor of flickering light.

'Following the transition to Japanese rule, games of this sort played by subject races will not be tolerated. This waiting and this choice of venue is a sad little effort to prolong the last moments of a defeated system. The murderer of the two Japanese soldiers will now be handed over for punishment, and, following an honourable interval, the Imperial Japanese Army will move into the Settlement to maintain order. Tomorrow. In the afternoon. In preparation, Japanese flags will be placed at various points along the Bund and Nanking Road. The triumphant entry of the Japanese forces will be recorded on motion picture film by Army photographers and it is further expected that groups of Chinese and European inhabitants of the Settlement will line the route with expressions of joy and welcome. The flags of the various nations will be left flying from the roof of the Shanghai Club and these will be ceremonially struck and replaced by the banner of the Rising Sun following the moment of actual welcome by a party of dignitaries and representatives of the civil and military authorities.' Isogai took out his silver case, selected a cigarette from it, and lit it unhurriedly, 'It is the custom of defeated peoples then to bow from the waist in respect.' He puffed at the cigarette carefully, 'I have considered the situation and it is my intention to install my Headquarters in the premises of the Shanghai Club so there should be no suspicion that an arrangement has been struck. There should be no resistance. Arms should be left in store for collection by members of the Ordnance and Quartermasters' sections of the Imperial Army.' He glanced at Edge's three piece grey suit, 'At the official welcome, full uniform will be worn,

213

together with all decorations and emblems of rank.' He asked again, 'Where are your people?'

Edge shook his head.

'You are witnessing a great moment in history, Sergeant Edge.'

'Am I?' Edge's hands felt tired and empty. Isogai's eyes fascinated him. They flickered back and forth with the light. Below the eyes his face was unmoving, like cast steel.

Isogai took a step forward. He stood ten feet from Edge. Edge saw his gloved fingers moving backwards and forwards on the hilt of the sheathed sword. His voice dropped, 'The International Settlement was built upon the power of one race over another. Based on the cravings of decadent Chinese for opium, for an escape from the world. Stronger, cleaner men took advantage of this weakness and they held this part of China with the snivelling consent of the Chinese ruling class for ninety nine years.' He paused for a moment. 'Ninety nine years. And now at last Japan's hour has come and now we are the superior race. Japan is not China. We will never become decadent. We will never be conquered like the Chinese.' He paused again, 'Your people may rely on that. I understand why they are attempting to make me wait, why they have chosen this place in which to meet me, but Japan is an irresistible force. They are not dealing with second rate bastard Chinese. They are dealing with modern men. Following the commencement of the new administration, this will be made clear to them.'

Edge said quietly, 'All you are conquering are a few burned out warehouses and an empty city.'

'The real Shanghai is—'

'These warehouses are the real Shanghai.'

'I know my history, Mr Edge. I know the history of commerce in the International Settlement. You characterise ninety nine years of history by empty warehouses because—'

Edge said, 'There is nothing more. There never was.'

'Your junior grade opinions do not interest me.'

'The Chinese—'

'Nor your reflections on a race clearly meant to be nothing more than a great unthinking market place for other, great nations. Shanghai is a great prize!'

'Shanghai is nothing but empty warehouses and streets full of refugees escaping from the war. It is not worth having. It never was.'

214

'You absurd man! You are wasting my time! Where are your people?'

'You cannot subject another race of people to domination! It's all up here, finished—even people like Moffatt have—the people here have finally realised that you cannot continue to—'

Isogai said with contempt, 'What are you begging me to do this time?'

'—ordinary people have realised that China is for the—'

Isogai looked away. 'Where is this murderer you have caught?'

'Can't you see that? Can't people like you ever see that—'

'Where is the murderer of the two Japanese soldiers? Reply!'

Edge indicated the darkness beyond the lights. 'He is there.'

'Where?' Isogai looked into the glow of the lights.

'There. In the darkness.'

'Ah, yes, the mechanic, Henry Chu.'

Edge said, 'He is dead.' He said with an effort, 'Every one of the people who—they're all dead.' He shook his head, 'Don't you understand? *There isn't anyone here any more.*'

'The *city* is here—the fact that the perpetrator of the crime is a corpse is a matter of no importance compared to—'

'You are getting nothing!'

'I am conquering a city!'

'You are conquering nothing! All you are conquering is land and buildings! You are conquering the Shanghai Club: a few rooms and marble floors, a few leather chairs and the right to say that you are in command of a speck of soil in a nation full of—'

'Full of *Chinese!*'

'Full of people you will never understand!'

'And you understand them, do you, Mr Edge? You are the spokesman for them, are you? Is that who you beg for? The Chinese? Oh, I understand the mentality of the Old China—'

'You understand nothing!'

'This is my victory, Edge!'

'All you are getting is a burned out warehouse! All this is over: one conqueror then another—it's all over!'

'Where are your people?'

'Where do you *think* they are!'

'You will inform them to—'

'I will inform them to do nothing!'

'You have been given an order! You will obey it! Instantly!'

Edge said quietly, 'I want you to allow the ship to depart. It is carrying away the last real remnants of European power in China and I want you to allow it to depart.'

'The ship will not leave. Arrangements will be made tonight and your people will inform the Master of the ship that—' He listened for a moment to the noise of the engines, 'There is still plenty of time to—'

'The ship will leave.'

'That is not a condition that was set on the orderly transfer of power.'

'There will be no orderly transfer of power.'

'Your people will fight?' Isogai said suddenly, 'Ah.' The smile appeared for a moment, 'This is to lessen the humiliation—this threatening. To make me feel the prize is worth having.' He nodded to himself, 'In return for future lenient treatment.' He raised his index finger to tap out the words, 'The theory goes that you were capable of inflicting damage on the Japanese Army but good sense and restraint prevailed. So I should feel obliged to them—to treat them a little more softly.' He smiled to himself, 'You have told them of my—of my interest in the Settlement and they have tried a game on me that has kept them safe and prosperous for their ninety nine years and although I am far from stupid enough to fall for it, I am well-versed enough in their methods to be flattered. I find it amusing. And nostalgic. I congratulate them. The technique is so well documented in histories of the Europeans in China. Unfortunately for them however, as a representative of the Japanese Imperial Forces, I have seen through it.'

'The ship will leave.'

'No.' He shook his head.

'I am asking you to—'

Isogai demanded abruptly, 'Who are you, Edge? What have you done in your life?'

Edge did not reply.

'Where does your glory lie? In being a servant and a messenger for your masters? As a minor character in one of the great events in—'

'This is not a great event.'

'Get your people here! I am tired of all this.'

'My people are not coming.'

'What did you say?'

Edge was silent.

216

'Your people are coming!'

'No, they are not.'

'They intend to *fight*?'

'They have nothing to fight for. This is not their city so they—How can you fight for something that was never yours? They merely lived here. They conquered it and they built their warehouses and their roads to remind themselves of their warehouses and their roads in their own countries and then they resided here. They put up borders and barbed wire and they built walls around their houses and their factories and they employed policemen to keep them safe. They built ships and banks and clubs. And factories. They built parks and gardens to walk in, roads and shops and entertainments for themselves. But it was all temporary, on lease.' He said fiercely to Isogai, 'Do you understand that from your histories? On lease! *They never intended to stay!* And as for the Chinese, the nation, the people around them: the ordinary people, the people who bought their goods and gave them their profits, the people who worked for them and served them, the people whose country they had plundered—most of them, most of the Europeans: the conquerors—most of them never even learned the Chinese language! Your "Old China Hands"—your models of virtue and romance—most of them are tucked up safely at home in bed thousands of miles away and they couldn't care less whether you or anyone else was in command just so long as they'd got out with their profits. And they have got out and they've taken everything they had with them—their profits—and now there's nothing left: they've taken it all away with them. This city—this place—is nothing! They've taken it all away with them—' Edge shouted at him, 'And in the final, last analysis it all belonged to the Chinese!'

Isogai's face was unanimated, hard. 'And you, Mr Edge, you are the saviour of that China, are you?'

'The ship will leave, with the last of those people on board. You are all that is stopping it.'

Isogai looked at him carefully. 'And you are the last man left—'

'I suppose I am. Yes.'

'Yes.' Isogai nodded. 'And you intend to fight me for your city. You. The Old China Hand who does speak Chinese. You are prepared to die here for your Chinese. Here, in a dirty warehouse.' He nodded again, 'You intend to fight me.'

'No.'

'Ah.' Isogai raised his hand and looked closely at his cigarette. He dropped it and tapped it out with the toe of his boot. He was nodding and smiling to himself.

Edge's voice said calmly and evenly, 'What I intend to do, Captain Isogai, is to kill you.'

He looked up to see Edge's pistol pointing at his heart.

61

In Japanese Headquarters, Shanghai sector, the fat Sergeant sat at his desk, waiting. The little lights on his switchboard were all out: he waited for the one above General Sakai's direct connection to suddenly light up.

The clerk's room was empty. He sat alone in a pool of light from an overhead lamp biting his lips. The bakelite plugs to the lines connecting the various tank commanders and platoons and company leaders were all inserted, ready: he only had to flick a single switch to activate them.

He looked at the wall clock facing him: twelve thirty-five—he heard it ticking away the seconds, echoing in the empty room.

Under his tunic, there was a thousand stitches *obi* wound about his stomach—he opened a drawer and took out a photograph of his wife and children and laid it on the desk. The ticking of the clock went on and on.

The fat Sergeant massaged the fingers of his left hand and brought the knuckles up to his mouth. He touched at his pebble thick glasses. The lights on the switchboard stayed out.

He heard his own breathing and the sound of the clock.

Just one white light . . .

He bit his lip and waited.

Twelve fifty-eight. Then . . .

One minute more to one a.m. . . . .

A light came on. It was the Corporal in charge of the artillery emplacement trained on the docks reporting activity on the ship. The fat Sergeant refused to hear him out. His eyes stayed on the single light above Sakai's connection.

He willed, 'Come on, come on . . .'

He ordered the Artillery Corporal, 'Hold your fire.' Unconsciously, the fat Sergeant glanced about the office for Captain Isogai. He was not there; the Sergeant had his orders from General Sakai. He ordered the Artillery Corporal, 'Wait—' He shouted at the man as he started to protest, 'Wait!'

The light went on. General Sakai's voice said very clamly and clearly, 'In exactly forty-five minutes from now, Japanese aircraft will be sighted over the major American naval base in the islands of Hawaii. At that moment, at exactly that moment—'

In the Pacific, at fifteen thousand feet, the formations of torpedo planes and fighters formed a triple column ahead. All over the Pacific it was a cool crisp day. Ten miles behind them was a second wave of aircraft.

Morning was coming up. The first wave of aircraft roared unstoppably eastwards towards the rising sun on the horizon.

Sakai's voice said conspiratorially, 'At that precise moment, no sooner . . .'

62

On the bridge of the Bocca Tigris Moffatt ordered the Portuguese Captain, 'Now! Go now!'

The Captain glanced at the First Mate. The tide still had an hour to flood. Moffatt drew a short sharp breath, 'It's totally on my head if I'm wrong.' He commanded the hesitating man, 'I order you to cast off now!' He said softly under his breath, unheard by the Portuguese, 'Fully paid up . . .' He said curtly, 'You are still in my city, Captain—*do as you're told!*'

Deep inside the ship the sound of the engines changed. In their cabins, the passengers heard it. The sound changed to a deep rumble. There was a lurching and then, a moment later, a heavy chopping as the propeller cut into the river and the mud and sent it spraying. They heard the bells: a ringing, then an answering sound, and then the rumbling halted, meshed, and shuddered through the ship.

There was a movement. Clean air flushed suddenly in through open cabin portholes. The vessel lurched again, seemed to stagger for a moment, and they heard the hissing of steam blown from the funnel.

Something turned: some great metal weight, and then there were more bells, the sound of orders being shouted from topside down to the docks, and then—in the sudden silence as they waited—they heard the hawsers crash into the water. There was a metal-upon-metal grating. They felt the bow move. The sound of the great propeller came again.

The ship moved.

Carefully, and with infinite care, unaided by tugs, the ship was moving. Early. People looked at each other.

They heard the stern line go.

63

Isogai's voice hissed, 'You damned *Sergeant*—!' There was a tic at the corner of his mouth. 'You inferior, second-rate, failed, damned *Sergeant*! You pathetic, threatening, sad, unsuccessful joke of a man— you cannot kill *me*!' His jaw and mouth trembled in rage, 'I did not come this far to have my destiny frustrated by *you*! You, you are a nothing!' His hand touched the scabbard of his sword and gripped at it, 'Your little pistol and your lanterns and your play-acting—' He drew the sword an inch from its scabbard, 'None of this makes you my equal! You have no nobility—this is not a great battle in which you are my—'

'I thought you people liked unequal contests!' He felt his hand hard on the gun butt, 'I thought you people liked standing men up against butts with targets over their hearts? Don't you? I thought that was the way you people preferred it!'

'Some scum of a Chinese! You knew personally some low scum of a Chinese!'

'No, I didn't know personally some low scum of a Chinese!'

'Some junior soldier, some—'

'They were human beings! Major Ling, and Singh and Hooper, and—their lives were important!'

'Not to the will of Japan!'

'To hell with the will of Japan!'

'Then shoot!' The sword moved out of its scabbard another

fraction, 'Then shoot me down like a Chinese!' His voice dropped, 'You cannot defy. You people are weak. We are a great tide of history, unstoppable, irresistible. I have trained myself! Japan is a single weapon—you—' He said quietly, almost encouragingly, 'It is pointless to resist. You should welcome us.'

Like a man coming out in his shirtsleeves with his arms out, or a woman in a white dress . . . Edge said softly, 'No. Not this time. Not twice.'

Isogai's eyes glittered at him in hatred. 'This . . . *charade*!' He paused and drew the sword six inches from its sheath. 'I tell you as a superior officer, as a man who has made his way in the world, that all this is pointless. You will not shoot, because it is not in my fates to be killed by you. My ordained fate is to die in a great battle—'

Edge said quietly, 'This is a great battle.'

'To *you*! This sordid place and—this is all you aspire to! A dirty little ship carrying cowards and women running away— is that the cause of your great battle? That is nothing!' He took a single careful step forward. The sword slid out another quarter of its length, 'The ship is nothing!'

'Then let it leave.'

'Is that all? Is that all your little pistol requires? That I nod to you as a gesture of humanity and let the ship go?'

'Your enemies are not on that ship. I am your enemy. People like me.'

'You are not my enemy! You are not worthy of the honour! People like you are objects! You cannot resist because it is not in your destiny! The ship will not leave because it should not! There is an ordination, a plan—'

'A secret harmony—' Edge felt his finger tighten on the trigger, 'There are no secret harmonies.'

'There is a plan for my life. There is a great plan for the nation of Japan—'

'Ordinary people will resist it. Ordinary men will take up arms and go to war against you and defeat you in your great battles—your great plan will be defeated by farmers and clerks—'

'Your American views on democracy!'

'If you like, yes.'

Isogai said evenly, 'You will not resist. You are already a carcase of dead meat. You will not resist.' He drew his sword its full length and held it loosely by his side, 'You have nothing to fight for. Can you kill in cold blood? Can you? Is your will so strong you can kill in cold blood? Or will your Western conscience make you hesitate? Your *democracy*—your *humanity*—'

Edge saw the condemned man kneeling by the grave. His head was turning, the eyes were looking at him. He stepped forward and—he saw his father going forward to meet the procession at the bottom of the hill with his arms outstretched—'Let the ship go.'

Isogai shook his head.

'Let them go. Please.'

'*Please?*'

'Let them go.'

'Why are you fighting, Mr Edge, when you have nothing to fight *for*? If you love those people so much, you should be with them.' He asked, cajolingly, 'Where is your cause? Your reason? And who, who do you defend?'

Edge felt the gun waver in his hand.

'Don't you know? In all your life have you made no loyalty to anyone? Will no one have you?' He opened his left hand to show a hollow palm, 'Look around you: there is no one here. You are alone. No one will accept you. You fight for nothing. You have no cause. Your gun is without purpose.' He said simply, 'There is no one who wants you to defend them. Where are the relatives of your dead Chinese—your target-practice soldiers, your friends? Where is anyone who will support you?'

'The ship will leave.'

'Will it?'

'Yes!'

'You will die here for nothing.'

Edge felt his hand grow heavy. 'That is not important to me.' He saw himself go forward towards the condemned man. He saw his father going towards the procession with his hands outstretched. He thought sadly, "Was I wrong? Was I always—" He heard the ship's engines gathering momentum and he thought, "It's going. The ship is going, and they're all on board and I'm—" He saw Isogai step forward, the sword swinging loosely in his hand, "All I—all I wanted to be—*there are no secret harmonies, there are only—*" He saw his own childish hands clenched against his temples in terror that day at the Mission, the spots on his father's shirt and on his mother's white— He shouted at Isogai as the sword arced forward in a sudden blinding movement, '*You people are wrong!*'

222

64

The aircraft raced above the first mountain ranges of Hawaii. The pilots' eyes were wide and staring. In the distance they saw the black shapes of the American fleet.

At the border the fat Sergeant in the turret of the lead tank ordered, 'Go!'

65

OH MY GOD—!!

He felt the sword skewer upwards through his stomach and hack through lung. He felt its sudden withdrawal out of his body, slicing and destroying him inside. There were gunshots in his ears, a terrible rushing sound as a torrent of blood surged out from the wound. He felt himself going backwards, falling back. He heard explosions and shots and Isogai—he saw his eyes. He saw him run to the road outside the warehouse. Falling backwards. His hand was covered in blood. There was a widening pool of it on the floor of the warehouse. He saw his hand covered in blood. He heard firing and someone shouting, lights outside, lighting up Isogai's back and legs, blossoms of yellow flame. He thought, "It's started:" He heard the ship's engines. He saw Isogai shouting at something. He heard him screaming. He saw him coming back.

He saw the sword dripping blood. Isogai was coming back. He saw the sword raised for a second thrust. Isogai's eyes. He heard him shriek, 'You have robbed me! You have robbed me of my destiny! The invasion has begun without me!' He tried to crawl towards something: the gun. He saw it through a haze of throbbing on the floor beside him.

Isogai shrieked, 'You kept me here! You kept me here!'

He saw the sword raised for a gigantic pinning thrust. He saw Isogai's eyes. Something was in his hand. He lifted it up.

Isogai shrieked, 'You have ruined me!' Edge thought, "The ship—the ship is out of range—" He saw the diamond point of the sword. The muzzle of the pistol was pointing upwards, its black snout—he raised it up and squeezed at the trigger.

The recoil of the gun thumped against his hand. He saw Isogai's face change. He saw his eyes stop with the sword in mid-air, grow blank, stare at him. He saw him stagger. The sword dropped. He held the muzzle of the gun up higher and pressed at the trigger and part of Isogai's head disintegrated in a spray of colour and he thought, "I'm doing it." He pressed at the trigger again and again. He saw the gun fall down through the air out of his hand, its slide open, and he thought, "I've fired every cartridge I had in the gun at him and he's dead." He saw the body on the ground. He thought, "I've done it and he's—" He thought through a haze of blood, "At last I—"

He began to crawl out of the warehouse.

66

The shells from the guns on the foreshore were falling short. The passengers on the ship were crowded along the railings. They saw the lights of the tanks moving into the streets. There were tracers from machine-guns whipping out from border emplacements manned by the American Marines, searchlights, then flashes and explosions as the defenders were killed and the posts were silenced one by one. A building in the centre of the city disintegrated in a flash of brilliant light; there were fires starting. They saw eruptions of flame as the giant buildings along Nanking Road took the full force of a barrage of shellfire, then a cacophony of sound as the tanks swept the streets with machine-gun fire. The passengers gripped the railings until their knuckles turned white with the effort.

They saw Shanghai falling.

67

He saw the ship going. Somewhere, from a church somewhere, from Duras' bell towers in the school, there was a
bell tolling. He heard explosions and firing from up near the
border moving into the streets. He heard the bell tolling. The
ship's siren began blowing over and over and over. He saw the
lights on its rigging—he saw it moving as a dark shape along the
river. There were tanks, and men, soldiers: he saw them
coming, and firing. There were lights and explosions and
chaos— He thought, "It's leaving. It's really leaving. They're
going. After a century, they're finally—" He heard the great
mass of China's humanity sigh. The ship's siren blew over and
over and over. Shanghai burned. The International Settlement
in Shanghai finally burned. He thought—

He heard the rumbling of the tanks—he saw the ship going.
He thought, "Well, good luck to them." Something seemed to
happen to his eyes. He thought, "At last. *At last.*"

He lay down in the street like a dog and died.

68

At 7:55 a.m. local time, people looked up. December the
seventh, 1941.

Pearl Harbour, in the islands of Hawaii.

For a single moment, the swarms of aircraft, like something
from a sepia, stiff-backed photograph, were frozen in time.